WAYNE STINNETT

SWIFT AND SILENT

A JESSE MCDERMITT NOVEL

Caribbean Adventure Series
Volume 27

DOWN ISLAND PRESS

Library of Congress cataloging-in-publication Data
Stinnett, Wayne
Swift and Silent/Wayne Stinnett
p. cm. - (A Jesse McDermitt Novel)
ISBN: 978-1-956026-94-8
Cover and graphics by Aurora Publicity
Edited by Marsha Zinberg, The Write Touch
Final Proofreading by Donna Rich
Interior Design by Aurora Publicity
Published by Down Island Press, LLC

If you'd like to receive my newsletter, please sign up on my website. WWW.WAYNESTINNETT.COM. Once or twice a month, I'll bring you insights into my private life and writing habits, with updates on what I'm working on, special deals I hear about, and new books by other authors that I'm reading.

THE GASPAR'S REVENGE
SHIP'S STORE IS OPEN 24/7.
There, you can purchase all kinds of swag
related to my books, and even my books themselves,
in whatever format you choose.
You can find it at
WWW.GASPARS-REVENGE.COM

Also by Wayne Stinnett

The Jerry Snyder Caribbean Mystery Series

Wayward Sons   Voudoo Child   Friends of the Devil

The Charity Styles Caribbean Thriller Series

Merciless Charity   Enduring Charity   Elusive Charity
Ruthless Charity   Vigilant Charity   Liable Charity
Reckless Charity   Lost Charity

The Young Jesse McDermitt Tropical Adventure Series

A Seller's Market   Bad Blood

The Jesse McDermitt Caribbean Adventure Series

Fallen Out   Rising Storm   Rising Tide
Fallen Palm   Rising Fury   Steady As She Goes
Fallen Hunter   Rising Force   All Ahead Full
Fallen Pride   Rising Charity   Man Overboard
Fallen Mangrove   Rising Water   Cast Off
Fallen King   Rising Spirit   Fish On!
Fallen Honor   Rising Thunder   Weigh Anchor
Fallen Tide   Rising Warrior   Swift and Silent
Fallen Angel   Rising Moon
Fallen Hero   Rising Tide

Non Fiction

Blue Collar to No Collar   No Collar to Tank Top

Dedicated to all my Tropical Author friends and colleagues.
Any time I can interact with my tribe is time well spent. Look forward to more drinks and cigars on the beach.

"I've begun to realize that you can listen to silence and learn from it.
It has a quality and a dimension all its own."
— Chaim Potok

Jesse's Island

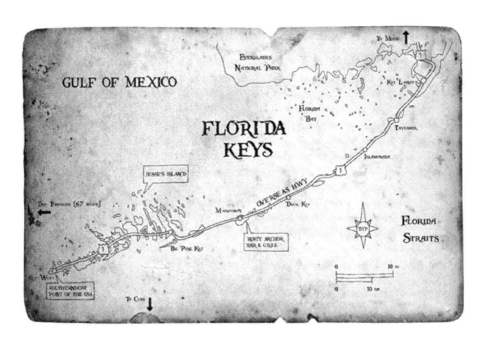

CHAPTER ONE

Thursday, January 25, 2024
Lower Matecumbe Key, Florida Keys

As anchorages went, the one Hoagie had chosen was idyllic, as well as convenient, with acres of shallow flats for snorkeling, and dozens of unspoiled little islands and sandbars to explore by stand-up paddleboard or kayak.

Snorkeling with a speargun, Hoagie had managed to add a few fresh snappers to the dinner menu over the last couple of days.

Other boaters had passed by, several times a day, mostly center consoles rigged for fishing, but they passed far enough away in the channel that the anchorage felt quite secluded.

The fact that it was only three or four miles from one of the busiest two-lane highways in Florida didn't diminish the tranquil setting at all—the road was too far away for the traffic noise to be heard.

Hoagie could reach a dock on Lower Matecumbe Key, not far from a grocery store, in ten or fifteen minutes, and be at the store after a five-minute walk.

It took longer than that just to drive to Kroger from their home in Jacksonville, Florida.

Ronald Hoagland, or Hoagie to his friends, had been recently "rewired," as he was fond of saying—not retired. At the age of thirty-nine, just over one year earlier, he'd hit the lotto numbers and had a sudden windfall that was well into the eight-figure range. More than enough to last several lifetimes.

In short, Hoagie and Amanda Hoagland were rich beyond their wildest dreams.

Once the realization of what their good fortune meant had started to set in, Hoagie and Amanda sat down and broke the news to their two teenage children, Ron, Jr. and Emma.

Then, after a lot of questions and answers, the family began to put together a list of things they wanted to do together before the kids left for college in two and five years. They were a close-knit, adventurous family and many ideas flew around the dinner table for several weeks.

Having been avid boaters all their lives, it didn't take long before the Hoaglands hit on the idea of a new boat. And not just any boat. To make things work, the boat had to have certain amenities and capabilities.

It took them weeks to come up with an idea of what kind of boat would be suitable for their wants and needs, and that would allow them to travel the U.S. coastline and eventually get out to the Bahamas without interrupting the kids' schooling.

Where they planned to cruise made a big difference in the type of vessels to choose from. Hoagie wasn't interested in crossing vast oceans but was very comfortable handling a boat near shore. So, the boat they'd choose would have to be a shallow-draft vessel.

What good was a boat if it couldn't go where they wanted?

Hoagie was a big man, standing over six feet tall and weighing over two hundred pounds. He didn't like the idea of having to work on or maintain diesel engines in cramped quarters, and nearly every vessel they looked at had the engine below deck, or under the steps, or inside a cabinet. An engine room big enough for Hoagie meant a boat too big for him to handle.

He'd grown up with small boats, jon boats, runabouts, and bass boats, mostly. So he knew outboard engines quite well, and leaned toward a boat with multiple big outboard engines.

Having more than one engine provided redundancy—if one, or even two engines failed, they could rely on a third, and possibly a fourth, to get them safely back to port.

Multiple outboards were more expensive to run, but Hoagie wouldn't have to learn a whole new skill set to *keep* them running.

So, the Hoagland's boat search shifted to shallow-draft yachts with outboard engines, and those proved to be very few and far between.

Summer travel would be easy to figure out— they could just pick a destination and go. They wanted to cross to the Bahamas for the summer, once the kids finished school. There were only a few summer vacations left before Ronnie would leave for college.

But if they wanted to cruise full-time, they'd need an extra crew member on board—a certified home-school teacher who had no ties and could travel with them. Another high hurdle.

Hoagie was quickly learning, however, that the family's new-found wealth made even the biggest obstacle seem a mere bump.

Having five people aboard meant an outboard-powered, shallow-draft boat with at least four separate staterooms. Most of what they found with four cabins tended to be far too large for Hoagie's taste and required deeper water.

Cabin size didn't matter a whole lot—cabins were for sleeping, but finding a boat with four of them that was still small enough to allow them to explore inland waterways and anchor in shallower waters, like the cove they'd found three days before, just north of Lower Matecumbe Key, had proven to be very difficult.

It couldn't be a *production* boat, as most manufacturers bent to the demands of the consumer—fewer and larger sleeping quarters. They'd have to sacrifice one need for another or hire a yacht builder to create a custom boat just for them.

So, Hoagie started looking at having his boat custom-built. Or at least finding a production boat builder that could offer more options. Building a new boat from scratch would take more than a year and eat into the time he and Amanda would have with their growing kids.

It'd taken a while, but they'd finally found a boat builder in the Chesapeake Bay area who was nearing completion of the hull for a new fifty-five-foot, shallow-draft inshore cruising trawler with four separate staterooms, though two were very small.

The builder had at first balked at the idea of triple outboards, but Hoagie had managed to talk him into it, and through the rest of the year, he'd watched it being completed, finally launching *Rewired* just before Christmas.

After an extensive shakedown in Chesapeake Bay, during which the builder corrected all the deficiencies they'd found, the family was ready, and they spent New Year's weekend back home in Jacksonville, preparing for their great family adventure.

There was a lot to do—plans to make, charts to check, and provisions to buy. *Rewired* had tons of storage below the pilothouse, in the area that had been designed to accommodate a diesel engine. Filling this "pantry" meant the family would be able to go for two or even three weeks without having to reprovision.

The beginning of the new year had brought the start of a new life for the Hoagland family. They'd planned to cruise South Florida and the Keys until late February, getting to know the boat and its abilities, and then head back up the East Coast in spring to begin the Great Loop.

It was something Hoagie had dreamt of since he was just a boy, and figured it'd be a great way for them all to become very familiar with *Rewired*.

The Great Loop was a circumnavigation of the eastern half of the United States, using either the Erie Canal or the St. Lawrence River to reach the Great Lakes from the Atlantic side and the Intracoastal Waterway, which ran the length of the Eastern Seaboard.

From southern Lake Michigan, boaters could enter the Illinois Waterway through the Chicago or Calumet Rivers, then pass through a series of canals and locks to reach the upper Illinois River. From there, they'd go south to the Mississippi, then into the Gulf of Mexico, looping around the Florida Panhandle to get back where they started. Once finished, a boat is said to have "crossed its wake," and those on the journey were called Loopers.

In the month since taking ownership, they'd cruised down the East Coast, stopping in several places along the way to refuel and reprovision, but moving steadily away from the cold of winter.

Even their home in Jacksonville was too cold.

The boat had performed admirably, but there were a number of system malfunctions. Nothing Hoagie and his son couldn't handle, and they mostly had to do with the electronics, which Ronnie was becoming somewhat of an expert on.

Now they were simply idling away the days, until a recent friend of Hoagie's and his wife would join them on their boat at the end of the month to begin the Great Loop.

In Hoagie's mind, starting in the Florida Keys, where it was warm in the winter, and moving slowly up the coast to follow the spring blossoms, then cruising the cool, deep waters of the Great Lakes through summer and floating down the great Mississippi, chasing the fall color change, and finally, wintering in the Gulf of Mexico sounded like the life he'd always wanted to live.

Just keep going, he thought, looking out over the subtropical waters all around them. *Just keep going around, and around, and—*

"Everything okay?" Amanda asked, as she joined Hoagie on the flybridge of their new, custom-built yacht.

Hoagie smiled at his wife. Being out in the bright sun for the last month, although the first part had been cold, had lightened her red hair to a beautiful strawberry blond. And while most redheads usually shunned sunlight, the last three weeks in the more subtropical climate had given Amanda's skin a glowing tan.

"Perfect," he replied, moving over to make room and waving a hand to the sky. "I was just sitting here... watching the clouds drift by, and experiencing such a feeling of true freedom. Like I've never felt before, you know. Anything we want to do, babe, we can now do. And right now, being here with you and the kids, away from everything, and free to have fun—this is like Nirvana to me."

"You're really looking forward to this adventure," Amanda said with a happy smile. "This is something we've both dreamed of doing, Hoag. I was afraid we might never be able to do it with the kids." She kissed his cheek. "I'm the luckiest girl in the world, married to the luckiest man."

He turned and kissed her back. "What are Destiny and the kids doing?"

Destiny Douglas was a recent graduate of the University of Michigan, where she'd earned a master's degree in education, along with a secondary teachers' certification to teach high school- and college-aged students. She'd also graduated with a strong yearning to escape the cold of Ann Arbor and see the world. She'd come highly recommended by a college friend of Amanda's, who was on the faculty at U-M.

"They just finished a lesson," Amanda replied. "I think they're planning to take the paddleboards to the beach."

"Want to join them?" Hoagie asked, taking his wife's hand.

"Kids need time to themselves," Amanda replied. "And Destiny isn't much more than a kid, herself."

"She's got a master's degree in secondary education," Hoagie scoffed. "Yeah, she's young. But all she's gotta do is get Ronnie through high school and Emma into it. Then we can look at one-on-one tutoring for Emma."

"You noticed it too?"

"What?" Hoagie asked, a bit confused by his wife's conversational change in direction.

It was something she did a lot, and for a long time, Hoagie had trouble keeping up.

"Ronnie's almost a man, Hoag," Amanda replied. "And Destiny is very pretty."

"She's seven years older than him," Hoagie said. "She wouldn't be—"

"Hush," Amanda whispered, hearing the thunk of the salon's sliding glass door closing on the deck below.

A moment later, their son, Ronnie, climbed up the ladder.

"We're going to a little beach over on the other side of that island," he said, pointing toward the north. "We'll be back in a couple of hours."

Hoagie nodded. "Look after your—"

The sound of a high-speed outboard cut him off as a center console boat came roaring around the tip of the island Ronnie was pointing at.

Hoagie was on his feet in an instant. "They're going way too fast."

The boat turned and started racing straight toward them, and Hoagie could see three men aboard.

One of them held a rifle.

"Get below!" he ordered his wife and son. "Find Emma and Destiny and get down in the pantry!"

Amanda rose and stood next to him. "What do you suppose—"

"Quick!" he shouted, moving his wife toward the ladder. "Get below!"

"Stay where you are!" an amplified voice shouted over the water.

Hoagie froze. What did these people want? Were they the police?

The boat slowed and the man with the rifle moved to the front, aiming the gun up at them.

"Do not move!" a man shouted through a bullhorn, as the boat came alongside. "We are going to board your vessel!"

A second man joined the rifleman, pointing a pistol up at them.

"We are coming aboard," the man at the helm repeated, putting the bullhorn down. "If any of you move, you will be shot."

These aren't policemen, Hoagie realized, slowly raising his hands and stepping closer to the rail.

"What do you want?" he shouted down. "We have no cash, no valuables."

The boat bumped the yacht hard, near the stern, and the man with the pistol jumped over into *Rewired's* cockpit. He holstered his gun and grabbed a line the helmsman handed him, then tied it to a handrail. His gun came out again as he turned and pointed it up at the three on the flybridge.

"Where are the others?" the helmsman demanded, as he and the rifleman came over onto *Rewired.*

He seemed to be the leader. He wore jeans and boots and had long, dark hair and several weeks' growth of beard. His actions were quick and jumpy, as if he were agitated.

"What do you want?" Hoagie demanded once more.

"If any of them move," the leader said to the rifleman as he went toward the flybridge ladder and looked up at Hoagie, "shoot the old man."

He mounted the steps quickly, then stood in front of Hoagie. "I am taking your boat," he said calmly. "*And* your women."

The color drained from Hoagie's face. "What are you going to do with them?"

The leader looked over at Ronnie, then back to Hoagie. "You and your son are free to leave," he replied. "Take the paddleboards and go to shore."

"What about—"

"I will call you about the ransom at precisely one o'clock. Now, where are the two girls?"

Many thoughts flashed through Hoagie's mind at once. The man knew Ronnie was his son, he knew his phone number, and last, Hoagie realized that with three of them, armed, he and Ronnie couldn't overpower them.

The man aimed his gun at Ronnie's chest. "You have three seconds to tell me."

"Please," Amanda pleaded. "Nobody has to get hurt. They're probably hiding in the cabin. We can pay the ransom. Just don't hurt anyone."

He stepped back and motioned with the pistol. "Down."

The leader followed them down the ladder, where the other two men waited. The man with the rifle wore a tank top and khaki shorts. His hair was long and disheveled, hanging menacingly over his face as he stared at Amanda.

The man in charge opened the door to the salon and called inside. "Come out of there now! Both of you!"

How did he know we had five people aboard? Hoagie wondered.

Through the open door, Hoagie saw Destiny, then Emma come up from the lower deck into the salon.

"We'll do whatever you want," Hoagie said to the leader. "You'll get your ransom. But I have to have your word that they won't be harmed."

The man turned and gave him a curious look, moving his gun up to aim it at Hoagie's face before speaking over his shoulder. "You hear that, Snake? He wants the word of a kidnapper who is pointing a gun at his head."

Both men laughed as the third man went up to the flybridge.

The leader pointed to the man who'd just gone up the ladder and was looking down, waiting. "He will need the key."

Hoagie thrust a hand into his pocket and suddenly had *two* guns pointed at his face.

"Real slow," Snake said, hissing the S sound a little. "Two fingers."

Hoagie pulled the keyring out of his pocket between his middle finger and thumb, feeling a cold sweat trickle down his back.

The leader snatched the keyring from Hoagie's hand and tossed it up to the man on the flybridge.

"You," he then ordered, waving the gun at Ronnie, "get the boards in the water."

The young man bowed his chest out slightly. "You better not—"

"Better not what?" the man snarled. "Do as you're told!"

Ronnie went down to the swim platform and lifted the boards down with him, one at a time.

"Get the paddles," the leader ordered Hoagie, waving with the gun.

Hoagie picked up two of the paddles, went down the steps to join his son and handed him one.

"Now get going," the man said, looking at his watch as all three outboards started. "You have a little over an hour before I call. You should easily make it to shore by then. If you call the cops, the women die."

Hoagie gulped, feeling the weight of his phone in his pocket.

How could he already have my number?

It was obvious that these men had done their homework.

Ronnie pushed his board into the water and stepped over, balancing easily as he paddled away a little to allow room for Hoagie to get the other board off the swim platform.

When he did, he stepped over and paddled one stroke to get beside Ronnie. "Don't worry, son," he whispered. "We'll get them back."

"Go and get the anchor up," the leader ordered Snake. Then he turned toward Hoagie, a few feet away from the stern. "Get moving!"

Together, the father and son began paddling, going past *Rewired's* bow, heading toward Lower Matecumbe Key in the distance.

The anchor windlass engaged, and the boat began creeping forward as they paddled harder.

Ronnie looked back at the man on the foredeck. "We could have—"

"No," his father said, cutting him off. "Too much risk to your mom and the girls."

They paddled harder, moving past the anchor, which Hoagie could clearly see on the bottom.

Suddenly, the water all around them began to splash as machine gun fire erupted behind them.

Horrified, Hoagie looked over and saw blood explode from his son's chest as the younger man spun and fell from the board into the water.

Something hit Hoagie in the back, then the leg, and he went down, grasping for his board.

The last sound Hoagie heard was the anguished screams of his wife, his daughter, and Destiny Douglas.

CHAPTER TWO

Monday, February 26, 2024
Riviera Beach, Florida

It was a cold morning as we headed out—colder than I like it, anyway. We had a twenty-knot wind dead out of the north, kicking up small whitecaps in the shallows off the Intracoastal just north of Peanut Island, where we'd just pulled anchor.

February can be hit-and-miss as far as chartering in the Florida Keys goes; one day it might be eighty degrees and sunny, and the next, cold and rainy. Which is why I'd planned this trip for this time of year.

The sky was gray, with low, thudding clouds all around. It wasn't a good day for casual boating, but it looked like a perfect day for the final shakedown ocean trial.

Cold is a relative thing. I don't get up to the Florida mainland very often, and almost never as far north as Stuart, so an air temperature of sixty-one felt downright frigid to me. Add to that, there was a one-hundred-percent chance of thunderstorms, and the stout north wind and Mother Ocean promised a real challenge for our new boat. The acid test would be comfort. And cold wasn't comfortable.

I glanced at the thermostat on the overhead multi-display and grinned. Maybe my blood was thinner from living and working just eighty miles north of the Tropic of Cancer for the last several decades.

To folks living up north, sixty-one degrees in the last few days before March might seem like a balmy, early spring day, but I'm not from there.

I grew up on Florida's southwest coast, and my home since the turn of the century has been a little island in the Florida Keys that's only accessible by water.

Or helicopter.

So, when I say it was cold, I mean that *I* found it cold. Don't hold it against me. I think hot, humid, South Florida summers are quite comfortable. It's simply a matter of perspective.

We'd done the first sea trial before Christmas, even before the interior was finished. Then she went back to the boatyard for a haul-out to finish the buildout *and* address the first of what would be dozens of malfunctions, or I guess "mis-functions" might be a better word—all minor problems.

The shakedown runs through late January and early February revealed more problems as interior work was completed, sometimes during testing, all of which were solved by the engineers aboard for the cruises.

She'd gotten a heavy workout since being launched, and now all the bugs had been addressed. So far, anyway. I anticipated more. It was a common thing with such an intricate piece of marine engineering.

The hatch to the master suite behind the lower helm opened and Savannah came around the wide helm seat to join me.

"It's horrible out there," she said, leaning against the seat beside me and looking at the low, gray clouds all around us. "This is the kind of day I would've just rolled over and gone back to sleep."

I glanced over, grinned, and did my best impression of Travolta in *Broken Arrow*. "Yeah, ain't it cool!"

"You *like* this slop?"

"Me, personally? No," I replied. "Much too cold out there for man or beast. But if anything else is ever going to break, it's going to break today."

Just then, the first sheet of cold rain passed over us, adding an ominous overtone to my words as it pelted the side glass of the lounge on the port side.

Alberto looked up from his laptop, where he'd been studying. "If it ain't raining..." he said, and paused.

"We ain't training," I finished with a laugh.

It was something an old platoon sergeant of mine used to say a lot during my first tour in Okinawa, Japan, that carried over to the troops in my charge years later.

No matter what was on the schedule, if it started raining, day or night, Sergeant Russ Livingston had us out in the field, training to adapt to whatever crappy conditions Mother Nature could throw at us.

We once completed a ten-mile force march in full gear, at night, during a full-blown Cat-2 typhoon.

"The Army only trains in spring and fall, Marines!" Sergeant Livingston would yell over the crashing thunder of a Japanese typhoon, while running back and forth along the barbed wire obstacle. "The Air Force only trains in sunny weather! Marines train in the mud! If it ain't rainin', we ain't trainin', ladies! Get your head down!"

I grinned, remembering Russ as he'd been back then.

"I was going to put on a fresh pot," Savannah said. "Want me to top you off first?"

"Thanks," I replied, reaching over, taking my mug from its holder, and handing it to her.

In my opinion, the last cup from a pot is the best cup. During my later years in the Corps, I was often the first one in the office, and would simply turn the hotplate on under the coffee machine and wait a few minutes for it to heat up the last dregs from the night before.

We'd only made about forty nautical miles the first day out from Stuart, running solely on the electric motors in the amas—the outer hulls—before we'd anchored early in shallow water off Riviera Beach, well out of the main channel of the Intracoastal. While we waited for the forecasted storm to arrive, we enjoyed a peaceful evening on the hook, completely unencumbered by the drudgery of life on land, which was just a quarter mile away.

Through the previous evening, several boats moving along the ICW had slowed down as they passed, the people on board no doubt befuddled over just what kind of boat we were.

Taranis was a custom-built trimaran, with three long, sleek, wave-piercing hulls. From the front she has a very imposing look, like a bird of prey swooping down on an unsuspecting fish. From the side, she looked like a typical blue-water trawler, built tall for heavy seas, with a windshield that was raked forward and was covered by a long brow.

But she was also a wolf in sheep's clothing.

The main hull in the middle housed a luxurious VIP stateroom aft the narrow, wave-piercing bow, with a short passageway to the mechanical room. Aft that was the garage for the jet-drive tender, fully enclosed below the cockpit.

In the two amas, or outriggers, there was more living area forward, a massive lazarette in the aft port ama and a full dive shop starboard. In the stern of each ama was a powerful electric motor, which is what we'd run on all the way down the ICW the previous day.

However, the bulk of the living area was the main deck above, which spread across all three hulls and included the salon, galley, forward lounge, and wheelhouse, as well as the master stateroom, which took up almost half the enclosed house directly behind the helm.

"Here you go," Savannah said, sitting next to me again and handing the mug back. "Any update from Kim?"

Our middle daughter, Kim, along with her husband, Marty, were sworn officers with FWC, the Florida Fish and Wildlife Conservation Commission. She'd called just after dusk, knowing we were moving *Taranis* from Stuart, and wanted me to keep a sharp eye out. She said there'd been a couple of yacht thefts in the last few months and two bodies had been found in the water off Lower Matecumbe just four weeks earlier.

They'd been identified as a father and son. The wife, daughter, and a tutor the couple had hired for the kids were still missing, along with their yacht.

The yacht thefts puzzled me. It wasn't like stealing a Corolla and taking it to a chop-shop to be disassembled and sold for parts. Yachts are large, easily spotted, and hard to get rid of.

"You mean about the boat thefts?" I asked, though I knew that's what she was talking about. I pulled my phone out and looked at the screen. "Nope, nothing new."

"How long before we reach the inlet?"

"About twenty minutes," I replied, glancing at the chart plotter. "Are we rigged for a rough sea state?"

"Everything except Alberto's laptop," she replied, looking over at our adopted son.

"It'll be smooth, Mom," Alberto said. "Dad's going to run the gyro when we get out there."

"Will it be that rough?" she asked me. "On a day like this, I'd be *adding* dock lines to *Sea Biscuit*, rather than casting them off."

"NOAA says seas are six to eight feet," I replied. "With a seven-second interval and a moderate chop. I just want to see how stable she is with and *without* the gyrostabilizer. It draws a lot of electricity."

I could see the apprehension in her face.

"If it's too rough," I said, "we'll come back to the ICW."

The name of our new sixty-six-foot trimaran came from the Celtic god of lightning and thunder, Taranis, who was worshiped all over Northern Europe. My parents and Savannah's mother were Irish, and her dad's ancestors were from northern France, and probably worshiped the same gods.

So it seemed an appropriate name for a vessel that could run indefinitely on electric power alone.

Slow, but steady.

She could cruise silently at five knots, while solar panels provided more energy than the motors used, keeping the batteries fully charged. At night, she could continue on, using the stored energy from the sun until morning, when the batteries would be half-depleted.

Rinse, lather, repeat, for as many days and nights as a person might want to cruise non-stop. Even the wide Pacific wouldn't be a challenge.

Or... I could just hit what I'd started referring to as the "thunder button"—the ignition switch for the 630-horsepower main diesel engine.

With it and both electric motors at maximum output, *Taranis* could easily outrun an approaching storm, with a designed top speed of twenty-five knots.

We hadn't been able to test that much during sea trials and shakedowns, but I hoped to in the calmer waters of Biscayne Bay tomorrow or the next day.

There hadn't been any problems at all the previous day on the ICW, so today, I wanted to take *Taranis* through Lake Worth Inlet and run outside all the way down to Miami, in conditions I wouldn't consider unless it were an emergency.

With three engines, I was certain of one thing—if there was a breakdown, we could easily limp into a haul-out marina from just about anywhere in the world's oceans, so we certainly wouldn't have any problem by staying within two or three miles of shore.

"Is it proper to refer to a boat as 'she' if it has a boy's name?" Savannah asked, a twinkle of amusement in her eyes.

Her boat was called *Sea Biscuit* and the name had nothing to do with the champion racehorse, Seabiscuit. But I always teased her about how the horse had been a male, and the two names couldn't be pronounced differently, even though one was a single word and the other two words.

"No different than Seabiscuit," I said, with a grin. "Or *Sea Biscuit.*"

"I didn't name her," she replied. "And I never felt like going through all the trouble to change it. And besides, I like biscuits. It's a Carolina thing."

"The marker ahead is for the inlet," I said, barely seeing it a half mile directly in front of us through the windshield.

The front glass of the wheelhouse was in four pieces and made of polycarbonate sheets, each one six feet by three feet. They spanned the whole front of the main structure of the boat and were inclined forward, tugboat-style, with a long brow above to help keep rain to a minimum. There were four wiper arms that kept the blades almost vertical across each six-foot windshield, clearing them with a single pass.

Alberto looked up toward the approaching marker, then closed his laptop and put it away. He came over and slid in next to Savannah.

The wide helm seat was something I'd insisted on, at the expense of more lounge area. All three of us could comfortably sit at the helm, which had redundant systems for everything.

"Local high tide won't be for an hour," Alberto said, looking at an app on his phone.

"For this inlet, that's a good thing," I said. "Imagine if we had a following current colliding with big, incoming waves."

"How fast will the current be?" he asked, ready to dazzle us with his math skills.

"Hit the thunder button, son," I told him. "The current through here is a good four or five knots."

Savannah rolled her eyes. "Didn't Hank say the electric motors alone could reach seven or eight knots?"

"Yes, he did," I replied. "That would only give us about three knots speed over ground, though. And if another boat is coming or going, we'd be a hazard to navigation."

Alberto looked up at Savannah, who nodded. "Start it, but don't use it unless we have to. I'd like to see how *she* handles it without diesel power."

Alberto switched on the ignition, checked the gauges, then pressed the starter button. The tach sprang to life, which was the only sign the engine was running. It was seven feet below and behind us, in an almost sound-proof mechanical room.

The double hatch to the port ama behind the lounge opened, and Jimmy came up the steps, stretching his arms.

"It's nine o'clock already?" he asked, going to the fridge and pulling out a plastic bottle of mango juice. "You shoulda woke me, man."

"Nothing to do," I informed him. "We didn't even need to step outside to rinse the mud off the anchor chain."

"Thanks to *another* torrential downpour an hour ago," Savannah added.

I nodded. "In hindsight, I think we should have added automatic spray nozzles to the pulpit."

"Now that's just plain lazy," Savannah scoffed.

I leaned forward and looked over at Alberto. "Mark that down for the next upgrade, son—auto chain rinse."

"Anything you need me to do?" Jimmy asked, standing comfortably between the helm and lounge, one hand resting on the rail in front of the steps.

"Extra eyes," I said. "The forward bolster and lounge seat flips back and raises up."

He fiddled with the bolster until he found the latch, then pulled the seat back toward the stern. The forwardmost section of the lounge seat rose with it, moving back a full eighteen inches to allow room for one person to sit, and another to slip past them to the port hatch.

"Looks pretty gnarly out there, dude," Jimmy said, gazing out at the inlet ahead and to the left.

I moved the two small controls for the electric motors all the way forward, giving us a full 50 kilowatts, or about 70 horsepower each.

While the power wasn't much, the torque and RPMs were high and each ama motor had a large folding prop, providing a great deal of thrust.

Taranis gathered speed against the oncoming current, quickly reaching a little over eight knots of actual hull speed through the water.

"We're half a knot over designed top speed on electric only," I announced. "Hull speed is 8.1 knots."

Alberto watched the chart plotter for a moment, then looked over at me. "We're only going 4.2 knots, speed over ground, and it looks like it's narrower up ahead."

Alberto seemed to have a natural grasp of hydrology. Without asking, he knew that if depth was consistent, water flowing through an opening would move faster when the opening got narrower. The only way it could continue at the same speed through a narrower opening would be if it got deeper. Water has no choice since it always seeks its own level and can't rise up. So, if the depth was the same, the current would be greater to move the same volume of water.

The inlet ahead narrowed by about a third, so it stood to reason that the flow would be a third faster.

"It will be, son," I replied, studying the water ahead. "This might get a little bumpy."

CHAPTER THREE

Reaching up to the overhead console, I switched on the camera system, with its four monitors spread across the visor above the windshield.

The two outermost monitors provided a view to the stern from just above the side doors of the wheelhouse, just like the sideview mirrors of a car or truck.

Second from the left was a view of the wheelhouse from the galley behind us, and the next one was a combination thermal imaging and infrared camera looking dead ahead from under the flybridge roof's brow eight feet above us.

In thermal imaging mode, the camera could pick up a swimmer's head in ninety-degree water, contrasting it sharply, even though the temperature difference might only be as little as five degrees if the person had been in the water for a while and was hypothermic.

The default mode was standard imaging, giving us a high-definition view ahead that could be zoomed in.

"Switch over to thermal on number three," I told Alberto. "And change number four to forward sonar."

With just those four monitors, we had a dozen different views and capabilities, which would allow us to travel or anchor securely under just about any conditions. And each monitor was capable of displaying multiple camera and sensor feeds.

The two monitors on the right flickered and changed.

"Okay to switch number one to weather radar?" Alberto asked. "I don't see anything behind us."

He'd gone with me to Stuart several times to learn about all the systems on our new boat while she was being built, and he had a much better grasp of her electronics than I did. Though only eleven, he'd made some pretty astute observations and suggestions during our visits, which were later incorporated into the build.

"Good idea," I agreed. "Anything coming up behind us will show up on radar, and we can switch back to the camera if we need to."

"I'd sure like to know when this weather is going to end," Savannah said, as I turned toward the second marker in the inlet.

I looked over at her and grinned. "Hopefully not for a while."

Leaning past her, I nodded at Alberto. "Start recording all cameras and sensors, son. We'll be able to review this later and get a lot of information from it. Everyone speak loud, so the galley cam will pick up what we're saying."

There was another camera in the wheelhouse, between the two overhead monitors, but it was more for video communication. The one behind us would show our movements and reactions to what was happening ahead. There was a reason athletes studied game films.

You're in charge of your effort and attitude, I remember Pap telling me many times. If the opponent, be it an enemy battalion, an opposing football player, or the elements can't be overcome by effort, then your attitude has to change, and that includes physical attitude as well as mental.

We were going to make mistakes. Studying our reactions when those mistakes were made could help avoid them in the future.

"It's eighty-nine nautical miles to Biscayne Bay," Jimmy said, working on a second chart plotter at the nav desk. "All day at eight knots, just on electric, but that'd mean running the generator when the batteries are more than fifty percent depleted."

"We'd need it anyway," I said, looking up at the weather radar. "I don't think we're going to see much sun today. The main engine's already running, though."

Jimmy looked over, surprised. "It is?"

I glanced at the tach and confirmed that the Cat diesel was indeed idling at 600 rpm.

"Just in case we encounter traffic," I replied. "It's not engaged, per the admiral's orders."

Savannah poked me in the ribs with her elbow.

The helm felt lively in my hands, the swirls and eddies in the water being transferred to the rudders in the amas, which were mounted just aft of each prop and engaged whenever the electric motors were on. When the motors were offline, the rudders folded into recesses in the hulls to reduce drag and the props folded into tapering points.

"The inlet looks clear," Jimmy said, standing and leaning against the nav desk. "Next marker's a mile ahead."

"You can *see* that already?" Savannah asked, straining her eyes, then checking the chart display in front of us.

Jimmy pretended to squint. "Can't quite read the number on it yet."

I knew his eyesight was good—better than good, in fact. But I was pretty sure he was just kidding about reading the number.

We were less than a quarter mile from the inlet's narrowest point, where it turned just a few degrees to the east.

"Speed over ground is down to just three knots," Alberto announced. "That means the current is—"

"Over five knots," I finished for him, putting my right hand on the Caterpillar engine controller. "It's okay to round off in a situation like this, son."

Alberto switched the far-left monitor back over to standard visual to look behind us, though, from his vantage point, closer amidship, he could just as easily have turned his head to look back through the glass doors at the stern.

"Nothing's behind us," he said.

"There's a big fisherman inbound," Jimmy said. "It just popped up, and a good two miles out of the inlet still."

I only spotted it by the crashing bow waves. Inbound, he had engine power, waves, and current all pushing him a lot faster than we were going.

"What's his speed, Alberto?"

He touched an AIS icon on the chart plotter, the only signature on it besides ours.

"He's going over twenty knots," Alberto replied, reading the information from the oncoming boat's Automatic Identification System. "We'll pass each other about the time we get to the outside of the jetties."

I kept my hand on the main engine controller, comfortable in the knowledge that we could accelerate to at least thirty knots in a matter of ten or fifteen seconds.

Taranis dipped and rocked as we encountered the larger waves rolling in off the Atlantic. It was far less than I would have expected, as the long, slender bow sections of each hull simply sliced through the oncoming waves, dispelling their energy outward. The starboard one disappeared under water for a moment, as the north wind pushed against the high port side.

Savannah looked out the sliding door beside me. "This is crazy smooth," she said. "But not very fast."

"Half a mile," Jimmy said, as another slash of rain peppered the windshield on his side.

"Experiment over," I said, engaging the main engine. "We gotta get out of his way."

I knew what it was like to come through an inlet with a crosswind in a big, heavy, sportfishing machine with the current and waves pushing from behind.

Dodging a slow-moving vessel in a narrow inlet increased the pucker factor exponentially. Especially if that slow boat was more than thirty feet wide.

As I pushed the throttle forward, *Taranis* gathered speed, seeming to ignore the hills of water piling up ahead of us.

"Fifteen knots, speed over ground," Alberto said.

I steered to the right side of the channel, clearly signaling my intent to the other vessel. I could ignore the channel for the most part, but he couldn't. With the way he was being tossed around, he'd need the whole width when he reached the bottleneck.

At anchor, *Taranis* only needed four feet of water. She was designed to have a draft of just over three feet when running at cruising speed on flat water under main engine power.

"Twenty knots," Alberto said, as the next marker flashed past. "Hull speed is twenty-five."

I could see that the oncoming boat was being piloted from the flybridge, which was only partially enclosed. I'd hate to be up there in this weather.

We passed the jetties, and I steered a little farther up onto the shallows.

"Depth is ten feet," Savannah said.

"Twenty-five knots, SOG," Alberto added.

"Five hundred yards," Jimmy announced needlessly.

The Viking sport fisher looked incredibly large from inside the comfort of the wheelhouse, but we were out of the channel and through the inlet, flying across slightly less choppy water, like a pelican riding the updraft created by a breaking wave.

Outside, whitewater splashed from all three hulls as the long, wave-piercing bows did their jobs. The boat rolled slightly from side to side, but with an overall beam width of thirty-two feet, the rocking was minimal.

"Thirty-two knots hull speed!" Alberto shouted, as I steered wider into deeper water. "And thirty over ground."

Out of the channel and clear of the inlet, I steered east-southeast, keeping the boat in the trough of the large rollers coming in from the northeast. The sea state immediately became calmer out of the current, and well out of the Viking's wake. But it was still nasty out there.

I slowly throttled back and turned more toward the south. At ten knots, I disengaged the main engine and shut it down.

"Bringing the electrics down to eighty percent output," I said, as I dialed the little handles back.

Heading due south, two miles off the Palm Beach coast, we slowed to just five knots. If the sun was shining, we could maintain that speed for a very long time.

The bows tilted downward as a quartering wave lifted us from behind. The boat began surfing along the face of the wave until it passed beneath the hull's midpoint, and we slid down into the next trough.

"Surprisingly smooth ride for such messy conditions," Savannah said. "I'd compare this to riding on the bridge of *Ambrosia*."

"And at a third the length and a tenth the price," I added.

"I could get used to this real easy, man," Jimmy said, putting his feet up on the handrail guarding the companionway down to the lower deck. Another slash of rain hit his side of the windshield. "High and dry, and climate controlled, *hermano*."

I looked around the interior. Aside from slight bounces and jerks, which were at complete odds with the white caps and big waves coming up behind us, it didn't seem any rougher of a ride than it'd been in the intracoastal.

"If we hold this speed," Jimmy said, going through the electrical analytics again, "we can make Biscayne Bay a little after sunset with about thirty percent of dedicated battery power left. The house batteries will probably only be down to fifty percent, thanks to getting a charge from that short run on the main engine."

"Make that thirty percent, as well," Savannah corrected. "If y'all want a hot lunch and dinner, that is."

"We'll need to start the generator before we get there," I allowed. "I want to get a good feel for how she acts at different speeds with different power configurations and settings, while we still have these rough conditions."

Savannah got up and stepped between Alberto and the console, picking up my and her coffee mugs. "More coffee, while the storm rages all around us?"

"You'll never hear me say no to coffee," I replied.

She easily walked back to the galley, both mugs in one hand and occasionally using the overhead grab rail with the other as the boat rose in the stern for another surfing ride.

"I'd call this stupid stable," Jimmy said, watching the triple bows plow through the choppy conditions with ease. "You could almost match the speed of the rollers and have only the slop to contend with."

As the next wave began to lift the stern of the port ama, I moved that motor speed up just a little, to eighty-five percent power, forcing the boat to try to pivot down the face as I steered against the turn.

Then I played with both motor controllers, trying to get the stern only slightly up as we raced ahead of the wave. I missed the first one, but got it dialed in half a minute later with the next wave.

"Like this?" I asked, as the boat settled into a slightly nose down attitude, tilting to starboard.

Jimmy jumped to his feet and shouted, "Off the hook, dude!" as he assumed a surfer's stance on the deck between the helm and lounge.

Savannah stepped past him, giving him a questioning look as she moved back to her seat between me and Alberto.

"What did you do?" she asked. "It's not as rough."

"We're surfing!" Alberto shouted and jumped up to join Jimmy, mimicking his stance.

"No droppin' in, little man!" Jimmy said, jostling for position on an imaginary wave.

"Hey, dude, that's my wave," Alberto said, getting a laugh from Jimmy and Savannah as he elbowed Jimmy. "There's room for two, so don't give me any of that 'locals only' stuff."

I couldn't help but laugh. "Okay, okay. Let's run some more tests. Alberto, you want to start up the gyro? This canted attitude is putting a lot of stress on the rudders."

He slipped quickly back into his seat and pulled up the gyrostabilizer control on the left multi-screen display and powered it up. "How high?"

"Let's give it full power and see what it does," I replied.

Amazingly, as the gyro's tach spooled up higher and higher, the starboard bow began to rise slightly and the whole attitude of the boat changed.

I brought the port motor speed back down to match the other, and there was no change in the ride and a much lighter feel to the helm.

The bows settled into a slight nose-down attitude compared to the horizon, but one side was higher in relationship to the surface.

It was an odd sensation in such a large vessel.

"We are quite literally surfing," I proclaimed. "Riding an eight-foot wave on a sixteen-ton, thirty-two-foot-wide surfboard. Both motors are at fifty-seven percent power. What's our hull speed?"

"Ten knots," Alberto replied.

Jimmy sat down and pulled up the electronics, then did some math on the calculator app on his phone.

"With both motors at fifty-seven percent and the gyro at a hundred," he said, looking up, "we're using the equivalent of 2.2 gallons per hour."

I looked over and grinned at Savannah. "That's damned good for ten knots."

"That's good at any speed," she agreed. "But can we count on riding a wave to outrun a storm on just electric?"

"More power!" Alberto exclaimed then grunted like an ape.

CHAPTER
FOUR

We ran at full power on the two electric motors, with the gyro on and off, slowly overtaking the quartering waves. Climbing up the backside seemed to take forever, but when we crested each one, *Taranis* would tilt slightly forward, then accelerate, reaching speeds a little over ten knots on two occasions.

We found we didn't need full power on the gyro in these conditions to maintain a comfortable attitude, which brought our equivalent fuel usage down to just one-and-a-half gallons per hour at ten knots while surfing a wave, which was unheard of in a conventional monohull trawler.

Hank's design specifications had been for a cruising speed of five knots for ten hours just on electric, and a top speed of eight knots for five hours.

Jimmy's calculations pointed more toward a cruising speed of six knots for ten hours and a top speed of eight for five hours, just running on the batteries. He sent the results to Hank via email, and the project manager and engineers were beyond pleased.

Then we hit *Taranis's* thunder button again and were able to run at just over twenty-five knots with the gyro on full power, and the ride was mostly comfortable, with a little throttle left. We experienced a slight hull slap coming over the tops of the big rollers, but nothing rattled, cracked, or broke off.

Two hours later, we were just offshore of Boca Raton, and we'd finished testing every possible speed and power combination we could think of. And the weather conditions were deteriorating. We were starting to see some sun and the sea state was calming, as we outpaced the storm.

Jimmy sent the results of those tests to Hank as well.

I started the Cat again and looked over at Savannah. "It's not a matter of *if* we can outrun a storm, but how *far* we can get ahead of it."

Pushing the throttle forward, as well as the electric motor controls, I brought our speed up to almost thirty knots, and we were no longer slapping the hulls.

The waves we were cresting were much smaller than they'd been earlier, and the choppy conditions continued to improve with every passing minute and half mile.

An hour later, with the sun shining fully and the clouds miles astern, I throttled back to just six knots, then shut *Taranis's* main engine down.

"You can stop recording everything, Alberto," I announced. "I think we've put her through all we can for one day."

He looked up at me and grinned. "I kinda want to turn around and play in the storm some more, *Taranis* is *fi*—um, *cool*."

"I felt absolutely safe," Savannah agreed. "This boat is a dream."

"Can you send all the video data to Hank from here?" I asked Jimmy.

"I'll start compressing the files, dude. Might take an hour to send, but yeah."

We continued at trawler speed as Jimmy ran another battery calculation.

"Looks like we'll make our anchorage before sunset, now," Jimmy announced. "And dedicated battery power will be better than fifty percent when we get there, now that we have Sol on our side again."

Savannah went back to the galley to get started on lunch and Jimmy went with her to help out.

"What do you think, little man?" I asked Alberto.

He scooted over closer and whispered, "*Fire*, Dad."

"I'm inclined to agree, son. Beyond cool."

"Will we ever have to outrun a storm like that one while we're cruising?"

I looked down at him and shook my head. "Not with proper prior planning," I replied. "But it's good to know we *can* if we have to, and by watching the weather, we can get out of the way of just about any storm."

"Even a hurricane?"

"I think the fastest moving hurricane ever recorded traveled at sixty knots forward speed," I replied. "But only a fool would try to outrun one in the same direction. We'd just move perpendicular to its course, move quickly out of its way, and just let it blow on by."

"What about pirates?" he asked.

Piracy still existed on the world's oceans. Not one-legged, eye-patch-wearing swashbucklers in galleons, though. Today's pirates used modern powerboats and sophisticated electronics in an attempt to thwart the law.

During our conversation, Kim had told me that boat thefts of all types, not just high-end yachts, were way up in South Florida the previous year.

I thought again about the father and son who'd been shot to death off Lower Matecumbe Key. The fates of the wife, daughter, and the woman crewmember were probably worse. By now, they'd likely been split up and shipped to different buyers around the globe.

"I think it's safe to say that *Taranis* can outrun most boats and definitely outmaneuver anything on the water."

"That's good," he said, checking the chart plotter. "There's a boat straight ahead about four miles."

He touched the icon on the screen. "It's a fishing boat heading into Haulover Inlet."

The boat was way too far away to see, and by the time we got there, it'd likely already be through the inlet.

"Something bothering you?" I asked, hearing Savannah laughing behind us at something Jimmy said.

Alberto looked back quickly at her, then up at me. "We hid a lot when we were in Mexico."

I hadn't considered all the cautionary moves Savannah must have had to make to avoid detection. While not every passing boater would have bad intent, there was no way to tell the ones that might from the ones who were just happy, laid-back cruisers.

While underway or at anchor, Savannah must have taken extraordinary steps to remain out of sight. That was likely even more true when she and Florence had been cruising on *Sea Biscuit*.

Drug and human trafficking were modern-day pirates' crimes of choice. Easy to handle and big profits.

"I've never been much good at hiding," I admitted to my adopted son. "My talents lean more toward being the seeker."

"What if a pirate has a faster boat?" he asked, a grave expression on his eleven-year-old face.

"Then they'd need to be a better shot," I replied honestly. "We're safe aboard *Taranis*."

I checked the weather station, mounted on the corner post of the windshield. The temperature outside was up to seventy-three, so I set the autopilot and said, "Why don't we go topside to eat."

With Alberto right behind me, we went aft through the galley.

"We're eating on the flybridge," Alberto announced, as I slid open the door.

"Go ahead up," Savannah replied. "We'll be right behind you."

I pushed the slider open and stepped out into the cockpit, instantly aware that the only sound I could hear was the soft swishing of water at the stern.

"Weird, huh?" Alberto said, following me outside. "I guess not hearing the engine takes getting used to."

He was right, it *was* weird. Traveling at just six knots in Savannah's big Grand Banks trawler, *Sea Biscuit*, or aboard my overpowered Rampage sport fisher, *Gaspar's Revenge*, the monotonous drone of the diesel engines could easily lull a person into unconsciousness during a long passage.

I locked the single door panel in place, open, knowing Savannah and Jimmy would have their hands full.

The entire salon wall was comprised of four polycarbonate sheet panels mounted in heavy aluminum frames, each three feet in width and running from the deck to the overhead in watertight tracks. All four could be opened to the full width of the salon by sliding the panels behind the stairwell going up to the flybridge. This completely opened the dinette area inside to the matching one outside.

Climbing up the steps, I unlatched the large deck hatch at the top, pushed it up on pneumatic pistons, and locked it into place. Then Alberto and I went up the rest of the way and walked across the upper lounge deck to the helm.

From the flybridge helm, I could see the sportfishing boat Alberto had spotted on the AIS. It was still two miles away and about to enter the inlet.

Though the sun felt warm, the air was chilly, so I opened the large, tinted sunroof over the helm, allowing warm sunlight in from directly overhead.

"I really like it up here," Alberto said, moving to the forward rail.

There was almost no apparent wind, since it was blowing from our stern and moving at about the same speed.

"Always my favorite part of a boat," I agreed, switching on the systems as I looked all around. "The view's a lot better."

The white sand beaches of some of the most expensive real estate in the country slipped slowly past, less than two miles to the west. The reef line ran very close to the high-priced shoreline in the Palm Beach and Miami areas, but we were well beyond that and only saw an occasional boat.

The Gulf Stream also ran very close to shore in that same area, bringing nutrient-rich water to the reef. We'd been motoring against the powerful current ever since we'd left the inlet that morning.

"I've always loved it there," Savannah said, as she and Jimmy came up, each of them carrying a large tray.

"Where's that?" I asked.

"Dominica," she replied. "Have you ever been?"

"Once," I said, leaving the autopilot on and turning the helm seat to face the table. "But it was a really long time ago. Russ Livingston and I flew there on leave once. Do you know how Columbus described it to King Ferdinand and Queen Isabella?"

Savannah put a tray of fish tacos on the table, then took a paper napkin, unfolded it completely, then wadded it into a ball and tossed it onto the table.

"That is Dominica," she proclaimed, attempting an Italian male voice, and failing.

The wind buffeted and picked up the napkin, and Savannah dove to catch it.

"What's that even mean?" Alberto asked, reaching for a fish taco.

"Dominica is the top of an underwater mountain," Savannah explained. "It rises straight up out of the ocean and all the deep crinkles in the paper are her steep valleys and mountains. We should go."

I started to turn back toward the helm. "Right now?"

She and Alberto laughed. "Not yet," she replied. "But soon."

"Is this the fish we caught last night?" Alberto asked.

The previous evening, when the tide turned and *Taranis's* stern was closer to the mangroves, I'd managed to coax a nice-sized snook out of hiding with my fly rod.

I bit into one of the tacos and nodded. "Uh-hum, yeah! These are great."

Savannah smiled. "Thank you. And thank Rufus for the seasoning."

With every passing minute, as we talked and ate, *Taranis* carried us farther and farther to the south.

We'd been up since before dawn, getting things ready to run offshore, and hadn't eaten since 0600, so the snook tacos didn't last long.

Jimmy'd had the last midwatch, so we'd let him sleep in, since he rarely ate breakfast.

South of Miami, a couple of hours later, the sun was low in the sky, and the clouds it painted with pastel colors of pink, orange, and red easily beat out the glitzy skyline.

Finally, just before sunset, we cruised past the Cape Florida Lighthouse and entered the calmer waters of Biscayne Bay.

I turned to starboard and swung around the point to a protected anchorage just north of the lighthouse called No Name Harbor. It was a small, natural harbor on the west side of the southern end of Key Biscayne.

We didn't need the safety of the harbor, though. The storm we'd outrun had moved ashore and dissipated over the Everglades. So, we anchored half a mile across Florida Channel from it, in seven feet of water.

Away from most of the noise of civilization, but close enough to reach it in an emergency, we dropped the anchor and started the two generators to charge both the house and dedicated propulsion battery banks. They were fully charged before we finished dinner.

"Care for a beer?" Savannah asked, as we relaxed on the large stern sun pad on the flybridge deck.

"Feet up, anchor down," I replied. "Thanks."

A moment later, she returned from the small galley area on the top deck and sat down beside me, offering a stubby little brown bottle of Red Stripe as we watched the sun dropping lower and lower.

Savannah took a sip of her white wine. "This is an absolutely amazing boat," she said, her voice soft in the last few minutes of daylight. "And today's conditions were the worst I've *ever* been out in."

Savannah used to run a shrimp trawler out of the South Carolina Lowcountry, so I was sure she'd seen some nasty weather.

"Don't forget that tropical storm that formed over *Ambrosia* off the Yucatan," I said. "That was a lot worse."

"And *Ambrosia* was three times as big," she said. "I meant in *Sea Biscuit*. I've seen worse on my daddy's shrimp boats, too."

"*Taranis* took everything the storm threw at her," I said, nodding, then taking a long pull on my beer. "When we're cruising, we'll avoid weather like that."

"Is that what you want?" she asked, looking over the rim of her wineglass at the setting sun. "Stay in the little latitudes and avoid drama, even from the weather?"

"No, not always," I replied. "I spent over four million on her, with one goal in mind. I want us to go all the way around the world—the old school route—in total comfort."

"Around Cape Horn and the Cape of Good Hope?" she asked. "What number is that on your bucket list?"

"Recently added," I replied, patting her bare thigh. "Along with a visit to Antarctica and doing a polar bear plunge."

"You know that means visiting two different places, right? At opposite ends of the earth."

"Remember, I told you a couple of years ago that I wanted to visit Antarctica? It was when I first told you about the idea for this boat build. It's the only continent I haven't been to. And since we'll be there, I might as well knock out one of the two oceans I haven't swam in. Is it swam or swum?"

"It's swum," she replied. "I thought you were just kidding. You, a devout tropical boat bum, want to go to Antarctica and go for a swim?"

"In the summer, of course," I replied with a grin. "Gets to minus one hundred there in winter. What's on the top of your bucket list to visit?"

41

"I want to see Indonesia," she said, as Jimmy came up the steps, Alberto right behind him. "This couple I follow on YouTube lives there and cruises the Indo-Pacific in their sailing trimaran."

"I just got off a video call with Mr. Kennedy and Tank!" Alberto interrupted, jumping up onto the sun pad with his tablet. "Look!"

On the screen was a closeup of our new puppy's face. Tank was a black Labrador Retriever and Tibet mountain dog mix, and he was just about finished with his initial training with Warren Kennedy, a retired Miami-Dade Police lieutenant, who now trained police dogs.

Tank's mother was a police dog—a bomb sniffer—and she and Tank's "stepdad," a big Rottweiler named Diesel, had both been stolen several months earlier, and we'd helped get them back.

"He's so cute," Savannah squealed, as Alberto swiped the screen for a full shot of the two-and-a-half-month-old pup, standing at heel with Warren.

"I can't believe how fast he's growing," I said. "He's already as big as a lot of full-grown dogs."

"Warren said he'd be big," Savannah reminded me.

Tank would be protection-trained starting in the summer, once he was old enough. And bigger. But he would soon be joining us on the island for a break from training as we prepared *Taranis* to cruise the Bahamas for the rest of the winter.

It would be our responsibility to train him for life on an island or on a boat. And several concessions would have to be made aboard *Taranis*, as well. He was part of the reason for the massive shower in the master stateroom. Tibet mountain dogs were heavy shedders and Warren wouldn't know how much Tank would shed but suggested at least a weekly shower. And he would need a "convenience area," as Savannah called it.

I hadn't figured that part out yet, but I did instruct the builder to install macerator pumps on all three shower drains. I just had to pick the one Tank was going to poop in. Or come up with something completely different.

With that very thought in mind, I pointed at the screen. "He's only ten weeks old and already to Warren's knees."

"He said he weighed twenty-two pounds, man," Jimmy said. "At two and a half months!"

Yeah, I thought, *gonna have to come up with something else.*

Alberto looked up, smiling. "And that was six days ago. He gets weighed every Tuesday, so he's probably over twenty-five now."

"Why Tuesday?" I asked.

"That's the day he was born," Alberto explained, looking at the picture. "Tuesday, December fourteenth. Remember? We went up there the next day."

I did remember the trip. And I also remembered it was in the middle of December. But even on a good day, I rarely knew what day of the week it was. It had just become less important over the years.

We'd gone up to Warren's training facility every week since the puppies were born, so we could get to know Tank and work with him in his training, and so he could bond with us. At just five weeks, he was already clumsily fetching a ball.

Molly doted over her puppies the first few visits. And Diesel was the perfect stepdad, following each pup through individual training and showing them what was expected for each command.

Having watched it, I was amazed at how responsive the puppies seemed to be, having Diesel's calm reassurance and example for them to emulate.

There'd been nine pups—four females and five males—eight tri-colored, and one black and white. We'd had the first pick of the litter, with a name already chosen, so we sort of had to pick a male. We only had to find the pup with the right attributes for his name.

The one we'd chosen that day was almost solid black, with four white feet and a patch of white on his chest, shaped kind of like an inverted, five-point star. It was similar in shape and location to where his namesake, Owen "Tank" Tankersly would have worn his Medal of Honor.

When we'd visited last week, Tank's paws were already massive—nearly the size of my closed fist. And most important of all, he had the same webbed toes as his mother.

Labs and other water sporting dogs had skin between their toes, which made them excellent swimmers. Tank's webbing was thick and probably not as efficient as his mother's, but coupled with their size, they'd get the job done.

Labs also had dense underfur, which trapped air when the dog went in the water, making them more buoyant. Warren said that all the pups had Molly's fur and feet.

He'd be a swimmer for sure.

And if the ratio of the size of his webbed feet to his weight remained the same as he got bigger, he'd likely be able to swim long distances.

It seemed the only attributes the pups had gotten from the mountain dog father were their saggy jowls and tricolor markings.

And of course, their immense size.

# CHAPTER FIVE

A beeping sound woke me suddenly from a deep sleep. Savannah and I both sat up in bed and turned toward the source of the sound.

The radar alarm at the helm.

A boat was moving within a half mile of where we were anchored.

I threw off the sheet and rose to my bare feet wearing only skivvies as Savannah got out of bed on her side, wearing an old *Gaspar's Revenge* T-shirt of mine.

We'd decided that a night watch wasn't necessary, due to the redundant systems aboard which would electronically "watch" everything for us and alert us of any danger.

I'd felt safe enough with the helm just a few steps from where Savannah and I slept.

She followed me out to the wheelhouse, where I noted the position of the radar contact on the screen and looked out the port hatch.

I couldn't see anything.

"It's half a mile away and heading toward us," Savannah said, taking a seat at the nav desk. "Moving slowly. Maybe a fisherman lost in the darkness?"

One of the screens on the overhead flickered, then displayed the image from the night optics camera on the flybridge roof.

Savannah turned it toward the west, across the flats, and I could see a center console with a bimini top coming head-on.

Center console boats were very popular with fishermen. With the helm centered in the boat, a fisherman could walk all the way around it while trying to boat a fish.

Coincidentally, the thieves Kim had told me about had used a center console with a bimini top.

I felt the hairs on my neck come to attention.

Savannah looked up at the monitor, trying to zoom in and stabilize the image. "Looks like three people," she said, then looked back down at the radar image. "They're making about four knots in water that's just a couple of feet deep."

"Turn the spotlight toward them," I said. "But don't turn it on yet."

"What are you going to do?"

"I'm not going to let them get within a hundred yards of our boat," I replied. "Use the camera to keep the light on them. I'll run 'em off."

I moved quickly and quietly through the salon, then slid the door open. In seconds, I was on the expansive flybridge and went straight to the helm. Savannah was probably right—odds were that the approaching boat was a lost fisherman. But I wasn't taking chances.

At the helm, I pressed down on both corners of the expansive dash area. The lid popped up slightly, then rose fully as the gas-loaded pistons expanded, driving the lid upward.

Inside was my new Sig Sauer XM7, a Christmas gift from my good friend, Billy Rainwater. I snatched it from its black foam cradle and, even though I knew there was a round in the chamber, pulled back slightly on the charging handle, just enough so the moonlight glinted off the brass of the Fury cartridge. Then I moved over to the port side and toggled the switch to open the large sunroof.

Sig recently got a ten-year contract from the DoD to replace the smaller caliber M4 with their XM7. They also made a civilian version, the MCX, which was chambered for the larger .308 round. The military's XM7, like mine, was chambered for the new Sig Sauer .277 Fury cartridge. Unlike the civilian version, the XM7 could be fired on full automatic.

Having already put over a thousand rounds through the barrel in the last couple of months, I felt that the .277 cartridge, which was equal to seven millimeters, was an excellent mixture of the best of both the standard NATO 5.56 and 7.62 millimeter cartridges.

It had the smaller caliber's muzzle velocity to be able to reach out and touch someone from up to half a mile away, but with greater mass to make them feel it—usually mortally—even wearing body armor.

In my opinion, the XM7 will one day prove to be the most significant upgrade to an individual fire team's lethality since the M1.

I stepped up onto the lounge seat with the rifle, which put my upper body above the rooftop in a comfortable stance with a nearly 360-degree view of the surrounding water. Only the radar arch behind my left shoulder blocked the view.

Though the sunroof had a truly aesthetic and functional purpose, allowing warm sunlight in when it was cold and letting the heat out for the other 359 days of the year, the reason for the design was exactly what I was doing.

I flipped up the covers on the night optic scope and searched through the darkness, easily spotting the approaching boat.

It was about five hundred yards away, and I could see the

silhouettes of the three occupants clearly, standing behind the center console's windshield. They were in the bimini's shadow, cast by a nearly full moon almost directly overhead, so I couldn't make out any facial features.

I stooped and toggled the intercom for the wheelhouse, then stood back up. "Can you hear me okay, Savvy?"

"Yes," she replied over the intercom. "The boat is five hundred and fifty yards away. Still coming straight toward us, but really slow."

"As shallow as those flats are," I said, "they have to go slow with the outboard tilted up. Hit them with the light when they're within three hundred yards and keep the light on them, no matter what they do."

I waited, the night scope's reticles just above the boat's windshield, and my finger alongside the trigger housing.

Suddenly, a narrow beam of light slashed through the darkness, putting two million candlepower right on the approaching boat and overpowering my optics for a second.

When it corrected, I saw the boat turn suddenly and come to a stop. There were no registration numbers on the bow.

"Turn off that light!" a man shouted from the boat. "We are going to board your vessel!"

It definitely wasn't a Coast Guard or Fish and Wildlife boat. It had no markings or emergency lights, and more importantly, it wasn't even running the required navigation lights.

"That's close enough!" I shouted across the intervening water. "Alter your course and move away!"

"I am giving the orders!" the same man shouted, stepping out from under the bimini top into the spotlight, shielding his eyes. "Turn that light off, now!"

I could see him clearly through the night optic scope, which adjusted automatically to the increased light. He wore jeans and a dark T-shirt with some kind of faded logo on the front. His hair was long, hanging past his collar, and he had a scraggly beard—definitely not law enforcement.

And he hadn't identified himself.

But he did have a gun sticking out of his waistband.

I fired a three-round burst on full auto, aiming just below the boat's waterline where the man stood.

He ducked for cover and a second man stepped out, raising a rifle.

"Gun!" Savannah shouted.

I didn't hesitate. The scope's reticles found center mass and I pressed the trigger, putting a bullet through the man's chest.

The boat's engine screamed, shooting a geyser of water up at the stern, as the helmsman attempted to accelerate away.

"Start the main engine, Savvy!" I yelled, as I tracked the boat trying to flee. "And get the anchor up! We're outta here!"

There was one thing we hadn't tested *Taranis's* ability at yet.

I'd noticed that the outboard on the center console was a big one, probably two hundred horses or more, and the boat was small, about twenty feet.

It could outrun us.

At least in the calm waters of Biscayne Bay. Our only option was to get to open water before they could. It's what *Taranis* was designed for.

Even a moderate chop on the outside would force the other boat to slow down. And I already knew *Taranis* could run full speed in even worse conditions.

But first we had to get there.

It was a drag race to the open ocean, and *Taranis's* "hole shot" capability hadn't been tested.

I continued tracking the boat as the anchor came up, and I could hear Jimmy asking what was going on through the intercom.

Savannah quickly explained what was happening and told him to take care of the anchor so she could keep the light on the now-retreating boat.

The beam stayed right on them as I watched the boat continue to move away to the west, toward deeper water.

"Jimmy, bring the ama motors online, *di di mau*," I shouted, as I put the rifle on the settee and dropped down into the captain's seat.

I quickly activated the helm controls. "We're heading outside, then south. I'll drive from up here."

I could see the boat, thanks to Savannah's steady hand on the spotlight control. It reached deeper water and the rooster tail disappeared as the driver lowered the foot of the outboard and their boat began to accelerate.

I was committed now.

I couldn't drive forward and shoot backward at the same time.

Jimmy could take the helm in the wheelhouse, if need be, but I knew that shooting at a moving boat *from* a moving boat was an exercise in futility.

Except I could go full auto and follow the tracers.

After getting one of their men shot, the sane thing to do would be to get the hell out of the area. But instead of retreating, the boat was turning north, following the channel.

"The wing motors are activated, Skipper," Jimmy said over the intercom. "Control switched to the flybridge, and the chain counter's at twenty-five feet."

It would only take a few more seconds for the anchor chain to be retrieved by the powerful drum windlass in the bow. I held my hand on the controls, visualizing what I was about to do.

The boat was on plane, circling around the flats in deeper water, and heading back toward us, hugging the shoreline of the cape.

Just then, I heard the clank of the anchor in the pulpit.

"Hang on!" I shouted, pushing the main engine throttle and both electric motor controls all the way to their stops—a hole shot in drag racing terms.

With the combined thrust from all three motors, *Taranis* lunged forward as giant water bulges erupted at the stern of all three hulls.

She accelerated quickly with almost no bow rise—just launching forward like a rail dragster.

I turned the wheel to starboard, and *Taranis* responded like a sportscar in a hairpin, turning sharply into the channel ahead of the oncoming boat.

When I straightened the wheel, heading due south for the cut, the center console was half a mile behind us, already at top speed, and closing in fast.

I reached over to the chart plotter and turned the AIS off, just in case the smaller boat had it installed.

Savannah turned the roof-mounted spotlight forward, illuminating our escape route as we gathered more speed, quickly reaching thirty knots, then thirty-one.

I looked back just in time to see the muzzle flash from a rifle, followed quickly by a cracking sound as the bullet zipped harmlessly overhead.

The boat was still gaining on us.

Turning slightly to port, we started encountering the small waves that wrapped around the cape.

"Give me full gyro, Jimmy," I shouted.

"Already spooling up!"

Jimmy was a wise man; I'd always known that about him. He preferred nonviolence at any cost and would always look for a way out of an altercation. Even if it meant running from a fight.

He always kept his cool, thinking ahead, especially in a tight spot but that usually had more to do with cooling down an angry fisherman than a barroom brawler.

In this instance, I agreed. I couldn't risk his safety and that of my family, yet I could feel the warrior inside me urging me to slow and pick up the rifle again.

If someone was trying to take something of value from someone else, they should be ready for a fight. They should expect it. But societal norms dictate that we shouldn't resist. Because of that, thieves get bolder. If they expected a fight every time, there would be less crime.

When we hit the first rollers, no more than two or three feet in height, the wave-piercing bows did exactly what they were designed to do, and we continued at *Taranis's* top speed, thundering into the waves, spouting great plumes of sea spray from all three bows.

A moment later, I glanced back to see the boat encountering the first waves just two or three hundred yards behind us. They were coming at a slight angle and, when the boat hit the second one, it came out of the water, rolling to starboard, and was forced to slow down.

There was nothing ahead of us but open water, and *Taranis* charged through the waves like a bull through a cornfield.

After two minutes of heavy pounding, the attacking boat fell far behind, then gave up and turned around.

I continued east until we were two miles offshore, then turned south and slowed.

"Do you still have them on radar?" I shouted, out of habit.

It was very quiet as we dipped into the trough between two waves and once more became a sixteen-ton surfboard.

"Until just now," Savannah replied. "It disappeared into the back scatter inside the bay."

"Is everyone okay?" I asked, taking one last look back.

"We're fine," Savannah replied. "How about you? I heard a shot."

"Missed by a mile," I replied. "I'm fine."

"Are you sure?"

"Yeah," I replied. "Why?"

"Because it's fifty-four degrees outside," she said, and I could hear the mirth in her voice, "you're in your underwear, and you're you."

I suddenly got a shiver. In the heat of battle, I hadn't noticed how cold it had gotten.

After advancing the controls of the electric motors to eighty percent, I shut down the diesel.

"I'll be down in a minute," I said, taking another slow look around at the horizon.

The night was clear, and visibility was excellent. A waxing, nearly full moon was high overhead and there was nothing in sight. The only sound was the slight swish of water at the stern.

Taranis had once more done what she'd been designed to do—bring us safely through the storm. I put one hand on the dash, feeling the warmth she radiated, and smiled.

"Stay where you're at," Savannah said. "We're coming up. I'll bring you some clothes."

A moment later, Jimmy and Alberto appeared. Jimmy took a seat at the lounge to port and Alberto stood at the forward rail looking straight ahead at the sea.

"It was the boat stealers," Alberto said. "That's who they were, right? I heard you on the phone talking to Kim."

I nodded, though he had his back to me. "The two I saw fit the descriptions Kim gave me, as did their boat."

He turned around and came over beside me at the helm, side hugging me. "He didn't give you a choice, Dad."

"You saw?"

"I saw your warning shots. Mom turned off the camera as soon as we saw the man with the rifle. Did you shoot him?"

I bobbed my head again. "I couldn't let him shoot at us."

Alberto nodded back. "He was inside the fence."

It was a saying of my grandfather's that I must have mentioned at some point. Pap always thought fences made good neighbors, but even good neighbors were outside the fence.

Only loved ones were allowed inside.

"Here, put this on," Savannah said, coming across the deck holding out a long-sleeved work shirt.

"Take over, son," I said, as I gratefully accepted the shirt.

Alberto's demeanor changed instantly.

We'd done our best to guard him from some things, often things that I did or was forced to do. We weren't always successful, and it seemed anywhere we went anymore, we encountered something else we needed to shield him from.

Alberto took the helm as I shrugged the shirt on, and Savannah looked down at him in concern.

Alberto was one-hundred-percent focused on what he was doing. It was his first time at *Taranis's* helm, yet he seemed calm and attentive.

But I'd shot a man just fifteen minutes earlier. He'd been a threat to my family, and I'd protected those inside the fence. But how does an eleven-year-old process that?

I had no reference point. When I was his age, my biggest concern was where the fish were biting and how far I could ride my bike or paddle Pap's canoe to get to them.

The man I'd shot wasn't the first, either. And in the same situation a hundred times over, I'd do exactly the same thing every single time.

"Why'd you want to come up here?" I asked Savannah, accepting a pair of black sweatpants with *Marines* written vertically down the left leg.

"Well, I figured we're going to be motoring all night after that," she replied. "And I don't think any of us can sleep right now."

"Are you sure they weren't cops?" Jimmy asked. "Cause they sounded like cops."

"Kim said that two witnesses last November had said the same thing," I replied, slipping a pair of well-worn boat shoes on my feet. "Besides, they weren't running nav lights."

"Then we should report it," Savannah said. "Or no?"

"Stealing big boats takes planning and organization, man," Jimmy offered. "If we report this and the press gets hold." He paused and looked up at me. "Do we really want people like that knowin' anything more about us, man?"

"I vote no," Alberto said, looking up at me. "Just walk away."

I turned and looked ahead as *Taranis* moved silently through the night. The murdered father and son Kim had told me about had probably wanted to just walk away, too.

And what about his wife, daughter, and the tutor?

# CHAPTER

SIX

Savannah and the others stayed with me on the flybridge until well past midnight, then I told everyone to go get some sleep. The adrenaline rush had worn off, and Alberto had been nodding. He was smallish for his age but too big to carry to bed.

Jimmy offered to spell me after a couple of hours, but I declined.

Savannah knew why and didn't question my decision.

A few minutes after they left, she'd reappeared with a Thermos of coffee and my chipped Marine Recon mug. She kissed my cheek, then quietly went down the steps to the cockpit.

I knew the wheelhouse would be more comfortable than the cool night air, but comfort wasn't what I wanted or needed.

It wasn't what I deserved, either.

Savannah and I both knew what would be waiting for me when I finally went to sleep—the demons of my past.

I knew they'd come for me—trying to drag me down to the depths of Hell with them. And now, they'd be one specter stronger.

They'd come when I slept, too afraid these days to meet me in the daylight. I'd long ago accepted this fact. The nightmares used to come a lot more often, and many times, I'd awakened in the darkness in a cold sweat, shaking with fear.

So, when I *knew* they'd be coming, I preferred to wait until daylight to sleep.

It wasn't that I was afraid of the dark; nighttime had always been my friend—protecting me in a way—safe in the embrace of its shadowy cocoon.

Leaping Panther, the father of my oldest friend, Billy Rainwater, had named me Night Crawler on the day of my birth, and in the Corps, that's what I'd become.

It just seemed easier to bounce back to reality in the daylight.

The specters would come when I slept. But *I* would set the place *and time* of the next battle.

With the boat on autopilot and nothing else to do, I switched on the stereo with the volume low, then navigated to Jerry Rice's new *Pirate Sessions V* album on my phone and clicked play.

The first song was upbeat, with a driving acoustic guitar. He sang about fishing and losing his way in a mangrove maze—"Keepin' It Low Key."

Since we were running only on the electric motors, the music from the speakers was the only sound I could hear.

I turned the volume lower, until I could just make out the swish of the bow waves, alternating from one hull to the next as the rollers came up under our stern, lifting the big boat at a slight angle.

Taranis surfed gently down the face of the waves for a moment, then the faster-moving swell would pass beneath us and she'd slide down into the next trough.

It was a little mesmerizing, which was another reason why I chose to stand watch on the flybridge. The song of the ocean was great background music for the soul.

The steady guitar music from the speakers and the quiet lyrics were accompanied by the sound of the waves rippling at the stern and transferring from one hull to the next as each wave overtook us. Then similar sounds reversed as the bows dipped.

Gazing up at the stars ahead, I could easily pick out several constellations and recognized the major stars that made them. I didn't need to look at my watch to tell the time.

When I was a kid, I never wore a watch. We didn't care what time it was, and we knew to head home when the sun was low. The first time I ever had a watch was when I had a kid of my own.

Nor did I need to look at the compass or chart plotter to know our direction. The stars would move across the sky just as the sun and moon did—east to west. Looking south toward the horizon, the paths the stars followed created a small arc if you watched them long enough.

Farther south, Crux—the Southern Cross—pointed toward a black area of the sky that was directly over the South Pole. At night, Crux turned around an imaginary twenty-four-hour clock face, its top pointed accurately to the local time. Lying on its side, with the top to the left, it was 1800, local time, and when it was standing straight up, it was midnight, and lying horizontal to the right, it was 0600.

I sipped my coffee and satisfied myself that nobody I loved had been hurt in the attack, and *Taranis* had gotten us out of a dicey situation before anyone else got hurt.

Leaning back in the helm seat, I ran my hand over the black, destroyer-style wheel, feeling the tiny course corrections the autopilot made.

She felt alive.

I could just as easily have emptied my rifle's magazine at the boat trying to approach us stealthily in the darkness. Then, without a thought for the men aboard, I could have hoisted the anchor and slipped quietly out of the anchorage.

Each of us is personally responsible for our actions, and the path we choose is ours, and ours alone. Most choose a path long before reaching legal adulthood.

The man I'd shot was bringing a rifle to bear. That left no doubt as to the intent of the men on that boat. I felt no remorse. He was a grown-ass man who'd started down his path a long time before he met me. Still, I felt bad. He'd had a mother and father, maybe siblings. For all I knew, he might have had a wife and kids at home. Had I widowed and orphaned a family?

He'd simply had the misfortune of attacking the wrong boat.

It was the one consistent flaw I'd found in every bully's DNA. They never considered that their intended victim might be even scarier than them.

It just never entered their minds, and the more innocent people they preyed upon, the more solid that notion became.

Until they picked on the wrong guy.

Jesse Rice started singing about washing his Jeep, a nostalgic tune called "Sand in My Seat" that brought back more memories of Russ Livingston, my mentor, and the father of my business partner, Deuce Livingston.

Russ used to have a CJ-5 that we'd take to the beach to go fishing, or tool around through the woods for miles around Camp Lejeune, looking for big bass ponds. Not big ponds with bass in them, but any pond or lake with *big* bass.

Jimmy'd been spot on in his assessment of the logistics required to steal not just one, but several yachts. It wasn't like they could be hidden in a container and shipped somewhere.

And they'd *have* to ship them overseas. There was no way a stolen high-end yacht could be operated for very long in U.S. waters. There were just too many people scrutinizing boats to keep one in the States.

Yachts often did travel by cargo ship, though. Normally, it was for delivery to a new owner, but they were almost always carried on deck, above the containers—visible to anyone who looked.

A stolen car, taken to a chop shop, was worth more dismantled and sold as parts than it would be as a whole car. But a yacht was worth far more than the sum of its parts, and I'd never heard of a yacht chop-shop.

Barring that possibility, how could the thieves get an intact, fully-functioning, million-plus-dollar yacht out of the country?

That would be where the logistics of a much larger smuggling operation would come into play, as Jimmy had alluded to. All it would take was some organization or someone with deep pockets, like Jack Armstrong, to buy a cargo ship or two to smuggle stolen yachts out of the country.

I could easily envision a container ship with a "false bottom" where several yachts could be loaded, a framework above them to support a cover of neatly stacked, maybe even empty, cargo containers. A really large container ship could probably carry a half dozen multi-million- dollar vessels, probably worth a lot more than what could be shipped in the containers.

But who ran it? The mob? An international crime syndicate?

The drug cartels had been moving to other crimes more lucrative than drug smuggling—human and animal trafficking. So, maybe it was them, branching out even more.

Whoever it was, they'd have to have a big operation, and that meant lots of muscle.

I reached for my satellite phone. Not the one in the base charger on the dash, but the one I'd stowed in the overhead before *Taranis* was launched.

I started to type a message, then thought better of it, and backspaced out before putting the phone back in the overhead charger.

Did I want to involve myself? My family?

Opening the Thermos, I poured another mug of coffee before standing to look out at the horizon.

The moon had passed its zenith and was now slightly ahead and to starboard, its reflection sparkling by the thousands on the choppy surface of the water.

It was cold and past 0300, so there weren't any lights from any other boats in sight. A quick glance at the subdued red glow of the radar confirmed that nothing was on the surface within eight miles—an hour at our current speed, or half that if another boat was coming toward us at the same speed.

Reaction time to trouble was completely dependent on speed.

Eight knots was about as fast as I wanted to go at night. Things happened with far less urgency when you went slowly. Over the years, I'd found the same to be true for most captains who operated their vessels in a safe manner.

I sat back down at the helm and put my feet up, letting *Taranis* do exactly as I'd designed her to do—quietly gobble up the miles using only the stored energy from yesterday's sun.

Taranis hadn't been the only one performing well under fire. Her crew had responded like a well-oiled machine in the face of the danger the men on the center console posed.

Savannah had aided me in defending ourselves, not only calling out the threat when the rifleman appeared, but also having the presence of mind to shut down the camera feed to the monitor in the wheelhouse's overhead, so Alberto wouldn't see.

It was one thing for a boy to know his dad had hurt someone in defending him, and a whole different thing to see it happen.

I'd gladly meet *that* demon head-on every night so Alberto wouldn't have to, and Savannah knew that.

She'd been in that position herself more than once.

My wife was no wallflower and had risen to possible threats numerous times. She was a whole lot tougher than she looked, and far more capable than most would think. The first time we'd met, she threatened me, and *I'd* taken her seriously.

My long-time chartering first mate had anticipated my commands flawlessly, feeding me information. Though he preferred nonviolence, I knew Jimmy Saunders could be a dangerous man when backed into a corner.

Jimmy was a high school dropout, but when it came to boat knowledge, the backcountry, Florida Bay, the Gulf Stream, or the fish that inhabited the waters anywhere in between, he was unequaled. He had a razor-sharp mind and an almost photographic memory. I knew many people with PhDs who he could run mental circles around.

I also had no doubt that even though he was only eleven, and I hadn't heard him utter a single word during the altercation, Alberto wasn't just standing around being in the way. I knew he'd helped us out of the situation as best he could and remained calm—of that, I was certain.

And then there was the aging warrior on the flybridge. In hindsight, I was always my worst critic—always rethinking what I'd done—trying to see if there'd been any other way. I often second-guessed my decisions afterward, picking them apart at the end of the day, studying each step of a decision to see if there was *anything* I might have done differently.

Especially if there'd been someone hurt or killed.

I'd stopped counting the targets I'd neutralized years ago in Mogadishu, but I knew the number was north of fifty.

That was my burden to carry.

The Somali warlord holding the kid as a shield had been my "boxcar," my twelfth confirmed kill in combat. But there'd been a few others that were unconfirmed, that only a handful of people knew about.

It was what happened after I'd neutralized the boxcar that had altered my perception forever, and I'd stopped keeping score.

I'd been ordered to stand down—to not take the shot.

"Do not engage," were the exact orders I'd received that day.

I took the shot anyway, knowing what the consequences might be.

My patrol had found the kid the next day with his throat slashed. A new warlord had risen to take the place of the man I'd shot from more than half a mile away, and the new chieftain had picked up where the old one had left off.

My decision to press the trigger hadn't changed anything. Not for the kid, anyway.

Two weeks after the shooting, I was put on a transport plane and flown back to the States to stand battalion office hours, or non-judicial punishment, for recklessly discharging my weapon.

Had I been charged with disobeying a lawful order, it would have been a court martial and possible discharge.

I'd been a Marine for over fourteen years when I went to the battalion CO's office; I'd been a gunnery sergeant for a little over three, and was on the short list for promotion to first sergeant. For as long as I could remember, I'd planned on a thirty-year career in the Corps and reaching the top enlisted rank—sergeant major. But that one blemish in my service record book nixed all that.

A couple years after the shooting, I'd been allowed to reenlist one more time. Then, after four years in the same billet, I was quietly retired with a partial pension after twenty years of service.

Unforeseen consequences to reactionary thought....

# CHAPTER SEVEN

The dark waters slipped quietly past *Taranis's* triple hulls. The sea state had calmed, meaning even less noise, and occasionally, I could hear other sounds—the blow of a dolphin or splash of a fish trying to escape a predator.

We continued steadily, inexorably south.

The stars moved across the sky, completely indifferent to anything that happened below. Mankind could destroy itself in a great nuclear war, reducing the entire planet to a smoldering cinder, and the stars wouldn't blink.

Timeless and predictable, as Rusty often said. Unchanged since our early ancestors had first walked upright, they'd be the same long after a million more generations passed.

I was alone with my thoughts.

It seemed that no matter what I did, or where I went, trouble followed. I'd never been one to seek it out; I didn't have to. Trouble always seemed to know right where I was, and as a result, the number of bodies left in my wake seemed to grow with each passing year.

I shivered against the cool night air, which came blowing through the enclosed flybridge through the open middle part of the windshield. The cool air kept me awake and alert.

I'd been conditioned all through my life—as we all are—by those who raised me and the outside world I encountered. But my conditioning was a little different than most. Having been brought up by grandparents rather than parents, I had a different outlook on life.

My grandparents tried to avoid the pitfalls that might be incurred by often taking me places where they were decades older than other kids' parents, knowing that if I had only their morals and values to rely on as I grew older, I'd be far more naïve in modern times.

But enough of their generation's attitudes about the world had rubbed off on me that I'd been old before my time, even in school. After that, the "split-generation Jesse" was molded even further by the Corps, where those old-fashioned morals and values were highly prized and had become the cornerstone of the structure that would be my life.

I knew my weaknesses—some doubled as assets. I was hard-headed but smart. Many times, I could have simply walked away, except my stubborn side sometimes didn't allow me to back down.

Okay, so most of the time.

Several hours earlier, I'd done what I had to do when those men chose to attack and put my family at risk. It really was that simple. At least in my mind. If someone tried to hit me, I'd hit them back. Harder.

Neutralize the threat. By whatever means necessary.

I sipped my coffee and looked over toward southern Biscayne Bay and the mainland, then slightly ahead, where Key Largo's glow filled the night sky far to the southwest. It was still well beyond the horizon, almost twelve miles away. Behind us, the glow of Miami was still there, though not as bright as it'd been two hours earlier.

Glancing at the plotter, I saw that we'd covered nearly forty miles since leaving the anchorage where we'd been attacked. Off to starboard far across the bay was mainland Florida, and to port, the wide-open Atlantic Ocean beckoned. Above were the stars and moon, and below, only water.

The sea was empty. I was alone.

Though the shooting in the Mog had cost me my career and, as it turned out, had made little difference for the kid, I'd do it again. I knew at least that much about myself.

They say the definition of insanity is doing the same thing over and over and expecting a different outcome. If that be the case, I'm insane. If I could go back and do that over, knowing the consequences, I'd still do it, hoping that'd be the time the kid would run.

I do not tolerate bullying of any sort. It flips a switch inside my head that's wired directly to my fists. Often, I react without planning. And in any battle, there was always a plan. Then there were contingency plans, and backup plans A through Z, all based on how the planners thought the enemy might react to each step in the plan.

The trouble was, once first contact was made with enemy forces, all that planning went out the proverbial window anyway.

Especially for the grunt on the front line.

For them, it just came down to staying alive by neutralizing the threat immediately in front of them.

I'd reacted to the cowardly warlord hiding behind an innocent boy in a way that was contrary to the plan. I'd deviated by not following orders, setting into motion a lot of things that couldn't be altered.

The unintended consequence of good intent.

The lingering echo of that single shot had played itself back in my sleep hundreds of times since then. Sometimes even when I was awake.

It wasn't the specter of the warlord that haunted me most. It was the mangled body of the boy I thought I'd saved, lying broken and bloody in the mud.

I'd seen his face at the instant I pressed the trigger, knowing that the warlord would step down eight inches before my bullet arrived.

He'd been a normal-looking kid, though terrified and beaten. He had dark hair and eyes and had probably been around Alberto's age.

After the recoil of the shot, my scope came back into position, and I watched with great satisfaction as the back of the warlord's head exploded in a pink mist of blood and brain matter, just as his foot found the next step.

That was my job. It's what I did.

I often thought about how my life might have been different had I chosen another path—one of nonviolence, like Jimmy followed.

Personally, I could take the abuse from any tyrant and my ego wouldn't suffer. But I drew a line in the sand where innocent people were concerned, and it was made with a Marine NCO saber when someone I cared for was involved.

The fastest way to the ER would be to threaten someone I cared for, and the second fastest way would be to threaten any innocent person in my presence.

And that'd only be a millisecond slower reaction time.

I knew this about myself. And I also knew it was something I had no control over. I disliked those who would hurt innocent people with a passion most wouldn't understand. Maybe it was just that I *refused* to put up with it—I took action.

A light on the radar screen began to blink and the unit started emitting a soft, beeping sound.

I stood and studied the echo for a moment, then retrieved the night-vision binoculars from the overhead.

Sweeping the glasses slowly along the horizon in the direction the radar echo indicated, I saw the reason for the return.

The lights of a ship could be seen, headed east, riding the Gulf Stream for added speed. It was at least five miles away and already across our bow, so it posed no threat.

I silenced the radar alarm and sat back down.

On the other hand, I posed a serious threat to those who would do harm. I knew that and accepted it as both a flaw *and* an asset. While I couldn't always control it, I could at least direct it.

My friend Rusty had told me long ago that it was always wise to carry a gun when on the water, and I took his advice to heart.

Taranis had multiple hiding spots for weapons, though currently there was only the rifle and two handguns aboard. There are those who don't like being around guns, and that's okay. But in my mind, I would much prefer to be judged by twelve than carried by six.

I was very proficient with them, and Savannah could handle a rifle or pistol with sureness of purpose. Alberto respected firearms and was getting better.

At his age, I'd already bagged my first buck, hunting with Billy and his dad. We'd dressed the deer ourselves and given most of the meat to his people to distribute among the poorest.

As we reached the next pre-programmed waypoint, three miles off of North Key Largo, the autopilot turned *Taranis* more westerly toward the last one, twenty-five nautical miles west-southwest—just off Rodriguez Key.

We'd be there in two-and-a-half hours.

"Slow is smooth," I whispered to my old friend, the darkness. "And smooth is—"

There was a click from the chart plotter and the screen went blank.

I tried to reboot, but it was toast, and finding the right breaker in the dark would be more trouble than necessary, so I turned on the backup plotter.

I'd expected there to be quite a few more bugs and mishaps during this last shakedown, but so far this had been the only glitch. And it was something I could address later, in daylight. On any boat, things stop working, and it's up to the captain to be mechanic, rigger, plumber, and electrician.

For nearly every system on *Taranis*, there were redundancies. If the main engine failed, the electric motors could get us home, or vice versa.

In the case of navigation equipment failure, we had quite a few backup systems to figure out where we were and where we were going.

There were two more chart plotters down in the wheelhouse, another in the master stateroom, as well as several laptops that could be plugged into various communication ports throughout the boat, and, in a pinch, Navionics on a cell phone was often better in small, out-of-the way places.

I'd even learned to navigate fairly accurately using only a sextant, knot-meter, and clock. If all else failed, and I had only a compass and a clock, I could still find my position within fifty miles, simply by aligning sunrise and sunset angles and times, and finding the corresponding location in a nautical almanac.

The backup chart plotter came on and the brightness was instantly reduced for night ops. The AIS was on by default. Before I turned it off, I touched the icon for the ship ahead, now off to port, and brought up the ship's automated information. It was a tanker out of Galveston, steaming at twelve knots, bound for a terminal in Chesapeake Bay.

I switched off the AIS and we were once more invisible to the outside world.

Taranis rode silently onward, oblivious to the passage of time, her speed, and what stars could be seen. Through StarLink and AIS, she was connected to the world and could navigate autonomously to an end point thousands of miles away with great accuracy and efficiency, by using predicted winds, waves, and currents in navigation and, given certain parameters to avoid, could automatically navigate around storms.

I scrolled through the systems display beneath the right-hand plotter to the dedicated battery system for the electric motors. They were still above fifty-five percent but would soon automatically activate the larger of the two generators.

I clicked the override button, knowing that we'd make Rodriguez Key with power to spare. I didn't want to wake the others.

Once there, I knew I could drop the anchor by myself an hour before sunrise, and have the boat secure by daylight. Even in winter, there was always a boat or two anchored on the lee side of the island and there was a decent restaurant on "Useless One," just a short dinghy ride from the anchorage.

I'd try to convince Savannah to take Jimmy and Alberto to breakfast while I rested for a few hours. We could still make the last fifty miles or so to our island in the Content Keys before sunset, even if we didn't get underway until noon.

Two hours later, we reached the waypoint just south of Rodriguez Key and I turned off the autopilot.

The moon was halfway down to the western horizon and provided enough light to make out the four boats in the anchorage.

I steered wide, and with the moon at my back, came up behind and between two large sloops that were a good three hundred feet apart. I reduced the power to the ama motors to just twenty percent and slowly, quietly, crept between the two sailboats.

I could hear nothing, not even a ripple at the bows, as they knifed cleanly through the water. I watched the depth finder, knowing it was a sandy bottom that rose steadily but only slightly. The flats surrounding the island dropped to waist deep just a few yards from shore, so I knew we could get close.

Taranis crept past the two sloops, headed toward even shallower water closer to the island. This was what she was made to do.

The first time Savannah and Alberto saw *Taranis*, she was on the hard, resting on blocks at the boatyard where she'd been built. The blocks under the main hull were only a foot in height and at the time, the waterline boot stripe on the hulls was at neck level, about five feet above the factory floor, giving her a designed draft of four feet. The first time she'd been splashed, with just lunch and fifty gallons of fuel aboard, the whole boot stripe, which was three inches wide, was clear of the water and Hank had promised that fully provisioned and fueled, the top of it would still be dry. I looked forward to loading her up and finding out.

That meant with a foot of water under her keel, I'd be able to stand on the bottom by the sugar scoops. This opened up a lot of gunkholing possibilities for us—getting into many places other blue water vessels couldn't.

In some places, we'd be able to beach her at close to high tide, step off the stern onto sand for a thorough hull cleaning, then ride her out on the next tide. In the old days, careening was what ship captains did, so the hull could be cleaned or repaired. But since those ships would "lay down" on one side, they could only work on one side of the hull per tide.

With just two feet under the main hull's keel, I reversed the electric motors and brought *Taranis* to a stop about fifty feet from shore, then toggled the anchor windlass and allowed the chain counter to reach ten feet before stopping it. The clatter of the chain over the rollers seemed quite loud to my ears.

As a light, easterly breeze slowly pushed *Taranis* backward, straightening the ground tackle, I slowly let out fifty more feet of rode. After I stopped the drum and locked the chain in place with a clamp, I looked around.

There was one other boat, anchored farther to the east. None of the three seemed to be lit inside, but all four had anchor lights at the tops of their masts.

I reversed the electric motors, backing down on the anchor at fifty percent power. There was no clunk of a transmission changing gears—just the quiet whir of the motors running in the opposite direction.

All done without having to leave the helm seat.

I stood and checked our position, then switched the electric motors to offline. *Taranis* sat a good hundred yards ahead of the two sloops and was centered between them, well beyond the swing of any of our boats' anchor rodes, should the wind direction change, which it wasn't forecasted to do. If the wind direction *did* change, I might have to move the boat. But that change would have to be greater than ninety degrees to what it was, and there was zero chance of that. It's why they're called Trade Winds. Early mariners, aboard ships that could mostly only sail downwind, followed the consistent easterly winds of the lower latitudes to reach the New World.

In the light breeze, and with no change in the conditions for several days, a bridle wouldn't be needed. The weight of the chain hung straight down from the pulpit, and that alone would hold us in place. A stiffening morning wind might put a slight curve to the chain, but not enough to pull the rode taut.

Besides, I was only planning to stay a few hours.

If the two boats were still there when we got ready to leave, I knew we could just raise the anchor, turn *Taranis* around completely inside her own length, and go out the way we came in.

Single-handing the boat had been a top priority in every facet of *Taranis's* design and build. I wanted to know that either Savannah or I could not only drive and anchor the boat, but even dock it without waking the other.

With joystick docking controls handling both of the ama motors, as well as the bow and stern thrusters in the main hull, bringing her into a tight marina would be easy, even with a strong current. She could be moved forward, backward, sideways, or at any angle using the joystick.

Hank had even boasted that with very little practice, I'd be able to move the boat in a figure 8, with the bow always pointed in the same direction, or even constantly outboard, spinning her around at the crossing of the 8.

I couldn't foresee the need for that maneuver, but it was nice to know *Taranis* had that kind of operability.

So, anchoring at night, in shallow, open water, was mere child's play.

I rose and used the night-vision binos to look slowly around, taking everything in. The boats in the anchorage all had mast lights on, and two had dim red lights glowing from inside, invisible to the naked eye.

The island itself was a rookery for dozens of bird species and was otherwise uninhabited. Up in the mangrove branches, I could see dozens of wading birds—herons, ibises, cranes, as well as a few pelicans and cormorants. Some moved from branch to branch, squawking as they started to wake up before the dawn.

Hundreds of smaller birds took shelter in the dense growth that covered the island's interior, and their "dawn chorus" was almost a cacophony of sound.

The anchorage was a favorite for birders, kayakers, and flats guides, due to being surrounded by expansive, shallow water that was as clear as it gets. It was a short paddle, only a mile from Silver Shore's pier, and a short walk from there to the highway, so it made for easy access.

Out on the Gulf Stream, the ship we'd passed earlier was far over the horizon, and nothing else could be seen out there. And to the north, the bridges and causeways of the Overseas Highway were mostly visible from Key Largo to Tavernier, the glow of the two cities causing the optics to darken.

A few vehicles moved on the highway, mostly trucks. The Keys depended on US-1 for just about everything, and most truckers I'd met hated coming down to the small islands, with their narrow roads and bridges. Especially during daylight hours, when traffic clogged everything. So, they drove at night.

We were safely at anchor, so I put the binos down and adjusted the radar alert to activate only if a vessel was moving and within two nautical miles, not including the quadrant toward the north, where trucks on the highway might set it off.

Then I poured another mug of coffee and sat back to wait for the dawn of a new day as I gazed out at the dim shapes of islands and boats around us.

Everything was secure, and I felt safe in the embrace of the darkness, with only the light from the moon and stars. And I felt reassured, knowing the Sig was right there.

I opened the dash again and retrieved my cleaning case, then settled myself at the table to field strip and clean my new rifle.

I didn't want music or company.

CHAPTER EIGHT

By the light of the moon and stars, I began to disassemble my rifle. Each part came away by muscle memory, was cleaned and oiled, then placed in the case under the dash for reassembly.

I worked quietly in the darkness, my hands on autopilot as I methodically cleaned each piece, knowing the job was done right by the feel of the metal parts on my fingertips.

Light was overrated. The moon provided more than enough for me to see what I needed to, and my fingers could feel what my eyes couldn't see, relaying the same signals to my brain, seeing each part by touch.

It wasn't the first time I'd cleaned a weapon in the dark.

When they came, I'd be ready.

Once finished, I put the rifle away and got down on my hands and knees to find the brass from the shots I'd fired. One had rolled down into a crack near the bottom of the low windshield, and finding it took a few minutes.

Then I moved aft and got comfortable on the sun pad to watch the night sky. The moon was behind us, halfway down to the western horizon, creating a V-shaped reflection of light from the tiny ripples in the water.

It was zero dark thirty, and I sat alone in the open aft section of the flybridge, looking at the multitude of stars over the southern horizon.

Millions of them spread across the night sky in a band, slightly east of directly overhead. The veil became fainter to the north, past the highway, and disappeared over the horizon. This wispy, almost invisible band of stars was actually the center of our own galaxy, the Milky Way, viewed from our sun's position far from the center, like looking at the spokes of a bike wheel from the perspective of the air valve stem's cap.

Knowing that our galaxy was just one of thousands of others, maybe millions, all swirling like pinwheels through the vast nothingness of space always made me feel very small and insignificant.

For one thing, you were looking back in time when you stared up at the stars. Some think light is instantaneous— you flip a switch and there it is. However, it moves through the vast vacuum of space at a known rate—186,000 miles per *second*. Still, it takes more than a second for the reflected light of the moon to reach our eyes and eight minutes for light from the sun to reach us here on Earth. The light from the nearest star, other than our sun, takes more than four years to reach us, and the most distant object we can see with our eyes, the Andromeda galaxy, is so far away, what we see happened two-and-a-half million years ago.

At 186,000 miles per second, that's a *long* way.

Everything we see in the night sky has already happened.

The early morning air was cool but not too cold. A light, steady breeze had been blowing out of the east since I'd dropped the hook, keeping the bugs at bay. On the wind, I could detect faint aromas mixed with the natural smell of the sea. Who knew? Maybe there were scents from some kitchen in the Eastern Caribbean being carried all the way to the Keys.

Or maybe even from a cookfire on a beach in Africa. Our Earth was so small. So fragile.

For the most part, only silence reached my ears, and I was quickly becoming a fan of it. The previous few days, operating *Taranis* from both the wheelhouse and the flybridge, I'd gained a new appreciation for all things quiet.

Without background noise, my brain could focus more clearly.

A loose halyard on one of the sloops lightly slapped a mast. Even if someone just turned over in their sleep, which would cause no noticeable movement of the hull, but sixty or seventy feet up, the masthead might move several inches to a foot. One or two more clicks on the winch would have prevented the slap.

There were occasional engine sounds from the road, but for the most part, the night was absolutely still.

After about an hour, more bird sounds began emanating from Rodriguez Key, becoming more pronounced as the rookery started to awaken. Faint cries from blue herons, sounding somewhat like small dogs barking, became throatier as others called back. Brown pelicans began to rustle and cry out.

With the first gray sliver of dawn, I moved to the helm seat to watch the sun come up. A moment later, lights came on through two deck hatches in the middle part of the starboard ama as a single rectangle of light from the porthole shone on the water.

Then another light came on, this time from the hatch over the shower stall in my and Savannah's head. The small vent hatch started to open automatically—it was wired to the light switch to allow steam to escape whenever the light in the shower was turned on.

Savannah was awake.

I heard the sliding hatch to the cockpit open and close and a moment later, Jimmy came up the steps and walked quietly across the flybridge deck in bare feet to stand beside me. He looked around, as if searching for something.

The rifle was in its place and all the brass had been policed.

"You're up early," I said, nodding toward the second seat.

"And you're up late, *hermano*." He sat down and looked back at the two sloops. "What time'd we get here?"

"A little over an hour ago," I replied. "She's a breeze to anchor solo."

The sound of the shower's rain head could be heard coming up through the open hatch.

"I don't want you to take this the wrong way," Jimmy began, then paused. I waited quietly while he organized his thoughts. "It's about last night, man."

I started to point out the obvious danger we'd been in, but he held up a hand as soon as I drew a breath and opened my mouth.

"No, man. It ain't what you think." Jimmy lowered his head, pulling his hair back over his scalp. He blew out a long breath. "I heard about what happened to that father and son," he finally continued without looking up at me. "And I can imagine what happened to the women."

I stared down at Jimmy's bowed head. The fate of the three women taken from their yacht was one worse than death, though that *would* be the end result, and much sooner than would come naturally. I wasn't going to let that happen to my family.

Jimmy knew this as well as I did.

Ask anyone when slavery ended in the United States, and some might recall the Emancipation Proclamation of 1863. A few might even remember it was on January 1st of that year.

But they'd all be wrong.

Slavery was alive and well in America today. Human trafficking had, in recent years, become one of the most lucrative forms of smuggling in the world. Hundreds of people are trafficked around the country and across America's borders daily, inhumanely confined in a truck or container, sometimes for days. Many are forced to work under horrible conditions to pay for what they thought would be a dream life in America.

Every year, more than 15,000 young women, girls, even boys, disappeared from the streets of America's cities and were sold into the sex slave business.

Finally, Jimmy raised his head and, as his eyes met mine, I could see the torment he felt.

"You shoulda lit them fuckers up, man," Jimmy said very quietly, but with great conviction. His eyes trailed off sadly to the west, toward Matecumbe Key, twenty miles away. "That's all I'm ever gonna say about it, man. Ya shoulda killed 'em all."

He rose then, and without saying anything more, shuffled barefoot toward the ladderwell.

I hadn't expected that kind of reaction. Not from Jimmy.

To think that laid-back, easy-going Jimmy Saunders would ever wish harm on someone was practically a foreign concept. He'd fight if cornered, but only to the degree we had the previous night—enough to open an avenue of escape.

Nothing more.

Maybe Jimmy wasn't the pacifist everyone thought he was—as *I* thought he was for many years.

Or maybe, like a valve on a teapot, his frustration at what he saw had reached its limit and he had to blow off steam.

Light spilled out onto the water from the galley portholes below, creating long patches of light on the still waters between the main hull and the port ama.

The shower was still running, so I figured it was Jimmy, getting ready for the day.

I waited a bit longer, not really ready to talk to anyone. Then, the sound of the shower stopped, the light in the shower stall went off and the little vent closed.

One of the generators came on, and when I glanced at the data display, I saw it was the dedicated system for the electric motors' batteries.

Jimmy had turned off the override to recharge them. It wasn't necessary, since by the time we got underway, the solar panels would likely top off the batteries, or we could just run the main engine and be home in a matter of hours, all batteries fully charged.

Finally, when I heard low voices from below, I rose and went aft to the stairs. When I slid the door open, warm air spilled out into the cockpit, and Savannah turned to me and smiled. Her eyes told me it was a ruse.

"I don't think I've ever slept more comfortably while underway," she said, and I knew she was lying. "I fell asleep watching Biscayne Bay go by in the moonlight. Did you get any rest?"

She knew I hadn't. And I knew she hadn't. But we each had a job to do and right now, hers was to feel me out about what'd happened, and be my rock, as always.

I gave her my best smile. "Rest, yeah," I replied, as Jimmy handed me a cup of coffee. "I stayed awake though, just in case something was floating in the water."

"So, you plan to stay up then?"

I'd sat bolt upright in bed on a few occasions over the years. She knew the reason for my nightmares and had always tried to protect me from them.

"I'll get a nap," I said. "Maybe you and Jimmy can take Alberto over to Harriette's Restaurant for break—"

A sizzling sound rose from the stovetop as Jimmy turned and dumped a whole package of bacon into a hot skillet.

"Eat something," Savannah said, taking my arm and leading me toward the bow. "I'll bring it to you in seven minutes—enough time for you to shower and get ready for bed. Jimmy and I have decided to spend the morning here."

"S'posed to be sunny all morning, *mi capitan*," Jimmy said, turning and smiling. "I was hopin' you might give us some time off to catch some rays."

Time off to catch rays?

Jimmy had a master poker face. But he'd let it slip just a moment earlier on the flybridge, revealing a darker side.

"That's it?" Alberto asked, coming up from the port companionway and looking over the settee. "We're not gonna do anything all morning?"

"*Exactamundo, hombrecito!*" Jimmy replied quite exuberantly. "At least for a few hours, so your dad can sleep." He paused, pulling a pair of sunglasses from his shirt pocket. "It's gonna be a Costa kinda day in February, man!"

"Go," Savannah said, pushing me toward the hatch to our stateroom behind the helm seat. "The shower's perfect."

Reluctantly, I went in, then down the steps to the head. I knew what Jimmy was doing, and I knew what Savannah was doing, as well.

For Alberto's sake, Jimmy was pretending that nothing of great consequence had happened the previous night. And he was hiding what I knew he truly felt about it.

Savannah was trying to stay close to protect me from what might come in my sleep.

Turning aft at the bottom of the steps, I went to the dresser and pulled out a clean pair of skivvies and some gray cargo pants, then went forward, stripping off sweatpants and shirt as I went.

The water from the rain head was instantly hot and felt good pouring down on my head and shoulders. I showered quickly and in seven minutes, I was pulling on a bright red Rusty Anchor T-shirt made of a stretchy wicking material.

Savannah was just coming into our stateroom with a tray as I came up from the head.

"Jimmy and Alberto are eating out in the cockpit," she announced.

I looked at her questioningly.

"Then Alberto said they were going to do some fishing from the 'back porch.'" She smiled. "Isn't that cute? The back porch. I'm still a little tuckered, so after we eat, I thought I'd skip the sunbathing and take a nap with you."

"You don't have to do this, Savvy," I said. "I'll be fine after forty winks."

Her smile started to fade, but only for a second. "I have enough here for both of us."

She placed the tray in the middle of the bed and went around it, climbing onto her side and sitting cross-legged.

"Come on," she said. "I'm starved."

 # CHAPTER
NINE

I woke with a start, sitting bolt upright when Savannah's hand touched my shoulder and called my name, as if for a second time.

"You were sleeping so deeply," she whispered, propped on one elbow beside me. "Are you okay?"

I blinked my eyes, feeling alert and fully refreshed.

Through the wide porthole, which ran the length of the exterior bulkhead, the tip of Rodriguez Key was visible, surrounded by turquoise water and golden sandbars.

Birds of all kinds hopped from branch to branch in the trees and the sky above them was a shade of blue that left no doubt as to the drop in humidity. There wasn't a whisper of a cloud.

"You were right," I said, looking over at Savannah. "The shower and bed *are* perfect."

"You...uh..."

"No dreams," I replied, honestly. "What time is it?"

"That's good, then," she said, relief in her voice as she sat up beside me in bed. "It's almost lunch time."

"Want to do it while underway at high speed?"

She cocked her head, seductively pushing a strand of hair back. "Do what, Jesse?"

"Lunch," I replied. "Jimmy can help me get underway."

"You just ate before bed," she said, swinging her long, tan legs off the bed and standing. "But I know what Alberto will want."

I grinned. "Fried baloney and cheese on toast."

"Why'd you ever make that for him?"

"Wasn't me," I protested. "Jamie over at the Spoon was responsible for that."

The Wooden Spoon was a breakfast and lunch restaurant in Marathon that catered to locals, opening well before sunrise, and staying open just long enough to serve lunch and clean up.

I'd stopped there with Alberto a couple of months ago, and Jamie's fried baloney and cheese sandwich had hooked him. He'd even insisted we needed to stock up and get her "recipe."

"What do you have in mind?" Savannah asked, looking at the small chart plotter in a console by her side of the bed.

"Cutting inside," I replied. "At full speed, we only need a little over three feet of water."

She spun around, her eyes going wide. "You want to drive your new four-*million*-dollar yacht through Florida Bay? Are you insane?"

"*Our* yacht," I corrected her, pulling my T-shirt back on. "And yes, it's been said by a few that I'm not quite right. Not many trawlers can do it, and *Taranis is* a trawler. Besides, Jimmy knows those backwaters as well as anyone. It's only ten miles of flats—we'll be in deep water in twenty minutes. I've done it on the *Revenge.*"

"*Gaspar's Revenge* only needs about two feet at speed," she retorted. "And this boat weighs a whole lot more."

"Not by much when empty," I argued. "And *Taranis* is barely stocked for a weekend."

We left our stateroom and went aft through the salon and galley, where we found Jimmy and Alberto out in the cockpit playing chess.

"Who's winning?" I asked.

"I think I got him this time," Jimmy replied, studying the board as he hunched over the table like a gargoyle.

Alberto moved his queen, unobstructed from all the way across the board, taking Jimmy's queen's knight, which was sitting on the back row, probably unmoved.

"Checkmate."

Jimmy's mouth fell open as he looked over at Alberto. "Wait. What? How? I had you in two more moves, man!"

"You have to play at least four counter moves ahead with him," I offered. "I want to get underway and have lunch on the flybridge."

"Good idea," Alberto said, putting the pieces away in the box. "I'm hungry and it's going to be dark when we get home now."

"Nope," I replied, heading for the ladder. "We'll be home in less than three hours."

"Your father's nuts," Savannah declared.

"What's the plan, skipper?" Jimmy asked, raising an eyebrow.

"We're taking *Taranis* through Snake Creek to Florida Bay," I replied, lifting my right foot to the first step. "Once we clear the bridge, I'll need you on the pulpit for about ten miles or so, getting across the flats on the step."

Taranis didn't have a planing hull, per se. The amas were rounded on the bottom to ease hull slap and the main hull had chines starting about a third back from the wave-piercing bow.

At speed, she was more of a semi-displacement hull with outriggers, as the flatter bottom of the main hull helped lift the whole boat.

I went up to the next step and paused. "There is one thing we haven't tested yet."

"What?" Alberto asked.

I continued up the steps and called back, "If we can make and serve fried baloney and cheese sandwiches at twenty knots."

I didn't know why I was in a hurry, but I was. Some preeminent feeling of doom, maybe. But from what, I couldn't tell. I just wanted to get back to my little island oasis as soon as possible.

And I had the means to do it.

Sitting down in the captain's chair, I brought the systems online, turned on our AIS, and started the main engine.

"Whatta ya need me to do?" Jimmy asked.

"Nothing, really," I replied, activating the big drum windlass in the pulpit. "To hear Hank tell it, *Taranis* can be single-handed with one hand tied behind your back. But double-check the bridge height for me."

"No need," he replied. "It hasn't changed since it was built in '81. Still twenty-seven feet, man."

"With the VHF antennas up, our air draft is thirty," I said. "But only twenty-four with them down."

"It's a rising tide," Jimmy said. "Be full in less than an hour, and it's a low high, so maybe a few inches under twenty-seven. Want me to get those antennas?"

"They're electric," I replied, as the anchor came up and seated itself in the pulpit. "We'll drop them when we enter the creek."

I turned the knob clockwise on the joystick and held it there. The helm responded, using bow and stern thrusters, as well as the ama motors, all in opposing directions, to turn *Taranis* completely around while staying in place.

I released the joystick and moved the ama motor controls to fifteen percent, and we started moving toward the gap between the two sloops, which I could now see were an older Morgan and a newer-looking Beneteau, both about forty feet in length.

The crew of the Beneteau was in the cockpit and all four of them stepped out onto the side deck for a better view as *Taranis* moved silently between the two boats.

Jimmy and I waved nonchalantly at the gape-mouthed crew as I turned toward open water and pushed the main engine throttle up to cruising speed, and the electric motors to an equivalent thrust.

More for the sudden acceleration than need. Like doing a burnout when another hotrod was beside you at a light.

Taranis lunged forward in what I was starting to think of as the ultimate change from displacement to semi-displacement hull—flat and level with barely any bow rise at all.

We reached *Taranis's* most economical cruising speed—twenty knots—and I took the electric motors offline, then bumped the main engine throttle up a little to 2,000 rpm.

"What's the hurry?" Jimmy asked, raising his voice above the wind.

I glanced over at him as I turned due west about a mile offshore.

"I don't know," I replied. "I just feel like I gotta get home."

With the gyro at fifty percent, and the three bows slicing cleanly through the small waves, we made it to Snake Creek in under half an hour. I slowed and turned toward the bridge, then toggled the switch to lower the radio masts.

Jimmy went to the back of the flybridge deck and stood on the sun pad to look over the roof.

"They're both down all the way," he reported. "Are you sure that radar is only twenty-four feet, man?"

"We designed *Taranis* with this bridge in mind," I replied. "As well as a few others just like it. The radar arch can also be lowered, and with *that* down, the air draft is only twenty feet."

I glanced back and nodded toward the sun pad. "Ever wonder why the roof doesn't go all the way aft?"

He turned around for a moment. "It's a sun area," he said with a shrug. "But yeah, a longer roof would give you room for more solar panels."

"The whole top can be lowered back and down four feet, leaving the helm exposed in the front." I reached over the long dash and put a hand on top of the low windshield. "This becomes the highest point of the boat."

"Seriously, dude?" Jimmy asked, looking around at the roof stanchions.

Savannah and Alberto came up the steps, carrying lunch.

"Cooking while we were moving wasn't difficult," she said, placing a tray on the settee. "It was a pretty smooth ride down there. But getting it up here might've been a problem. I'm glad you slowed down when you did."

"I was just explaining to Jimmy about the roof," I said, reaching around her and grabbing a sandwich.

"What about it?" she asked.

"It goes all the way down," Alberto replied. "It'll look like a Romulan warbird with the top sealed closed."

"A Romu... What in the world is that?"

"Star Trek, *chica*," Jimmy replied, hawking his arms out like a giant bird of prey. "Romulans are an alien race who like to fight."

"Why would the top need to go down?" Savannah asked, putting a bottle of water in a holder for me.

I bit into the sandwich, chewed, and swallowed. "Some of those bridges in Europe are fixed. At sixteen feet, we can get under a lot of them."

Savannah smiled. "But at thirty feet wide, can she fit between them?"

"That will limit us more than air draft," I replied. "But I think the ride makes for a good tradeoff."

Jimmy looked over, then at the windshield. "Wouldn't your head be higher?"

I nodded. "But I can duck."

"Europe?" Savannah asked, sitting down next to me. "I thought you wanted to go to the South Pacific."

"There, too," I replied, slowing further as we approached the bridge.

Jimmy turned on the monitor for the camera mounted on top of the radar arch. "Plenty of clearance," he said. "Nothing hanging down that I can see."

As we passed under the bridge, the air pressure changed, and the noise of cars above us seemed only inches away.

When we came out the other side, I bumped the speed up slightly, staying in the middle of the channel.

The radio in the overhead crackled, and I glanced up. It was on scan, searching all channels, and had stopped on channel nine.

"Beautiful multihull, Captain," a voice said. "Have a pleasant trip."

I looked back and could see the bridge tender at an open window on the upper level of the small house. He waved.

I took the mic from its holder and keyed it. "Thank you kindly," I replied. "Hope you have zero excitement today, sir."

I put the mic back and turned to Jimmy. "I'll need you on the bow in a few minutes. There's mostly five feet of water, here to home—two feet under the keel—but keep an eye out for sandbars and trap floats for me."

"On my way," he replied, taking the last bite of a sandwich and grabbing another to take with him.

A moment later, he appeared on the foredeck and moved all the way out to the pulpit forty feet away, munching on his sandwich.

Though I was higher and would have a more commanding view, his being lower allowed him to "read" the water differently, determining from the ripples where it got shallower. With Jimmy's sharp eyes farther forward, standing just a few feet above the water, he could also see anything sticking above the surface better, like a partially submerged tree branch snagged on the bottom.

Alberto joined us at the helm and switched on the forward scanning sonar. "Better to have it and not need it."

Savannah laughed. "Is there anything this boat *doesn't* have?"

I grinned over at her. "Well, like I said, we're still working on the escape pod."

I stood and yelled down to the pulpit. "Point at anything you see, Jimmy and which way I should go to avoid it."

"You takin' a rhumb line then?" he shouted back.

"Two-six-zero," I yelled, as I slowly accelerated across Lignumvitae Basin. "Straight for Harbor Key Light!"

I remained standing, wondering just how observant the other two men on that center console had been.

And how vindictive they might be.

CHAPTER
TEN

Taranis reached eighteen knots quickly, rising half a foot higher as the hull design lifted her, reducing the amount of surface area in contact with the water. I felt a surge in speed as drag decreased and I throttled back to hold her at twenty knots.

I kept one eye on Jimmy and one on the digital depth gauge on the dash, which bounced erratically from 1.9 to 3.2 feet, mostly hovering around two-and-a-half.

That indicated how far the bottom was below the keel, not the actual depth of the water, and the lowest point of the keel was still three feet below the surface. That meant it was shallow enough that I could stand flat-footed on the bottom, and not get my chin wet.

We flew across the shallows like a pelican riding a pressure wave over the surf. The exhaust sound from the big diesel far below us in the encapsulated mechanical room was barely audible. Loping along at a conservative speed, the sound of the water, now a third of the way back from all three wave-piercing bows, was louder than the exhaust.

If I pushed it to twenty-five knots, the main hull would lift the boat a couple of inches higher still, further reducing drag on the hull. But a sudden stop at twenty-five knots was a lot more serious than at twenty.

After a few minutes, Jimmy pointed straight ahead with one hand and extended his left arm straight out to port, letting me know which way to steer to get around whatever he saw ahead.

I turned the wheel slightly, and his pointing arm started to move to starboard as we avoided the obstacle. I couldn't see it, but I had complete trust in Jimmy.

He dropped his right hand and brought his left up, bent at the elbow, as if giving a hand signal for a right turn in a car—clear to resume course.

I turned the wheel back to starboard slightly, until the compass pointed to 260 degrees again.

We encountered several more obstacles, mostly trap floats, and when the depth gauge showed eight feet under the keel, Jimmy turned and gave an umpire's "safe" signal before heading aft to return to the flybridge.

"Whoa, man!" he exclaimed, as he came hurrying up the steps from the cockpit. "What a rush! That big diesel's so quiet and the water so calm, I could barely even hear the bow waves, man. It was like flying in a glider!"

"Can I go up there?" Alberto asked.

"Not alone, son," I replied.

"I'll be Rose, if you want to be my Jack," Savannah said, smiling down at Alberto.

"Who are they?"

"They're from a chick flick from a million years ago," I told him with a wink. I turned to Savannah. "On tether, portal to portal. Both of you."

"Come on," she said, taking Alberto's hand and leading him aft toward the ladderwell. "The harnesses are just inside the wheelhouse."

Knowing it would take them several minutes, I took my phone out and found Kim's text from before, then handed it to Jimmy.

"Ask Kim if she's heard anything more," I instructed. "But don't say anything about last night."

Jimmy typed with his thumbs on the small screen, far faster than I could with all ten digits on a keyboard. Then he paused and looked over at me. "Sent. Why do you want to know, man?"

I glanced over quickly. "Just curious."

"Yeah, right," he said, "When you get curious, people have a habit of gettin' dead, man."

My phone blew a boat horn sound in his hand, indicating an incoming text.

He started to hand my phone back, but I waved him off. "What's she say?"

He read the text and looked up at me, some of the color draining from his face. "There were reports of gunshots last night on Biscayne Bay and a man's body was found floating this morning."

My daughter, Kim, and son-in-law, Marty, both worked days and were usually up before the sun.

I'd anchored at Rodriguez at least two hours before they woke and had turned off the AIS when we'd left Biscayne Bay in case the men who'd attacked had it on their nav equipment. And I'd left it off until I started the engine less than an hour ago.

If Kim had tried to check our position between those times, she wouldn't have found it and wouldn't know we'd stopped in Biscayne Bay.

I wasn't worried about the police getting any ballistics from the bullets I'd fired. At that range, I felt certain that the one I'd put in the rifleman's chest had come out his back and been lost to the sea. If it didn't, the ballistics wouldn't identify any registered rifle.

The barrel, as well as two others that came with my new rifle, were custom made by someone Billy Rainwater dealt with. That meant they weren't ballistically traceable.

"Tell her thanks," I said, as Savannah and Alberto moved out onto the foredeck. "And tell her we pressed on to Rodriguez Key last night and are in Florida Bay now."

His thumbs tapped the screen again for a moment. "Sent."

Alberto turned and waved as Savannah moved their tethers around a stanchion, clipping them back onto the top rail. Both tethers were short and probably wouldn't even allow them to fall onto the deck. If either went over the rail, or under it, they'd dangle at deck level, and probably get wet, but even doubled over, hands and feet wouldn't reach the water.

The boat horn sounded from my phone again and Jimmy looked down at it.

"She wants to know if you know anything about it."

"Tell her no," I replied, looking at him sternly. "I just woke up an hour ago and hadn't heard anything."

Ahead, Alberto was leaning against the forward pulpit rail, with Savannah standing behind him. She bent and said something in his ear, then they both extended their arms like wings.

I couldn't help myself. Even though part of my mind was on other things, the sight before me made me smile.

The phone in Jimmy's hand rang and he looked up at me. "It's Deuce Livingston."

"Take the wheel," I said, reaching for the phone.

I scooted over and stood as Jimmy slid in behind the helm, then I went around the helm seat and leaned against the upper galley, out of the wind.

After touching the *Accept* button, I put the phone to my ear. "Hey, Deuce," I said cheerfully, wondering why he was calling. "We just tucked inside a little west of you, through Snake Creek."

"But Rodriguez Key wasn't where you guys spent the *whole* night," he said, a bit of severity in his tone.

"We lost a chart plotter, too," I said, a bit too defensively. "Are you tracking me?"

"Your AIS disappeared at about 2300 from the northern part of Biscayne Bay, Jesse. Then it reappeared at noon, down off Rodriguez Key. Shots were reported being heard from the water in Biscayne Bay last night. Did you do it?"

He knew it'd been me. It would be pointless to deny it.

"Yes," I replied honestly. "It looked like the three guys Kim described to me a couple of days ago as part of a yacht theft ring. The one I shot had a rifle and was bringing it up. We were at anchor—sitting ducks. Are you working on anything along those lines? Or Jack?"

"You're out, Jesse," he said, coldly. "You made it clear. Just how long after I found out you were there do you think it will take Miami-Dade PD to figure the same?"

Deuce and I were business partners, among other things. We jointly owned a private investigation firm in Key Largo, but I was the silent and *majority* owner.

That meant there could only be one reason he'd sounded off the way he had. Armstrong Research's Mobile Expeditionary Division, or ARMED, was investigating the thefts.

"We need to talk face-to-face," I said, matching his tone. "My island. Sunset. Bring Tony and Andrew and plan to stay the night."

"You're no longer—"

"These guys saw us, Deuce," I stated flatly. "*Taranis* is a one-off design—no other like her anywhere. And they could just as easily have gotten the same info from AIS as you did."

"But—"

"I'm back in, Deuce."

CHAPTER ELEVEN

I'd been in a hurry since waking up, though I didn't fully understand why until Deuce had called. It was when he'd mentioned the possibility of the police finding that our AIS had been turned off shortly after the shooting that I realized the danger we were in.

The automated identification system not only gave information about heading and speed, using an interface between the VHF radio and chart plotter, but also gave the vessel's name, home port, and registered owner's name.

We kept the speed up and the AIS off all the way to the Content Keys.

When we reached Harbor Key Light, I throttled back, activated the electric motors, and then shut off the diesel before turning into the mouth of Harbor Channel. The electric motors made maneuvering easier, and the props on those motors were about a foot shallower than the one on the main engine.

Hitting something with the main prop could not only damage the prop, but cause catastrophic damage to the shaft or transmission, or even seize the engine by damaging internal parts, like piston rods and other precisely machined parts.

Stopping an electric motor suddenly wasn't nearly as disastrous.

We passed Mac Travis and Melody Woodson's island at the opening to Harbor Channel, then entered the shallow basin just west of there, headed toward the north side of my island.

The channel I'd dug years ago for *Gaspar's Revenge* on the south side of my island was cut through water that was only three or four feet deep. It connected Harbor Channel with the dock area under my house and wasn't wide enough for *Taranis's* thirty-two-foot beam.

And she was far too long to fit under the house.

With other small islands and mangrove clusters surrounding the small basin to the north, the view from beyond them was partially blocked, so docking *Taranis* on the north side would draw less scrutiny. The water at the end of the floating pier on the north side was over five feet deep and there were no obstacles that would come close to our four-foot draft, except a couple of sandbars that I was very familiar with.

There'd been a time when I could sit on either pier all day long for several days and not see another person. But in the past year, I'd had two incidences where people just tied up to my dock to explore, not realizing it was a private island and inhabited.

I'd put up "No Trespassing" signs on both docks.

These days, on weekends, and especially during lobster season, we often saw several boats a day.

The damage was visible everywhere—straight line scars through the turtle grass, where reckless boaters had run aground.

I had to let Savannah know what was going on. And, out of an abundance of caution, I probably should have her and Alberto go stay with Chyrel up on Grassy Key, or at my friend Rusty Thurman's place in Marathon.

But I also knew she wouldn't go for it.

We tied up, I shut all the systems down except for the solar charging, and we locked up *Taranis*.

Savannah walked beside me as Alberto hurried ahead toward the foot of the pier.

"What happened?" she asked, once he was out of earshot.

"Miami PD received reports of gunshots on Biscayne Bay last night," I replied. "And they found a body this morning."

"Sound travels a long way over water," she said softly. "And that's a heavily populated area. I'm sure a lot of people heard it. How did you find out?"

"Kim," I replied. "And a call from Deuce." I looked toward the sun, now halfway down the western sky. "He and a couple of the guys are going to be here by sunset."

She stopped and held my arm, turning me to face her. "Why?"

"Our AIS was on last night," I replied. "At least until we started to run. I switched it off then and didn't turn it back on until we got underway this afternoon. When Deuce called, I turned it back off."

"And you think they might have had AIS on that little boat?"

"It's a possibility I can't ignore."

She turned and we continued walking toward the two houses beyond the foot of the pier. "I guess we should put sheets on some of the beds in the bunkhouse, then."

She was taking the news better than I would have thought, so I pressed my luck. "Maybe you and Alberto should—"

"Not on your life, Jesse!" she hissed, grabbing my arm again and spinning me around to face her once more. "I'll have Maddy come and get Alberto, but I'm not going anywhere, bud."

I grinned and looked down at her bare feet and long legs. "Bud?"

She took my arm, and we continued walking.

"I'm sorry," she said. "But I'm all through running, Jesse. You do tend to attract trouble like a moth to a flame, but I'm pretty good at handling logistics and research—you know that better than anyone. We work pretty well together, I think."

I nodded. "Okay, call Maddy. See if she can come out before sunset."

Madison Thurman, or Maddy, as she'd preferred to be called since arriving in the Keys, was a very distant cousin of Rusty's. She'd sold her family's ranch in the Big Horn Basin of Wyoming very soon after her mother died, and had arrived unexpectedly at Rusty's bar. Since then, she'd bought a beautiful, three-bedroom condo at Key Colony Beach, just across Vaca Key Bight from the Rusty Anchor, and it seemed she was going to be a permanent resident.

And Alberto adored her.

"I'm sure she can," Savannah replied, typing on her phone. "Or I'll take him there and come back."

Naomi met Jimmy and Alberto and they started putting driftwood in the fire ring to get a fire going. I also needed to warn Jimmy and Naomi—without worrying Alberto.

When Savannah's phone beeped as we approached the fire ring, she looked down at it, then up at me. "Maddy will be here in thirty minutes."

Thirty minutes? What was she doing? Waiting beside her new boat?

"Alberto," I called out. "Maddy's on her way out to get you. She wants you to spend the night at her new condo."

He turned to face me, arms at his sides. "Why?"

Jimmy knelt and put a lighter to some palm fronds. "You know why, little man."

The boy turned to look down at Jimmy. "Because of what happened last night?"

I sat down on an old palm log and Savannah sat next to me, pulling Alberto between us.

"Yes," Savannah replied honestly. "There's a chance those men might know who we are and where we live. It's just a precaution until we're sure there's no danger."

"Then we should just leave," he argued. "All of us. *Taranis* can go anywhere."

"What's going on?" Naomi asked.

We all sat down and had a frank and open discussion about what had transpired the night before, laying it all out, including the recent killings of the father and son off Matecumbe and the man's missing wife, daughter, and the kids' tutor, and the fact that reinforcements were arriving before sunset.

Naomi visibly shuddered and took Jimmy's hand. "We'll go to my place."

Jimmy shook his head. "Not this time, *ma chérie amour.*"

"What do you mean?" Naomi asked, her eyes wide.

Jimmy looked over at me as the fire took hold, light dancing across his features. "I'm stayin', man."

"Then I'm staying, too," Naomi announced firmly.

"Me too," Alberto echoed.

Savannah patted his hand. "No, you're going to stay with Aunt Maddy for a while. No argument."

"How long?" he asked, hanging his head dejectedly.

"I don't know," I replied. "But maybe we'll find out more when Deuce gets here. A day... maybe two."

He looked up at me, eyes wide. "But Tank's coming day after tomorrow!"

 # CHAPTER TWELVE

The driftwood in the fire had barely started to ash over and the coals at the bottom were still few when I heard the buzzing of an outboard motor in the distance, and immediately recognized the sound of the old Evinrude.

"That's Rusty's boat," Jimmy said, rising from his seat by the fire. "I thought you said Maddy was coming. Did her new boat break down already?"

I rose with him, turning toward the sound. "Not that I know of."

Savannah, Naomi, and Alberto followed us as Jimmy and I headed for the south pier beyond my house.

As we walked out onto the long pier, I could see Rusty's boat zigzagging through several natural cuts in the sand flats to the east to reach the upper part of Harbor Channel.

There were quite a few people on board.

Savannah took my hand. "Who all does he have with him?" she asked.

"Looks like five people," Jimmy said, gazing toward the boat, nearly a mile away. "Looks like Julie and Maddy in front."

He was close. There were six.

As Rusty's boat got nearer, I saw him at the helm, with his son-in-law and my business partner, Deuce, standing beside him. Maddy sat on the front bench seat with Rusty's daughter, Julie, and Tony Jacobs and Andrew Bourke stood on either side of the helm, each of them with a hand loosely holding the uprights of the bimini top.

The former Coast Guardsman and Navy SEAL were no strangers to small boats and had no trouble hanging on.

I'd been expecting them to arrive by helicopter.

"Thanks for coming," I said to Deuce, as I took a line Tony extended. I quickly tied it off to a deck cleat as Jimmy did the same with the bow line.

Then I extended a hand to Tony. "Good to see you again."

"Good to be seen," he replied, shaking my hand.

Turning, I caught Andrew's extended hand and pumped it as well.

"Been a while," the burly former chief petty officer said in a deep baritone. "You're looking fit as ever."

"I knew there was trouble brewin'," Rusty said, then jerked a thumb at Andrew. "Just as soon as I saw these two showed up with 'em. Figured ya might need some help."

"I thought you'd be coming by helo," I said, shaking hands with Deuce.

"It would have taken longer to get Charity and her chopper from Bimini than to drive."

Julie stepped lightly to the dock and hugged me. "And I knew there'd be plenty of boats at Dad's."

More handshakes, hugs, and greetings were exchanged, as well as introductions to Naomi, who'd never met the two men and only knew Deuce and Julie through the Rusty Anchor.

We walked together toward the end of the pier, where Alberto stopped and allowed everyone else to go ahead.

Then he trotted up beside me and exclaimed, "Wow! There's eleven people on our island! I don't think there's ever been that many."

"Not often," I said, getting a knowing look from Andrew.

Many years ago, my island, and more specifically, the two bunkhouses beyond the fire ring and tables, had, from time to time, housed Deuce's spec-ops Homeland Security team. There'd been upwards of twenty men *and* several women staying on my island, training to confront possible terrorist threats coming out of Central and South America by water.

The team had consisted of some of the best the military special operations commands had to offer, as well as a number of civilian police personnel, and even people from the FBI and CIA.

The Caribbean Counterterrorism Command had been dissolved more than ten years ago, and many of the team had returned to their parent commands in the military, or whatever alphabet agency sent them.

When the team was broken up, Deuce had already decided to leave the Navy after he and Julie got engaged, then he'd served for a while up in DC, as an assistant director of Homeland Security.

Andrew, Tony, and a few others from those days now made up my and Deuce's investigative agency, and some were still loosely attached to Armstrong Research.

"There were more people here than this before?" Alberto asked, as we reached the fire ring.

Tony crossed his ankles beside Alberto and mimicked pushing a button and making an elevator ding, then slowly lowered himself to the ground with a hushed hum.

Alberto grinned at him.

"I remember one time when something like twenty of us had a race," he said to Alberto. "We were all staying here for a few days and your dad had the crazy idea of a race. All the way to that little island at the end of the channel and back. Probably before you were born."

"That's Mac's place," Alberto said, sitting on the ground beside Tony. "Actually, it belongs to his girlfriend, Melody, but she doesn't stay there all the time. Who won the race? I bet it was my dad."

"Nope," Tony said, shaking his head, and holding up three fingers on his right hand—or two and a half, that is. "Jesse came in third place."

Tony had been captured by a terrorist cell in western Cuba while conducting surveillance. They'd tortured him, beating his face to a pulp, but he never gave them anything. I suddenly realized that had been more than fifteen years earlier.

Deuce and several members of his team, including myself, had gone into Cuba and rescued Tony shortly after the terrorists had taken the torture up a notch and cut Tony's trigger finger off at the first knuckle using a pair of pruners.

Alberto looked up at me, surprised. "Third place?"

"Well, in his defense," Andrew said, sitting on the ground next to Alberto, "the two who beat him were both Olympic swimmers."

Seating wasn't a problem. There were three wooden chairs, two long palm logs, a handful of folding beach chairs, a couple of milk crates, and lots of sun-bleached sand.

"Are you, uh..." Deuce's eyes cut to Alberto, and I nodded for him to continue. "Are you sure the men who attacked you were the same ones witnesses described?"

I nodded. "Kim gave me a pretty good description, knowing we were going to be cruising in the area. Not just their looks, but their mannerisms, too."

"What mannerisms?" Rusty asked.

"They sounded like cops, man," Jimmy replied.

Deuce cupped his chin in thought. "And there's a good chance they know who you—"

"Uh, guys," Tony said, scissoring himself up from a cross-legged position. "I hear a boat. Are you expecting more company, Jesse?"

I was on my feet quickly. "No, I'm not! Savvy, Naomi, take Maddy and Alberto to the battery shack!"

Savannah didn't hesitate but took Alberto and started quickly toward the little bridge that went over four or five feet of water to another small island where our electrical system was located. There was a shotgun over the door, just inside the shack.

"It's headin' into the channel from the Gulf," Rusty said, looking in the direction of the sound.

"Tony, take the eastern shore!" Deuce shouted. "Andrew, get down in the rocks beyond the garden!"

"Rusty, you and Jimmy go up to the house," I said, as Tony and Andrew tore off toward the east and south sides of the island. "Door's open. Arm yourselves."

I knew Jimmy would know where my hiding places were located, and I knew Rusty would be able to use what they found there. I didn't have to ask Deuce if he, Andrew, and Tony were carrying.

"Already armed," Rusty said, as the four of us started toward the house. "Legged, too."

"Then get up there and keep us covered," Deuce ordered.

A boat coming into Harbor Channel from the Gulf wasn't an unusual thing, especially lately. But I was on edge and so was Deuce.

Knowing probable murderers might know who I was and where I lived was an uncomfortable feeling. It was possible they could know where my island was located—it was public record—and if the organization behind the yacht thefts was what I was thinking it had to be, they could get that information easily.

"It's headed straight up the channel!" Tony called out from the treeline. "A center console! Maybe twenty to twenty-four feet!"

The sound of the outboard was growing louder. There was no chance anyone on the boat could hear us.

"Leapfrog Andrew," I called out to Tony. "And take cover by the southeast corner of the house!"

Deuce and I continued around the west side of my house, toward the foot of the pier, then we stopped and waited. I heard the door above open and close, then Rusty and Jimmy's footsteps on the deck.

"We're in position," Rusty reported.

We could see the boat approaching in the low light of the late afternoon sun. It slowed, coming down off plane, then turned toward my channel.

Blue lights flashed on the hardtop of the center console for a second or two, then stopped.

"Kim and Marty?" I asked rhetorically, as I stepped out onto the pier, Deuce right behind me.

The twenty-four-foot boat with the Florida Fish and Wildlife Commission markings turned into my channel and idled slowly toward the dock. My son-in-law, Marty Phillips, stood in the bow, ready with a dock line.

He handed it to me, standing ten feet behind Rusty's boat, and I quickly snugged it to a cleat. Kim reversed the outboard, stopping the boat, then handed a second line to Deuce.

"Now I know I was right," she said, coming over the gunwale and looking back at Deuce before facing me, hands on her hips. "You were in Biscayne Bay last night."

CHAPTER
THIRTEEN

In the last hour before sunset, we gathered everyone aboard *Taranis* at the north pier. With her radar arrays twenty-four feet above the water, she could "see" over everything on the island, except the houses, which were about the same height.

Savannah and Jimmy slid the doors all the way open, creating a large seating area for up to fourteen people, using the adjacent indoor and outdoor tables.

I looked around at everyone as they were all talking to one another and felt a mixture of both pride and apprehension at having my friends and family come so readily.

It wasn't that I didn't *want* a reunion, but this wasn't the best time, and the mix was bound to cause controversy.

Kim and Marty were sworn law-enforcement officers.

"Can I make a request?" Savannah asked, sitting at the far end of the interior table with Alberto on one side and Kim and Marty on the other.

I nodded for her to continue, and she turned to Kim. "We will be talking about certain things that you might not want to hear," she began. "At least not while wearing the uniform of a law enforcement officer."

Marty stood and removed his belt and holster, then pulled his shirt tail out, unbuttoned and removed his uniform shirt and placed it on his holstered sidearm. He wore a lightweight tactical vest under the uniform, with a white T-shirt beneath that.

He looked down at my daughter. "It's not like we haven't been down this road before, Kim."

My daughter stood and removed her belt and blouse, then they both pulled the Velcro loose on one side of their body armor and pulled the vests over their heads.

Kim stared at me. "What'd you do, Dad?"

"He had to," Alberto said, looking up at his adoptive big sister. "They were bad men."

Kim gazed down at him for a moment, then let her shoulders sag as she let out a long breath.

"Everyone, please," Deuce said, raising his hands, palms out. "Let's all sit down and discuss this situation, okay?"

Kim sat back down, but Marty stayed on his feet. "I know you both work for Armstrong Research," he stated flatly. "And I know what ARMED does."

"Okay, so we can skip the preliminaries," Deuce said, then sat down at the corner in the cockpit next to Julie and Rusty.

"What is armed?" Maddy asked.

"That's Armstrong Research's Mobile Expeditionary Division," Alberto bragged. "We used to be on the flagship, *Ambrosia*. Dad was the captain."

"So, it's a research company?" she asked, looking at me and Deuce.

"They do a little more than research," Marty replied, finally taking his seat and looking me in the eye. "What I know, I keep to myself, unless it involves an innocent bystander."

"This wasn't any innocent bystander," Jimmy said. "I don't know if they were pretendin' to be cops, but the one guy sure talked like one."

"And just how does a cop talk, Jimmy?" Kim asked.

Though he'd known Kim for a long time, since she was a teen, Jimmy involuntarily sat back in his chair, distancing himself. "Well, kinda like you are now."

"They spoke with authority," Savannah said. "Or maybe arrogance."

"These men came to take Jesse's boat, man," Jimmy continued, becoming more impassioned. "We heard what happened last time. Has the law found the wife and daughter? Where's the teacher, man?"

Jimmy was rarely outspoken when police were around, even if one of them was my kid. His long history of smoking and probably smuggling pot made him more than a little paranoid where uniforms were concerned.

"You don't know that, Jimmy," Kim said, leaning over the table.

"Okay!" I stated loudly, slapping the table with both palms and rising to my feet. "Let's lay all the cards out, so everyone can see."

Everyone's attention turned toward me, and I continued. "Armstrong does things governments don't want to dirty their hands with. Things that make the world a better and safer place, without all the bureaucracy and bullshit of government. And yes, we are"— I cut my eyes to Savannah—"or once *were*, connected to them."

"Still, we are all connected to each other," Savannah said softly, while looking down the length of the two tables at Rusty. "Your daughter and son-in-law directly"—she turned and locked eyes with Kim— "and Jesse will always stand with Rusty, as Rusty would with him; they're two peas in a pod. And, Kim, you know as well as I how they both feel about protecting family. That includes Marty and Maddy, too."

"And me," Alberto added.

"Of course you," Savannah said, touching his hand. "We're all family here."

I crossed my arms and looked down at the table. When I looked up, I gazed around at all of them. "Last night," I began, my tone even, "three men approached my boat in Biscayne Bay. Savannah, Alberto, Jimmy, and I were aboard, sleeping. The three in the boat were armed, and they had no navigation lights on their vessel, nor any registration number on the bow." I paused and looked directly at Marty. "One of them stepped out into the light and I saw him clearly. He had a handgun tucked in his pants. When they wouldn't turn away after a verbal warning to do so, I fired a warning volley in the water. When that man took cover, another guy rose up and aimed a rifle.... I shot him."

Maddy gasped.

"At the end of the day," I continued flatly, "it comes down to who mourns. I chose his friends and family, rather than mine."

Marty glanced down at his uniform blouse, then slowly brought his gaze back up to meet mine. "Before leaving to come down here," he began, "I filed paperwork with our captain." He paused for a moment, then added, "Kim and I are both on vacation."

Kim's head snapped around. "Wait! You didn't say anything about doing that."

Marty turned toward her and shrugged. "I've told only you what I've heard about who your dad works for. And now he's confirmed it. I want to know more. And I might want to be a part of it."

"You want to join Armstrong?" Deuce asked incredulously.

"Maybe," Marty replied, looking him in the eye. "If only a tenth of what I've heard is true, I think I could make a bigger difference."

"That'd be a discussion for another time," Rusty said, steering the conversation back on course. "Right now, it looks like we got some bigger fish to fry."

"What do you know about the thefts, Deuce?" I asked point-blank, as I sat back down.

He looked over at me, then scanned the faces of the others. "What I'm about to say doesn't leave here."

Everyone nodded, including Kim.

"Yacht thefts have exploded in numbers recently," Deuce said. "Not just here, but in many other parts of the world, as well—South Florida and the Caribbean seem to be the hotspots."

"More high-end boats," Rusty said, nodding.

"The one place there doesn't seem to be a problem," Deuce continued, "is in the Mediterranean, specifically, the Eastern Med."

"The Mediterranean?" Rusty asked. "Next to South Florida and El Caribe, the Med's gotta be right up there with million-dollar boats."

"Why's that important?" Naomi asked.

Tony looked over at her. "An operation this big requires a lot of money and manpower. The kind you'll only find in organized crime."

"We believe, as does Interpol, that the Greek mafia is at the heart of these thefts."

"The *Greek* mafia?" Savannah asked. "Not to split hairs, but isn't the word *mafia* Italian?"

"Mafia, mob, syndicate," Jimmy said, "Semantics, *chica.*"

"In this case, you're right," Tony said, nodding his head. "Organized crime in Greece is, for the most part, confined to small organizations, or families, with no ties to the others. They come together for something that might be profitable for more than one family, dissolve the association when the deal or crime is finished, and partner up elsewhere. Interpol has a tough time keeping track of who's playing with whom on a daily basis."

"And Jack's working with Interpol?" I asked Deuce.

"Who's Jack?" Maddy asked.

"Jack Armstrong," Savannah replied. "One of the wealthiest men in the world."

"Jack's not," Deuce said. "But Colonel Stockwell is. ARMED is providing logistics and if necessary, manpower."

"They can't possibly steal boats in the U.S. and continue to operate them here," Savannah surmised. "So, they'd have to be shipped elsewhere, right?"

"Can't they just drive a stolen boat somewhere else?" Maddy asked, obviously intrigued.

"Too visible," Savannah replied. "And not very cost-effective."

"Exactly what we're thinking," Andrew said, his voice resonating through the salon and cockpit. "More than seventeen percent of all the world's merchant vessels are Greek flagged; more than any other country, including China."

"What's Interpol doing about it?" Savannah asked.

There wasn't any doubt in my mind that Armstrong Research was already doing more than just providing logistical support or investigating this. Innocent people were being killed or kidnapped, simply because they'd worked hard to get ahead and enjoyed a boating lifestyle.

ARMED had been created in response to the terrorist attack on the World Trade Center. Jack had lost his wife and son there. Like me, Jack didn't like bullies.

"Until now," Deuce replied, then looked at me, "Interpol hasn't come up with squat. They've asked for our help."

Savannah pressed him further. "What do you mean?"

I held Deuce's gaze as I replied for him. "Until now, Armstrong hasn't had a big enough carrot to dangle in front of the Greeks."

CHAPTER FOURTEEN

As sunset approached, we all made our way up to *Taranis's* upper deck. I needed time to think, and though it was open and air-conditioned, the cockpit and salon had gotten a little heated when Deuce laid out his thoughts.

Everyone spread out to the various seating areas on the flybridge deck, and Jimmy broke out the chessboard for another rematch with Alberto.

I wasn't overly concerned that the men from the previous night would come looking for payback so quickly. If they had seen my AIS signal, they knew only the boat's name and home port. They could get my mailing address if they dug deep enough, but *Taranis's* home port was listed as Marathon, and my mailing address was the Rusty Anchor.

We were safely hidden in the backcountry, and even the Coast Guard would take days to find us with what little information the attackers might have.

Unless they searched deed records.

Savannah and I passed out drinks from the upper galley, then stood by the aft rail watching the sun go down.

Deuce joined us and stood next to Savannah. "None of this was planned, Savvy."

"I know," she replied softly, as Rusty and Julie joined us. "If Jesse was alone in a rubber raft in the middle of the Pacific, the first person to come along would be someone who wanted to steal his dinghy."

"I don't go looking for it," I said in my own defense.

She smiled and took my hand, but it was a sad kind of smile. "I know you don't, Jesse. You're a good man."

"But ya do kinda have a knack for bringin' out the worst in some folks, bro," Rusty added. "Not that I consider that a character flaw or nothin'. Just sayin'."

I glanced down at my old friend and nodded. Over the years, he and I had gotten into some unfriendly territory more than a few times, and I always knew he'd be there when few others would.

And Rusty knew he could expect the same from me.

"How are things progressing with the *Three Twenty*?" I asked him, changing the subject.

Last fall, our mutual friend and fellow jarhead, Billy Rainwater, had found a German U-boat buried in the Everglades. We'd later discovered that it was the U-320, which was reported scuttled after its first engagement.

"The last and biggest hurdle," he replied, "gettin' the state to sign off on buildin' a new dam, looks like it might go through."

"You still haven't opened it up again?" Savannah asked.

"Ain't no hurry," he replied. "Not once we found out we could do it all legal-like. But, yeah, we'll be openin' her up again next Monday. The permanent caisson's all in place."

Kim stepped up beside me, taking my other arm and getting back to the business at hand. "You always told me to follow my gut, Dad. What's yours telling you?"

"It really pushes the limits of family protection," Savannah whispered. "Going after hardened criminals wasn't what I meant about you taking on an occasional investigation for Deuce. But I will support you either way, Jesse."

As the sun reached the horizon, it grew silent on the flybridge deck, and everyone moved aft, gathering around me and Savannah at the rail.

The sky around the sun began to darken to a burnt-orange color, and it and the sun were reflected off the calm water. There wasn't a cloud in sight to catch the last of the sun's rays as it slowly started to disappear over the horizon.

I closed my eyes for just a moment to make a wish, then opened them again, just in time to see the sun wink out.

Another day done.

What had I accomplished? What could I have done differently?

"We'll assign watch here on the flybridge," I said quietly.

"And another over on the deck of your house," Rusty added. "To watch the southern approaches."

Savannah turned to Maddy and Rusty. "It's too late for you to leave alone," she said to the young woman, then glanced at Rusty. "Or were you planning to return as well?"

"I'll be stayin' on," Rusty replied. "Mind if Maddy borrows one of your smaller boats in the mornin'?"

"Of course," Savannah replied. "She and Alberto can go back tomorrow in the Grady-White."

There were a lot of things to consider, and my mind was ticking them off one by one, adding contingencies to each, and ticking *them* off, as well. A younger me would have come to the same conclusion, but a lot faster.

I had others to be concerned about.

"Your thoughts?" Deuce asked me. "On my idea?"

"Let's get something to eat," I replied, still looking off toward the western sky. "Then we can all get some rest, and I'll sleep on it."

I turned to face the man who was not only my friend and business partner, but the son of one of the men who'd helped mold me as a Marine infantryman many years ago. "When I said I was back in, I wasn't thinking *that* far in."

What Deuce had proposed was dangerous, and not just for those who would take part. There was a very real chance as well that we could lose *Taranis* or get her all shot up. Neither of which was very appealing.

"Tony and I can handle the watch from here," Andrew offered. "We can just tag team when we get drowsy. It's more than twelve hours till daylight this time of year."

"Gimme a pillow and one of your recliners," Rusty said to Savannah, "and me and your ol' man can handle the watch on the deck."

"What do you have here to eat?" Maddy asked. "This is a lot of people."

"Thirteen!" Alberto said. "But we have plenty of food."

Savannah sat down next to Alberto. "Why don't you run down to the galley and get that big cobia fillet out of the refrigerator?" She glanced up at me. "That's fourteen pounds of fish tacos, right there."

"I'll go with ya, Alberto," Rusty said. "I been wantin' to see some more o' this tub. We gonna cook out there at the grill?"

"Yeah," I said, my mind still sifting through all the "what-ifs" in Deuce's idea.

"We'll meet ya out there," Rusty said. "Alberto can show me around while you get the fire goin'."

"Bring that bag of tortillas from the crisper, then," Savannah said, rising and heading toward the steps.

Following her, Alberto shouted, "Let's get this show on the road!" which made Savannah snicker.

"What about toppings and stuff?" Maddy asked.

Savannah stopped at the steps and let Alberto and Rusty go down ahead of her. "Come on, Maddy. We have everything we need over by the house."

"Guac?"

"We'll have to make it," Savannah said, as everyone else started toward the stairs. "The avocado tree is next to the garden, and I have several ripening in the window basket."

I hung back at the rail as the others left and Maddy started asking excitedly about our garden.

Only Andrew remained on the flybridge deck, sitting at the helm and familiarizing himself with the radar and communications systems.

As I started to turn to follow the others, he approached me.

"It's crazy enough to work," Andrew whispered. "You know these types as well as I do. It's not a matter of *if* they'll come gunning for you, but *when*. Better at a time and place of your own choosing, right?"

I looked over at him, my mind flashing back to earlier that morning, when I was getting ready to go to sleep—to meet my demons at the time and place *I* chose. But they hadn't come.

Andrew's thick mustache was grayer now, and the lines in his face were deeper. But the fire in his eyes still burned with the same intensity as when I'd met him.

"Yeah," I replied, knowing he was right. "I just hate it when the officer comes up with a solid plan before me."

# CHAPTER FIFTEEN

After dinner, we'd taken Alberto up to the house and gotten him ready for bed, then Savannah and I had gone to sleep. Rusty and I had agreed on two-hour shifts and he promised to knock on the door at 2200.

When Rusty woke me for my first watch, a waning gibbous moon was just starting to rise over Harbor Channel to the east.

I went outside and sat alone on the deck chair I'd built from leftover debris after Hurricane Irma. There were five similar chairs around the island—all made of treated mahogany without a single nail or screw. There was one over on the north side of my deck, two on Jimmy's porch, plus the three over by the fire ring.

We'd had plenty of scrap lumber after Irma. And the majority of it had been hardwood from South America.

Occasionally, I talked to Tony, using a pair of low-power, hand-held VHF radios. But mostly, I just let my eyes wander across the night sky.

I gazed at the stars to the south as the moon slowly began to dominate more of the eastern sky. The waters out on Harbor Channel, as well as on the cuts to the west of Howe and Water Keys, were like a mirror, reflecting everything with equal brilliance.

Minutes turned into an hour, with nothing of note happening to the south, except for a fish that kept jumping in a line down Harbor Channel, some predator below making it seek safety in the air.

"Hey, Jesse?" Tony's voice came over the radio just before midnight.

I pressed the button on the side of the little radio and held it to my mouth. "I'm here."

"I'm looking at the top here," he said, curiosity in his voice. "In particular, the supports holding the roof up. Does this whole thing *move* or something?"

"It can be hydraulically lowered back and down," I replied. "It seals off the whole aft flybridge deck at the rails, leaving the helm area exposed for low clearances."

There was a moment of silence, then he said, "Badass."

At midnight, I went inside to wake Rusty for his second watch. He sat up as soon as I walked into the living room, nodded, and moved the handle on the recliner to return it to a sitting position, facing the window.

"This setup's kinda familiar," he whispered, looking out at the water to the south.

I knew what he was talking about without him saying it. The old rum shack also had a window that looked out over the water, *and* two recliners facing it.

"No need to mess up a good idea," I whispered back.

"Everything okay?" he asked softly, as he rose from the chair.

"All quiet," I replied, as I headed to the bedroom in back. "See you in a couple of hours."

I turned the knob slowly, so as to not make a sound, then pushed the bedroom hatch open. I did the same thing in reverse, gently closing it with the knob turned to avoid the click of the latch.

I needn't have.

"Rusty's on watch now?" Savannah asked, sitting up.

I nodded. "Go back to sleep."

She pulled the covers back on my side and patted the mattress.

I stretched out beside her, closed my eyes, and was instantly asleep.

It felt as if I'd only napped a minute or two when I heard the outside hatch open and close. I reached the bedroom door before Rusty knocked and woke Savannah. I hadn't even taken my shoes off.

He only nodded as I walked past. No words needed to be exchanged, since we'd both done this a million times before. If anything had happened during his watch, he would have awakened me and everybody else on the island.

I went outside and sat down in the mahogany deck chair, again facing south. Teak would have been better, though mahogany was good outside for decades and impervious to bugs. It was also heavier than the Asian hardwood. But teak wasn't what we'd had on hand.

After Irma had done her damage, Jimmy and I had scrounged all the mahogany siding that was broken, and had cut, planed, and joined the planks, using only joinery, glue, and wooden dowels. Each chair weighed a hundred pounds.

Then, once Jack Armstrong had sent *Ambrosia* to help, and when things were moving in to Marathon again, he'd brought material and skilled craftsmen out to my island to rebuild. The unbroken mahogany planks were reused for the siding.

Unconsciously, I rubbed my hand along the smooth armrest of the chair, remembering all the work we'd done. Then I noticed that the Thermos was still sitting on the table. When I hefted it, I realized Rusty must have made another pot.

My mug was still where I'd left it, so I poured a little coffee in and swished it around before swallowing the dregs. Then I filled the cup to the brim and sat back.

My deck's view of the night sky to the south was as spectacular as it was large. I'd never found a better place to stargaze than eighteen feet above the water, sitting on that deck.

It was more than four miles in a straight line from my island to the northernmost road on Big Pine Key. Any lights on that road were over the horizon and invisible.

The more populated part of Big Pine was ten miles away and Marathon was over twenty, so even the glow from the more densely packed areas was minimal. Almost no man-made light reached my island to contend with the stars.

The moon was nearing its zenith, reducing the number of visible stars due to its brightness. It shone down almost perpendicularly on the water and islands to the south from just slightly behind me, and I could easily pick out familiar details on the surrounding islands and mangroves.

Looking east, I spotted my trap floats along the channel and was reminded I needed to pull them soon.

An ibis stood alone in a high branch to the southwest, and I clearly saw a faint echo of a wake in the water as a large predator swam south into the maze of cuts Harbor Channel flowed into and out of twice a day.

A mile to the south lay Water Key and just east of it was Howe Key, both uninhabited. Farther away and just east of Howe, I could easily make out Cutoe Keys, and to the southwest, the mangroves that fringed the flats around Crane and Raccoon Keys were visible.

Deuce's idea had merit, I decided.

Lay a trap for the would-be thieves, using *Taranis* as bait. One look and they'd come after her, if nothing else, just for vengeance.

The problem with his idea was that if the same guys came—minus one, of course—they'd know at least one person on *Taranis* was armed, and they could easily come charging in, guns blazing.

They might also be wary.

But they'd have no way of knowing just *how* armed we could make *Taranis*. Our ace in the hole would be what they might consider to be their strong suits—their blood-lust desire for revenge and their feeling of invincibility, having met very little resistance in previous acts of piracy.

Their goal would be the boat.

Our goal would be to capture at least one of them alive.

In the past, we'd used physical pain to extract information from non-cooperative terrorists and criminals alike. I didn't lose any sleep over it.

And Tony was very good at it, having learned firsthand.

"We can work our way up the food chain," Deuce had suggested.

The trouble was, the apex predators in this particular food chain were a bunch of Greek "godfathers," or whatever they were called, and they were nearly six thousand miles away.

Then Deuce had dropped the bomb about *Ambrosia* being in the Med already, supposedly doing oil field research off the Tarragona coast of Spain.

The Med was over a thousand miles west to east, but with the ability to run at fifty to sixty knots for hours on end in the calmer waters of the Mediterranean, *Ambrosia* could be off the Greek Islands in less than a day.

But how far would Jack Armstrong be willing to move the needle?

Taking down a terrorist cell in Mexico or Cuba, or even a Miami street gang, was nothing compared to going after a crime syndicate in Eastern Europe, and one that I would assume had its foundations in ancient times and often had the backing of the local populace.

Did Armstrong Research have *that* kind of tactical manpower? Few countries could boast the *technological* advantage at Jack Armstrong's disposal. But could he assemble an army?

Because that was what it would take. And Stockwell's security team on *Ambrosia* was good, but not nearly big enough.

Having been the captain of *Ambrosia*, I'd had almost unlimited access to Armstrong's technology, but information on the number of assets at our disposal had been above my pay grade, and Jack had never discussed it with me.

I knew his reach was almost limitless and whenever I'd worked in the field, whatever hardware was needed seemed to appear out of thin air. But a force large enough to take down a well-entrenched crime syndicate?

Even if he could put together an army, how far would he go to help such a small community of mostly affluent people?

CHAPTER SIXTEEN

Behind a luxurious home in a gated community on the shore of Biscayne Bay, soft blue light spilled out onto a patio through a set of floor-to-ceiling sliding glass doors.

The light from the television pulsed and danced on the marble tiles and nearby plants and statues.

A nearly full moon hung high over the bay, adding its own bluish-gray hue, and creating dark shadows among the foliage around the edges of the property.

The small courtyard was tastefully appointed with a classical Mediterranean vibe. There were several nude statues among the potted palms, ferns, and flowering bushes.

Parts of the yard where there were no plants, vases, or statues became stone pathways weaving through the small area that was devoid of grass.

The focal point of the terrace was a kidney-shaped swimming pool, where the soft glow from underwater lights mingled with that from the TV, creating a hypnotic, pulsing ballet of subdued brilliance moving playfully across the nearby statuary.

The lights made the nearer ones almost appear to be moving, dancing naked and unashamed in the moonlight.

Farther away, the marble and terra cotta sculptures, illuminated only by the moon, seemed to watch on with eerily stoic features, frozen in peaceful repose.

From a neighbor's tree, the soft sound of a mourning dove could be heard, signalling that dawn would be coming soon.

In the great room of the house, the sound on the giant 85-inch television was low, barely audible. No other lights were on in the great room, but in the kitchen, a soft glow from the hood over the stove provided some illumination.

A middle-aged man sat slumped in a deep leather chair, staring at the screen. The arms and backrest of the chair were equal in height and boxy, leaving his head and shoulders barely visible.

His arms rested on the sides of the chair, and dangling in his right hand was a glass tumbler, which he gently swirled.

Slowly, he raised the glass to his lips, grimacing as the dark amber liquid went down his throat.

The same footage was playing back in a loop on the giant screen, the light flickering across the man's features changing from blue, to red, to green, then a momentary dazzling white, before going back to blue again, and repeating.

The reporter's face was in a small window in the corner of the screen, where he was talking into a microphone. What he was saying wasn't important to Ray Belsus, who already knew more about what had happened than the talking head.

The macabre footage—about eight seconds long and looping continuously—was of a wheeled stretcher being brought up from a dock by a pair of EMTs. On it, a sheet covered the body of a man, obviously dead, and very wet.

Ray Belsus was a businessman. He'd made his fortune, lost it, and then made it again in the shipping industry before he was forty.

He'd never really warehoused much of anything, though he did own a small warehouse on the Miami River.

Belsus had gotten rich by watching not just the prices of commodities being produced, but the upstream shipments of supplies to make the products.

When he saw a stoppage of one thing or another, even if just a short-term delay, he bought up the finished product, knowing that its value would go up while in transit. When production slowed, due to the delayed materials, supplies dropped, demand rose, and prices went up, all within the four weeks it took a container ship to reach the Port of Miami.

Sometimes, prices only went up a little, but his investments always fell in the black. But every now and then, the loss of a much-needed resource caused a massive slowdown in production, and his ship landed with a thousand percent uptick in retail.

And he couldn't sell it fast enough.

Belsus had always had his ear to the ground about what was being shipped where, what merchandise was in high demand, and where those commodities could be obtained on the cheap.

He never asked where something came from when it was available to purchase. What did he care if something he bought and sold was hot?

Caveat emptor, he thought. Let the *buyer* beware. He was just the middleman, the shipper.

One of Belsus's associates, the team leader in his new and quite profitable Miami operation, had reported to him earlier in the day that he'd lost a man in an exchange of gunfire late the previous night.

That wasn't supposed to happen.

People on yachts weren't supposed to have guns, and definitely not automatic weapons, which Manny had said had been used.

How Manny came to possess the items Belsus bought from him was none of Ray's concern. He knew the boats were stolen and without documentation.

But this was troublesome.

The two killings last month and now one of Manny's guys getting it could bring more light to his operation than Ray was willing to have shed.

Until now, the risk had been easily remedied when the inventory reached its destination, a shipyard owned by the husband of one of Ray's cousins.

Manuel "Manny" Woods had been a drug-dealing street thug when Belsus had found him. He'd grown up on the mean streets of Liberty City, one of Miami's most dangerous neighborhoods. His mother had been a crack addict who'd supported her habit by prostitution, and Manny's father had been her pimp, up until the day he'd just moved on when Manny was three years old.

"How did they get the drop on you again?" Belsus asked, without turning his head.

"I still ain't figured that out," came a voice from the kitchen. "We had the lights cut off, man. It was like they could see in the fuckin' dark."

Manny's slight Cuban accent and gutter language only came out when he got angry or excited, and at the moment, he sounded like the street urchin he'd been three years earlier.

When Belsus had first hired Manny, at the age of seventeen, he'd already boasted of four killings, and had a very long arrest record for possession and assault.

None of that had mattered to Ray. What mattered to him were results and loyalty.

This time, Ray did turn his head, staring at Manny in the shadows of the kitchen. "And they shot at you first?"

Manny nodded his head, then his eyes strayed up to the ceiling for a second. "Right after I told 'em we were going to board. But whoever it was, he was a lousy shot, *jefe*. Just hit the water on full auto."

"A lousy shot," Ray echoed, his dark eyes boring through the darkness at the hoodlum. "Until he put a single bullet right through the middle of Harvey's chest! Did it ever occur to you that the first shots might have been a warning?"

Manny glanced down at the tabletop, averting his boss's stare. "Not at the time."

Belsus looked back at the TV, now cutting to a drug commercial. *Not at the time?*

The kid was tough, no doubt about that, and he was aggressive, which was what Ray wanted. But could he have let his overconfidence cloud his judgment one too many times? Ray knew full well that no matter how big and tough a man was, there was always someone bigger and tougher.

That meant he had to be smarter.

Had the guy been a lousy shot, like Manny claimed? Or had Manny not yielded to the warning signs?

Either way, Ray couldn't let it go now. Not a boat like that.

"I have the information on the boat's owner," Ray said quietly, turning back to the television.

"Where does he live?" Manny asked, lustful retaliation evident in his tone.

"Marathon," Ray replied, then finished his Scotch. "I already checked, and his address is a bar, just off the highway. There's a marina there, too, so he probably lives on the boat."

"*That* boat sure won't be hard to find."

"I want you to send someone down there," Belsus said, in a tone that left no doubt that he meant immediately. "Have them ask around about this Jesiah McDermitt and see if they can locate the yacht. That thing will bring at least two million to our people in the old country."

"Snake was with us," Manny said, his eyes cutting to the ceiling again, as if anticipating something. "He knows what the boat looks like."

Ray's eyes also drifted upward, staring at a spot above the television.

"Give him my private number, Manny," he said, as he got to his feet, still looking up. "I want to hear something every hour." Ray turned and stared at his underling with menacing eyes. "Don't fuck this up, Manny. I want that boat on the next cargo ship to Piraeus."

# CHAPTER SEVENTEEN

During my last watch of the night, starting at 0600, there hadn't even been any fish jumping. It seemed the whole world was in a slumber, but I knew that wasn't true.

The natural world didn't follow clocks.

But there were people moving around out there. Some were getting ready for a hard day's work, while others were just ending their shifts, going home to safe families.

Far to the south, cars and trucks moved steadily back and forth on the Overseas Highway, commuters going to and coming from jobs, happy visitors getting a jump on the long drive home, and supplies coming in for the next batch.

Thousands of decent people out there, on the move before the sun even peeked over the horizon, just to earn an honest buck.

None of those sights or sounds reached my ears. Even Finn, with his highly sensitive ears, couldn't hear them, or maybe he'd just ignored any sound that wasn't within two miles, which was when he'd usually let us know someone was coming.

I missed the big doofus.

Out here in the backcountry, during the quiet, predawn hours, you could hear a manatee yawn from a mile away.

I knew there were also people out there who wanted to do harm, and even a few who would like to hurt me. Those on that boat weren't the only ones, but most of my enemies were either incarcerated, dead, or just gone—vanished like a puff of smoke.

Turning, I looked back over the island. *Taranis's* flybridge was visible over the mangroves.

I had the means with which to take Savannah, Alberto, and anyone else who wanted to join us and completely vanish for months at a time, to find a place where the filth of civilization hadn't reached.

Savannah and I knew these places existed. We'd been there. But we'd always been limited as to how much fuel and food we could take. *Taranis* though, was a floating gear locker, powered by the sun, with room carved out for humans.

And dogs, I realized.

I still hadn't come up with a viable solution for the toilet needs of a really large dog, and Tank was arriving in a little over twenty-four hours.

How could I plan or execute anything with a twelve-week-old puppy jumping and barking to play fetch?

Would Tank even fetch?

I could throw tennis balls into the water off the north dock until my shoulder was numb and Finn would shove a ball in my hand for one more throw. Even at the relative age of one hundred, a year before the cancer, he could leap fifteen feet off the end of the dock and swim for miles.

We'd often come out to the deck at this time, to watch the predawn light show. Finn would lie quietly at my feet as I explained to him what we were going to do that day, where we'd heard the fishing was good, how we fit into the cosmos we were looking at, or even how we fit into our tiny little part of the world.

Finn was a good listener.

I had tomorrow—or today, I realized, glancing to the east—to figure out the problem, since the biggest part of Tank's coming here was to acclimate him to boat life.

Gunkholing around the Bahamas had always been easy with Finn and Woden. They could just swim ashore and find a patch of grass beyond the dune, and we were rarely more than a few minutes from land, except during passages. Then, the swim platform was an option, and sometimes we'd just stop and drift while the dogs went for a swim.

As dawn broke, I could hear others moving around on the island, and lights started to come on in both bunkhouses, as well as over in Jimmy's place.

The hatch opened and Savannah came out, carrying two mugs.

"Want another cup?" she asked, placing one in front of me.

The coffee in the Thermos was getting cold, so I picked up the hot mug and took a drink. "Thanks."

She sat down at the table beside me, holding her cup on her knees with both hands, a sign that she had something on her mind.

"Have you made a decision?" she asked quietly.

"*Taranis* isn't safe in South Florida," I replied.

"So, we have two options," she said, without looking up. "Leave and never come back or hunt down the pirates." She took a sip from her coffee, then looked up at me. "This is our home, Jesse. Yes, I want to see more of the world, and *Taranis* is the perfect way to do it. But I don't want to give up our home."

I looked over at her. "What would we *really* be giving up? We can't even go into town without some—"

"I know," she said, quietly. "Trust me on that. It's risky, but if anyone can stop this, even on a small level, it's you and Deuce. With a little help from Jack."

"Another den of snakes is just gonna rise up in their place."

"Then you cut that head off, too," she said with finality, then turned her face toward the rising sun. "Eventually, we can win back our town, our islands, our state, and our nation. I've heard you say a million times that the only thing evil needs to win is for good people to do nothing."

She turned back to face me. "You *are* a good man, Jesse. This is what you do. There's a reason God gave you both the ability to *continue* making a difference, and the intelligence to do what is right when the time is right."

I met her gaze, searching her eyes. What I saw was conviction and resolve.

"This doesn't sound like Savvy from a year ago."

Her features hardened. "I've seen and been through a lot since then, Jesse. It's gotten worse out there in the real world."

"So... what?" I asked. "Are you telling me I should start stomping the crap out of every degenerate I meet? I'm a retired grandfather, for crying out loud. That'd be a full-time job."

She laughed. "You're hardly an 'old man,' and *retired* is a state of mind. I *know* you can still run, swim, or fight harder than men half your age. And so do you."

"What happens if they charge in with automatic weapons and start chewing up the fiberglass?"

"Aluminum, titanium, polycarbonate, and carbon fiber," she replied. "Which can all be repaired. Besides, having Deuce and his team aboard would mean they'd never get close enough to hit the broad side of a barn."

"You're serious," I said flatly, seeing Deuce coming across the yard from the north pier.

"As a heart attack," she replied, her tone matching my own. "If we don't, who will? The police? They're as hamstrung as the military by government bureaucracy."

Jimmy came out of his house with a large bowl, heading toward the outdoor kitchen and tables. Naomi was right behind him, carrying a box.

Deuce mounted our rear steps, and as Savannah and I rose, he strode across the deck toward us.

"Get enough time to sleep on it?" he asked, never one for beating around the bush.

"Tell him, Savvy," I said, looking over at my wife.

The hatch opened and Rusty held it as Alberto came out in his pajamas, yawning. He stopped when he saw the three of us together.

"Go get dressed," Savannah told him. "Jimmy's starting breakfast and probably needs you to help break the eggs. Then you and Maddy are going to her place for a while."

Rusty looked me in the eye, understanding instantly, as Alberto reluctantly went back inside. When the hatch closed, he nodded firmly at me. "Whatever ya need, I got your six, bro."

Savannah turned to face Deuce. "We're in," she said, her blue eyes as cold as Arctic ice. "I'll need Chyrel and Chip to help with logistics. I'm in charge."

"You're not in—"

"Yes, she is," I replied softly, meeting Deuce's gaze. "My boat. My op. Savvy calls the shots, working from the comm shack here on the island. Chyrel can be here in less than an hour with one phone call."

Although it'd had little use in several years, when we'd rebuilt the structures on the island after Irma, we kept the configuration the same, creating a small office or communications center in the left third of the western bunkhouse. And thanks to Star Link, we had our own orbiting satellite and didn't need to rely on Armstrong's. Chyrel would be able to connect to my account using encrypted software on her laptop to give us almost worldwide video communications.

But no eyes in the sky.

"We have a lot of work to do on *Taranis*," I said, heading toward the back steps. "Not the least of which is finding a place for Tank to poop before he arrives tomorrow morning."

"You're not takin' the pup, are ya?" Rusty asked.

"No," I replied with a grin. "But since the manpower's here, I want to take advantage of it."

Jimmy and Naomi had a line going, with Alberto's help, and they were turning out pancakes at a rate of about two per minute.

The others came from the boat and bunkhouses, and we all sat down for pancakes, eggs, and bacon.

"I'm not leaving," Alberto announced after wolfing down a stack.

Savannah turned toward him. "That's not open for dis—"

"Yes, ma'am. It is," Alberto said calmly, cutting her off for the first time that I could remember. "You, Rusty, Jimmy, and Naomi are staying here." He looked up at Rusty. "It's safer here than anywhere."

Rusty looked around at those who would be remaining on the island when we put Deuce's plan into action, and he, of all people, knew what kind of firepower we had on the island.

"He's right," Maddy said, seeming more worried than she should. "I think it's safer here, too."

Rusty nodded his head in agreement. "I reckon the seven of us could hold off anything better here than in town."

A buzzing sound out of the north rose quickly and turned suddenly into a roar as an airplane buzzed the trees, then banked up and to the right.

CHAPTER EIGHTEEN

Everyone instinctively ducked as the plane exposed its pale blue underbelly to the morning sun, but my brain had already recognized the sound.

"That's Billy!" Rusty shouted, as we all jumped to our feet.

I bolted for *Taranis* with the others chasing me. After I stepped down into the cockpit, I opened the portside dock-maneuvering station built into the gunwale and grabbed the handheld VHF radio.

Quickly switching it on and changing it to channel 68, which I knew Billy would be monitoring, I stepped over to the port side deck and moved forward. We both used marine radios in our planes to talk to boat traffic on the surface.

As I tracked the plane out over Raccoon Key, I keyed the mic and held the radio to my mouth. "That you up there, Billy?"

"You were expecting the Lone Ranger?" came his voice from the little speaker. "Got someplace we can land this bird?"

"Keep heading due west for three miles," I replied, moving over to the port side. "Then make a lazy one-eighty, about a mile wide, and line up on Harbor Light. You'll have a wide expanse of water to land on just north of where we are. I keep it clear of debris. Come in low over Content Passage, the deep channel you can see under your starboard wing right now."

"Got it," he replied.

"What's he doing here?" Savannah asked, joining me at the rail.

"I don't know," I replied. "It's not like Billy to arrive unannounced."

"A better question..." Rusty suggested, following us. "Where ya gonna tie him up?"

"The wings are higher than the port ama's foredeck rails," I replied. "We can tie her off on the bow."

"Yeah," Rusty agreed. "But what about the wing *struts*."

"It'll be close," I agreed, as I opened a deck hatch. "Help me with a couple of fenders."

I descended the ladder into the massive deck storage area in the bow and went forward to where the larger fenders were stowed, one above the other, in the very front part of the bow.

"Here," I called up, pushing a giant barrel fender up through the hatch. It had a single line attached to both ends. "The line's already adjusted so it'll ride horizontal at water level, just loop it around the recessed cleat four feet back from the bow. There's a bigger cleat right on the pulpit for Billy's aft dock line."

He took the fender, and I climbed back up, hauling another one behind me. Billy was banking right, out beyond the passage, as we got the giant fenders in place.

Each one was three feet long and would hold Billy's plane's float a good two feet away from the hull, so I felt confident the wing struts would clear the low aluminum rails.

Rusty and I stood and looked toward the west. Billy was over Content Passage already.

Keying the handheld's mic, I spoke into it. "You're too high and too hot, Billy. Drop your airspeed to seventy knots and come over those mangroves ahead of you at fifty feet."

"Roger that," Billy said.

The nose came up slightly as Billy reduced power, and the plane descended over the last fringing island.

"Okay, you have a mile of unobstructed five-foot-deep water ahead," I told him. "Once you're down, taxi south until you're east of us, then turn downwind toward us. We'll catch you here on the bow."

He waggled the wings as an acknowledgment, then flared the Beaver like a giant water bird and settled her onto the water.

Billy revved the engine, keeping his plane's floats up on the step as he turned south and then west, coming toward the bow. He approached at an angle so that when we slowed the wing, the momentum of the plane would naturally turn toward the side of the hull.

When he was about twenty yards away, he killed the engine.

The floatplane drifted quietly toward the port side as I moved all the way out to the end of the long, wave-piercing bow. I caught Billy's left wing about a third of the distance to the tip and began walking backward, past Rusty, slowing the plane's forward momentum and allowing my resistance to turn it.

Billy's port float came to rest neatly against the fenders, just as the rear hatch opened and Trish Osceola appeared, tossing a dock line up to Rusty, who quickly tied it off to the forward cleat.

Trish disappeared inside, then came out again with another line, climbed down onto the float, and moved forward.

I met her at the front and, after she tied one end of the line to a cleat on the plane's float, she tossed it to me, and I secured the other end to a deck cleat near the wheelhouse hatch.

The plane was snug against the giant fenders, and the wing strut had at least a foot to spare. But the plane's float was a good three or four feet down from *Taranis's* deck, and three feet out from her hull.

Trish looked up at me and Savannah. "I don't suppose you have a gangplank or boarding ladder?"

The front hatch opened, and Billy climbed out.

"If I'd known you were coming," I said, "I would've moved the boat."

Billy's eyes measured the distance, cut to the wing strut, then he shrugged. "The Slide for Life in reverse," he quipped, referring to an obstacle on Parris Island's Confidence Course.

One which he, Trish, Rusty, and I had all conquered.

He leaned out toward the strut, caught it in both hands, then swung his legs up and over the low bow rail, locking his toes around a stanchion.

Tilting his head back, Billy looked at Trish, upside down, with his long black hair dangling.

"Grab my belt with your left hand and swing over," he instructed her. "Jesse will catch you."

She didn't hesitate for a second and reached out to grab Billy's belt as he clung to the strut. Then she flew through the air, hanging on with one hand as the other came up to my extended right arm.

As her feet found the edge of the deck, we caught one another's wrists, and I pulled her up to a standing position, holding her with both arms. She got her balance, then easily stepped over the rail.

"Welcome aboard *Taranis*," Savannah said, hugging Trish. "It's so good to see you again. Both of you."

"But why the surprise visit?" Trish asked, hugging her back as Billy walked his hands up the strut and stepped over the rail.

The others gathered along the side deck and Billy's knowing glance paused on Deuce, Tony, and Andrew before turning to Trish. "I told you we were needed."

Trish looked at the others and then back at Savannah. "He came rushing in the door, telling me we had to go. And suddenly, here we are."

"I was with father," Billy said to me. "He told me that you needed my help."

"He's talking?" I asked, very surprised.

William "Leaping Panther" Rainwater, Sr. was in his eighties and hadn't spoken a word since his wife died in a car accident more than twenty years earlier.

"He doesn't speak *verbally*," Billy replied. "But I could tell, and seeing these men with you confirms my suspicion. What is going on?"

"And how can we help?" Trish added.

"It's a long story," I replied, then turned to Deuce. "Did you make that call?"

He nodded. "Chyrel will be here in thirty minutes. Charity, Paul, and Tom will arrive by helo in two hours."

My phone vibrated and chirped in my pocket.

"You might want to get that," Deuce said.

I pulled my phone out and looked at the display, then tapped the *Accept* button and held the phone to my ear. "McDermitt."

"I'm with Jack," Colonel Stockwell said without preamble. "You're on speaker."

I switched my phone to speaker also. "I'm with Savannah and more than a dozen family and friends, Colonel. Also on speaker. What's on your mind?"

Marty stepped closer and whispered to Savannah, "Jack Armstrong?"

She nodded as Kim moved up beside Marty.

"We know," Jack replied. "And Deuce told me you have more assets on the way?"

"Four more and a helo, sir," Deuce replied. "Chyrel will be here shortly by boat, and Charity is bringing Paul and Tom. Plus me, Julie, Tony, and Andrew already here."

"It sounds like you're starting your own little war, Jesse," Armstrong said.

"We didn't *start* it, Jack," Savannah replied, leaning toward my phone. "They attacked the wrong boat."

CHAPTER NINETEEN

With so many people on the island and more expected, just feeding everyone was going to be a big chore. Fortunately, nobody needed to be told what to do.

Rusty took Tony and Andrew in his boat and went down to Boot Key Harbor to get some needed equipment from *Gaspar's Revenge.*

Jimmy and I were back to chartering a couple of times a week and it just made more sense to keep her at the marina for the convenience of the clients.

Billy and Alberto got to work cutting up an old remnant of artificial grass to attach to the large bottom step of the port ama's sugar scoop. As big as Tank would likely get, Billy strongly advised against using one of the showers, even with the macerators attached.

Fortunately, thanks to the reverse osmosis units, *Taranis* had no shortage of potable water, and the shower hoses at each sugar scoop had plenty of pressure.

Poop problem solved.

When Chyrel arrived, we pulled her boat up under the house, and Naomi and Maddy helped her get set up in the comm shack. She and Savannah would be working side by side on two separate encrypted laptop computers.

Jimmy and I took the Grady to lay six more lobster traps along the channel and then pulled and rebaited the three that'd been soaking for a couple of days. I got thirty lobster trap tags every year, but rarely used them all. Lobster tags were like Monopoly money in the Keys: you could trade them for all sorts of favors.

We'd easily be able to provide everyone on the island with a fresh lobster or fish dinner every day without ever dipping into the big deep freezer, which currently held provisions for *Taranis*—over a hundred pounds of filets, at least a hundred lobster tails, twenty pounds of steaks, forty pounds of hamburger, and eighty pounds of chicken. And that didn't even count what was in my and Jimmy's refrigerators.

Not to mention the massive dry goods locker Jimmy'd built under the western bunkhouse and had been stocking for months.

Nor did it include the fresh fruits and vegetables we grew on the island, or the live Louisianna crawfish and catfish we raised in the aquaponics garden.

If we had to, thirty people could hole up on our island for several months, completely off the grid and isolated. And with a little planning and stocking up, more than a year.

And, with the added power of *Taranis's* nine hundred square feet of solar panels producing nearly twenty kilowatts of power to charge her house batteries, our guests would have an air-conditioned place to sleep.

But everyone on the island had to work—that was a given, whether it was just two of us or thirty.

"You really gonna do this, Skipper?" Jimmy asked, as he pulled a fourth legal bug out of the last trap.

"You know as well as I that the cops are a reactionary force," I replied. "Sure, Monroe County has a detective, maybe two, assigned to the case. But they're just looking for leads to find the killers, and these guys haven't left many."

He rebaited the trap, using a big grouper's head, and dropped it over the side, letting the line out hand over hand. "I said you should've blasted them, man, and I meant it." He bent over the gunwale to rinse his hands, then leaned back, pushed his hair back out of his face, and looked around. "I'd hate to see trouble come out this way."

"Same here," I agreed, putting the throttle control in forward and turning the wheel. "Which is why we're taking the fight to them."

The stern kicked around smartly, and I straightened the wheel, keeping the engine at an idle as we headed back up the channel.

"I can't go with you," Jimmy said softly, standing beside me at the helm and looking toward the island. "Too much to risk, man."

"I wasn't going to ask," I said. "The only ones on the boat will be me, Deuce, Andrew, Tony, Paul, and maybe Marty."

"I'll help out any way I can, man," he said. "I won't fight, but I can understand your reasoning to."

"You remember Tom Broderick?"

He nodded.

"Tom will be here with you and Rusty," I continued. "He can't hear, so he's no good on night watch. But I've never known a better tactician, and he's deadly if anyone gets within arm's reach. And don't forget Trish, Billy, Kim, Julie, and Charity."

"Alberto was right, man. Our little island is safer than Fort Knox."

As we turned into my channel, I heard the familiar and distinctive whump-whump of a Huey approaching from the east, and Charity landed in the clearing in the middle of the island before we got the boat tied off.

Jimmy and I carried the cooler full of lobsters straight to the cleaning station and set it on one side.

"Go ahead, Skipper," Jimmy said. "I'll get these cleaned and in the fridge for tonight's dinner."

"Thanks, Jimmy," I responded. "And thanks for understanding why this has to be done."

I strode on past my house and spotted Paul and Tom unloading the helicopter even before the rotors had stopped turning.

Charity climbed out of the pilot's seat and removed her hat, shaking her hair out. It'd grown longer since the last time I'd seen her.

Then Savannah came down the back steps and joined me as we approached the others.

"Thanks for coming," I said. "I hope we don't need you, but having a quick reactionary force in readiness will be a good thing."

"Aw," Charity said, pouting. "Does that mean I won't get to have any fun, then?" She turned and hugged Savannah, then me. "It's good to see you both again. Here, together, I mean."

Charity had been instrumental in finding Savannah last year, and they'd worked together to bring down a kidnapping ring in the Yucatan. I hated to think what might have happened had Charity not been there.

"Don't you worry," Savannah said. "We'll have plenty to do."

Alberto came running toward us. "Wow! Now there's nineteen!"

"Nineteen what?" Charity asked, dropping to one knee to face him.

"We have nineteen people on the island!" he exclaimed.

"I remember a time when we had about that many here," she replied with a smile. Then her smile faded as she remembered one of the men who'd been here at that time—Jared Williams.

He'd been killed in an explosion meant for me and Deuce, and he'd died saving countless other lives that fateful day.

Savannah and Naomi helped Charity get her things to the comm shack, which, as it had been before, was set up with a pair of desks and two sets of bunk beds. But unlike before, it was air-conditioned, on stilts, and had a great view of the basin over the mangroves.

The comm shack would take priority over the rest of the island, as far as energy usage. The computers *and* their operators needed to stay cool.

"Good to see you again, Gunny," Tom said, as he and Paul put a long case down and approached us.

Tom Broderick had been my company commanding officer when I'd retired from the Corps. But we'd known one another for ten years prior to that, since he was a boot second lieutenant, or "butter bar," fresh out of Officer Candidate School, and we were on a WestPac cruise, with Battalion Landing Team, First Battalion, Ninth Marines—the famed "Walking Dead."

Six months later, Tom was with me when I returned from Panama to find my house empty, wife and kids gone. Then six months later, during Operation Desert Shield, he and I had been transferred to Special Operations Force, and he'd been my direct connection to Colonel Eric Litaker, the head of Intelligence with U.S. Central Command, as I'd spent a month alone in the desert, moving at night, to identify fixed targets and troop strength. Colonel Litaker answered only to General Stormin' Norman Schwarzkopf, commander of American forces in the region.

I'd always liked a short chain of command.

Tom was nearly my height and weight, and had always been athletic, but he'd been injured in an IED blast shortly after he'd been promoted to major. The attack had killed three of his men, flash-fried his ear off, and left him deaf and barely alive.

He'd been horribly scarred on one side of his head and face. The scars had been reddish pink and had contrasted greatly against Tom's ebony complexion. Multiple plastic surgeries and skin grafts had helped restore his looks and evened out the color of his skin to the point he no longer frightened small children, but no hair grew on that side, so he shaved the other side every morning.

I took Tom's extended hand and pulled him into a bear hug.

"Great to see you again, Skipper," I said, after stepping back so he could read my lips.

Then I turned and shook hands with Paul Bender. "Thanks for coming, Paul."

"Deuce gave us a briefing," the former Secret Service agent and forensic psychologist said. "For what it's worth, I think his plan's solid, and fully exploits the enemy's weakness—their own over-confidence."

"Glad you agree," I replied. "But I can't emphasize it enough—this *will* be dangerous. From what we've dug up already, these guys are ruthless."

For the rest of the morning, we worked at getting the comm shack and *Taranis* set up for what we planned to do.

Rusty returned with Tony and Andrew, and rather than tie off at the main south dock, they went around the island so Rusty could dock his boat at the floating dock at *Taranis's* stern. Then they began unloading several large, unmarked boxes and moving them aboard *Taranis*.

When we gathered everyone for a lunch of lobster-bite tacos and a large fruit salad, Chyrel brought us up to speed on what she'd learned from Chip, who was aboard *Ambrosia*, off the southern coast of Spain.

"We've managed to identify the most likely shipping companies being used by this cartel," she said, looking around the tables.

"Cartel?" I asked. "I thought this was the Greek mob."

"It is," she replied. "But organized crime in Greece is different than here in the States or even Italy. What we're dealing with in this case is a loose... association or collaboration of several family-run organizations, more akin to a cartel than anything else."

"Do we know how many organizations?" Kim asked. "And how big they are?"

Whether she used the word "we" out of habit, working with other law enforcement officers, or something else, I couldn't be sure. Marty had made it clear that he not only knew of but was interested in learning more about Armstrong Research.

Had the two of them discussed it further?

I decided the obvious. Of course they had. They were married.

Some of the assignments Jack's operatives and investigators conducted were dangerous. But then, so were the occasional stops of suspected poachers and drug runners.

"At least three organizations are working together," Chyrel replied. "And possibly a fourth and fifth, but those are as yet unidentified. We've been working closely with Interpol, but like the police anywhere, they have regulations and rules of engagement to follow and so far, these Greek organized crime families have been untouchable. The three primary families involved in this case number between thirty and fifty people each, nearly all related."

Kim nodded, knowing full well the restrictions put on law enforcement.

"How much is known about 'em?" Rusty asked. "And how are they connected to what's happening here?"

"It's believed that a member of one of the families involved in moving the stolen yachts immigrated to the States, or perhaps his parents had, and he's running the operation in South Florida. He's a ghost, though. Just a blank picture on the wall. But he will eventually be identified."

"That's not good," I said. "You'd want to move against him at the same time. What about the organization in Greece? Has Matt come up with any intel over there?"

Matt Brand had been my first officer when I'd commanded *Ambrosia* and was now her captain. He came from a long line of Cornish watermen and fishermen. He had a military background, was slow to anger, and smart as a whip. The perfect captain of a ship engaged in covert operations.

"Not very much, I'm afraid," Chyrel admitted worriedly. "Even the three primaries are shrouded in centuries-old secrecy."

# CHAPTER TWENTY

W e toiled through the afternoon, with Billy working diligently to make things work on *Taranis* the way they had on *Gaspar's Revenge*.

Some of the equipment was easily interchangeable or adaptable, but he had to fashion a mounting bracket in the main hull's forward-most storage compartment without altering the integrity of the hull or interior.

While they were down in Marathon, Rusty had stopped at the Anchor and picked up a bunch of stainless-steel square tubing he'd scrounged here and there, as well as long, straight pieces of one-inch stainless tubing from wrecked boats he recovered.

Fortunately, Billy always had a portable welder on his plane. Since we were teenagers, he'd been able to look at a pile of rusty, twisted metal and see how it could all be cut, bent, fastened, and welded together to create what he wanted.

Over the last few years, he's turned a lot of scrap into statues and moving wind vanes in his backyard.

Marty acted as a runner, going back and forth from the tool shed to *Taranis*, and to the pile of tubing in the back of Rusty's boat, carrying whatever parts, pieces, or tools Billy asked for. They'd also scrounged through a large spare parts bin under the front steps of the house.

I stood on *Taranis's* flybridge, watching everyone move around the island like a colony of worker ants.

Jimmy and Naomi were in charge of food and, with help from Alberto, Trish, and Maddy, were already getting things ready for dinner.

I hardly saw Savannah for most of the afternoon as she worked with Chyrel, primarily doing research for now. But once we got underway, she'd have full control of all assets.

Hearing someone coming up the steps from the cockpit, I turned as Tom strode across the deck toward me.

He leaned against the starboard rail beside me and looked out over the island. "I wish I could go with you, Gunny."

I waited until he turned to face me. "I need you here, Tom. With my family. We have plenty of able troops, but no leader."

He chuckled. "You're a lucky man, Guns. To have so much family, and a wife devoted to supporting what you do."

Tom knew my history. When we'd returned from Panama, it was Tom who'd waited at the curb until I'd opened the door to my empty house, then had quietly put an arm around my shoulder as I'd sobbed.

Years later, Tom's own wife had abandoned him while he was recuperating in Bethesda, unable to deal with the reality of war.

It happened. I knew that.

People fell in love and got married. They started a family. All was sunshine and roses. Until it wasn't. But not everyone managed extreme stress in the same way and sometimes a spouse couldn't handle it.

I understood it. But I didn't have to like it.

We sat down and faced one another, and I looked my former CO in the eye. "To be honest, Tom, I'm scared shitless."

One corner of his mouth turned up—the good side. "I don't

believe that for one second, Jesse. And neither do you. It's just pre-op jitters."

He jerked a thumb toward where Deuce stood on the bow. "What was it you and his dad always said to lighten the mood before jumping out of perfectly good aircraft? Saturday night, rock and roll?"

I looked over Tom's shoulder. Deuce was holding a large metal contraption over the forward hatch, talking to someone below.

"I wonder what *Ace* would think of all this?" I asked rhetorically.

Tom and I had first met when he'd been a newly assigned infantry officer with 1st Battalion, 9th Marines, and I'd been a staff sergeant. It was during that cruise that my second daughter, Kim, was born and I wasn't there for the birth.

Shortly after our return and meeting Kim for the first time, just five days before Christmas, we both deployed again, with no warning.

That was when my first wife Sandy took the girls and left nothing behind except a toppled tree, and a crushed Marine Corps ornament I'd received from Tank and hung on the tree the night before we suddenly shipped out to Panama.

Tom and his new wife had helped me get through those dark days, though fraternization between officers and enlisted was frowned on. We became friends.

Tom turned and looked over his shoulder toward the foredeck. "You know what, Guns? I think he'd be right here with us. Just like his son, and Thurman and Rainwater."

"Semper fi, sir," I said, tossing down the cold dregs in my mug.

"*Always* faithful," he said. "To God, country, and Corps. But mostly to one another." He paused and looked out over the island again. "I'll stay here with Thurman and take care of your family.

Why's Rainwater not going?"

"His vision's declining," I replied, hearing Billy cursing down below.

"Oh?"

"Advanced glaucoma," I replied, knowing that Billy would tell him if he wasn't busy. "It's most noticeable at night. He and Rusty, along with Billy's girlfriend, Trish, will be in reserve, flying his plane in if we need them. Trish is also a Marine. Odds are, they'll be here to help you out."

Tom chuckled again. "The deaf leading the blind."

I turned to face him. "Either of whom is better than any two ordinary men. I appreciate you doing this."

"What else am I going to do on a Thursday night?" he said, grinning crookedly once more. Then he snapped his fingers. "Oh, yeah! It's ladies' night at my club. If I wasn't here, I'd be serving Miami's hottest and finest."

Tom owned a small, but very successful dance club in South Beach, where he also tended the bar, kept the books, managed the staff, and was also the "cooler" or head bouncer.

Being deaf and able to read lips, he had no trouble at all "hearing" customers' orders over the loud music.

Or an argument that was about to start all the way across the room.

"That's too bad," I offered. "I guess some 'po thang' will just have to go home with second best tonight. How many women do you juggle these days?"

"I beg your pardon," he said, sitting back in mock indignation. "I am an officer *and* a gentleman, and a gentleman *never* tells."

I laughed. To say that Tom was lucky with the ladies was an understatement. Aside from the now minor scarring, the prosthetic ear, and a long scar on the back of his shoulder, the guy looked like a Zulu warrior even now in his fifties.

His face turned critical. "Seriously, though. You be careful and watch out for *you* first. You taught Deuce and his guys well over the years. I see your influence in them every day—the way they interact and communicate. They can handle themselves."

There was a sudden blast from an air horn, and I turned to see Alberto handing the familiar red-and-yellow compressed-air canister and horn to Jimmy.

"Dinner's ready," I relayed to Tom.

"Jesse!" Deuce shouted from the bow. "We'll be along in a few minutes. Don't let your kid devour everything."

I waved down to him as Tom and I turned and headed for the steps.

Over dinner, Savannah updated everyone on what she, Chyrel, and Chip had learned. Jimmy, Naomi, and Maddy had taken Alberto over by the fire pit—out of earshot—to eat. Alberto knew why but didn't argue.

What Savannah had to say wasn't much.

Stockwell had assigned three more analysts to the team, a woman named Helen whom I'd never met, and who worked in shifts with Chip, along with two other analysts aboard *Ambrosia* whom I also didn't know, and Savannah didn't identify, each alternating during the other's midwatch, so information could be more efficiently shared.

Four analysts, plus Chyrel and Savannah.

"Travis will have two analysts aboard *Ambrosia* on call at all times," Savannah told us. "And either I or Chyrel will be in constant contact with them and *Taranis* until the situation is resolved."

Stockwell seemed a bit over the top in his response to our being attacked. But knowing the man as I did, I'm sure he probably took any attack against anyone he knew as a slap in his own face.

"The body recovered in Biscayne Bay has been identified," Savannah continued, keeping her voice low, reading her tablet. "Harvey Martinez, age twenty-four, of Miami. A few arrests for gang-related crimes. Cause of death was ruled a homicide. Manner of death was a gunshot wound in the chest." She paused and looked over at me. "The medical examiner reported that there was no water in his lungs."

It was a small concession. I'd killed the man and I'd do the same thing again in the same situation, but I felt some moral relief that I couldn't understand. It allowed me to breathe a little easier, knowing the man I'd shot had died instantly, before entering the water. He'd never heard the shot that killed him.

Swift. Silent. Deadly. The Force Recon motto.

Savannah went on, looking down at the electronic tablet she held in her hand. "Martinez was a known associate of a man named Ramon Martel, aka Snake Martel, aka Raymond Martin. Both men have long police reports, including drug possession and trafficking, burglary, grand theft, and several assaults."

"Is this Snake Martel the ringleader?" Marty asked.

"We don't think so," Chyrel replied. "At least not the top man."

"Martel is a known associate of Manuel Woods," Savannah continued, reading from the device. "Aka Manny Woods, aka Monty Woodson. He's twenty-six, born in Liberty City, never left the country."

She paused and looked at me again, concern in her eyes.

"Similar records to the other two, but Woods was also charged with two murders, and is a person of interest in two more that are unsolved. He was acquitted both times he was tried."

"We feel certain Woods is the top dog in the theft ring," Chyrel added. "But he has a boss, and we think *that* guy has ties to Greece."

"These men are a menace to society," Deuce said, standing beside the stone grill. "They are to be considered armed and dangerous."

# CHAPTER TWENTY-ONE

After dinner, everyone pitched in to clean up, and as the sun started its descent toward the horizon, most made it out to the end of the north pier, where *Taranis* was docked.

It'd been a long day.

With the number of people we had, Tom assigned night watch to twelve people—six teams doing two-hour shifts with one on *Taranis's* flybridge and another on the south-facing deck of my and Savannah's house. Two people would be on constant watch from dusk to dawn.

Since Charity and I, and possibly Billy, would be driving the next day, we were exempt from the night's watch, along with Tom, of course, and he utilized everyone who would be staying behind on the island, so those who were or might be involved would be plenty rested.

As I headed toward the north pier, Chyrel came out of the comm shack and met me at the bottom of the steps. "Savvy's picking this up really easy," she said, with a slight Alabama drawl. "I think she'd be a first-rate analyst, too."

I looked down at her. "When this is over, we're going cruising."

"She told me," Chyrel replied. "I'm just sayin'."

Tomorrow, we planned to take *Taranis* back to Biscayne Bay with six of us aboard. We wanted to arrive at dusk and the crossing would take half a day, so we'd be leaving at noon.

Savannah and I had no plans beyond what we would do tomorrow to find the killers and with any luck, help bring down an international theft ring.

After that, we would disappear. At least for a few months. We'd have to be back in the spring for our daughter, Florence's, graduation from University of Florida.

"Thanks," I said to Chyrel. "I'm sure she's very good. But like I said, after this is over, our lives are going to be nothing but sun, sand, and relaxation. I promised her I wouldn't involve myself in other people's squabbles anymore unless it involved family."

"And these guys are in the way of your and your family's vacation?"

I glared at her. "They'll keep coming," I said, my voice low. "These people hold a grudge forever. Better here and now, than some time in the future, when we might be surprised."

"You think I don't know that, Jesse?" she hissed. "There are a lot of good people out there who want nothing more than to get on with their lives after a brush with the dark side, but they can't for fear of someone finding them."

"And what?" I asked, getting a little heated. "Am I supposed to solve everyone elses's problems, and never have a life? I think I've earned it!"

"I'm sorry," she said. "I didn't mean to get you pissed off. But I've been on the inside a long time. I see what's going on out there and I hate to see someone give up, especially people with the talent you and Savvy have. But I get it. I apologize and won't bring it up again."

I breathed out slowly. "I'm sorry, too. I didn't mean to get angry."

She smiled. "Go on, ya big lug. Go watch your sunset."

I continued out to the pier, going over the details in my mind, while a small part of my brain played with what Chyrel had said.

Tomorrow, about the same time we'd leave on *Taranis*, Charity would fly up to Homestead with Kim and Marty and join a couple more of Armstrong's assets there, ready to move by air or ground to where they were needed. They'd stay in contact with Chyrel and Savannah, with Savvy calling all the shots.

Billy, Trish, and Rusty would be backup, ready to take off in Billy's plane at a moment's notice, either for extraction or with Rusty manning a rifle in the back door for suppressive fire.

Like all good plans, ours was rudimentary. We didn't even know who the primary target was yet. But we had a really good idea of how to flush the ones we *did* know toward him.

I joined most of the others on *Taranis's* flybridge deck, where it was more comfortable, and the cool breeze kept the bugs at bay. Once more, Jimmy and Naomi had diverted Alberto's attention with a late swim.

Maddy was interested in what Chyrel and Savannah were doing, and from what Savvy told me, she'd been quietly observing and getting them anything they needed.

I unlatched the backrest of the helm seat and flipped it forward, turning it into an aft-facing sunset seat. Tony joined me, and I looked around the fly deck.

Those who were going to accompany me tomorrow—Deuce, Julie, Tony, Andrew, and Paul—were scattered around the deck, along with Rusty, Billy, Trish, and Charity.

"I have a lot of confidence in Chyrel," Andrew said, leaning back in the settee on the port side. "She'll figure it out. And your wife's turned into a first-rate handler."

"Thanks to Stockwell," I said, maybe a bit too gruffly.

165

Tony nodded. "There is *that*," he said slowly, softly. "And I understand you not wanting to involve your wife. But it started with her long before Mexico, man."

"He's right," Julie agreed. "She's had it in her since before you two ever met. She's chill now, but we both know she could be hell on wheels back then."

"And she got *better*," Charity whispered softly, her back to us. "She became stronger and smarter during those years she and Flo cruised alone on her boat. Good, bad, or indifferent, she's always been able."

Charity slowly turned, her eyes falling on each person in turn. "Now she's calmer, more focused, and confident. But that woman has *always* had the heart of a warrior."

Charity's gaze finally met mine. "I'm not just talking about Savvy's confidence in herself, Jesse. She's more confident in *you*—in all of us. A lot more than you give her credit for. Don't go and fuck that up, boss."

She hadn't called me that in a long time, since the training days here on my island and up in Homestead. With no actual designation as a government employee, she and a couple others had used that.

To hear her, as well as the others speak so highly of Savannah wasn't unexpected. I'd seen it too. But I knew she didn't *want* to be the hard-ass covert analyst, even though she'd been through the training aboard *Ambrosia*. Everyone aboard had to pull their weight and that was what she'd chosen.

"Jack's put the full resources of Armstrong at her disposal," Deuce said. "Even the colonel is under her command on this one. And if you or she think it necessary, he can have a lot more people brought in." He paused and looked around at everyone. "But I think, as it is, with officers from FWC working in conjunction with DHS and Miami-Dade PD, we can make this happen."

"Maybe all the way down to its roots in Greece," Rusty added.

I was feeling pressured from all sides. All Savannah and I talked about was getting away—ditching the rats to run their races without us.

The sun reached the horizon, and I turned to face it, releasing a slow breath. "Yeah, and all I have to do is find *one* little center console boat in all of Biscayne Bay."

"We don't need to find *it*," Savannah said, crossing the deck with our son, who was wrapped in a towel. "Tell everyone goodnight, Alberto."

He gave me a hug and Tony a knuckle bump, then said goodnight to the others. Jimmy and Naomi waited at the top of the steps for him.

"He's gonna spend the night with us, man," Jimmy said. "Rusty and Maddy, too."

Knowing he meant more than just *this* night, I nodded. "Thanks, Jimmy."

When they were down the ladder and headed away from the boat, Savannah turned toward me. "As I said, you won't have to find one boat out of thousands. They'll find you. We're close."

She sat down between Tony and me, scooting close against me as we watched the sun disappear out of sight.

"Another day done," she whispered, then turned to face me. "I think we're onto something and should have an answer soon. Chyrel's taking first watch, along with Helen and Troy."

"Troy?" I asked. "And Helen? Who's the other two? Aristotle and Plato? Are those even their real names?"

"Probably not," Deuce replied. "Not with people outside the organization involved."

"They're smart," Savannah said. "And yes, we are technically outside of Armstrong. But I'm comfortable working with them. We'll find Mr. X."

"If he's Greek," I said, "that'd be Mr. Ten."

"You're thinking *Roman* numerals," she corrected me. "In Greek, X is one thousand. But in this case, it's just an as-yet unknown variable of a person we're calling X."

"We should all turn in," Deuce said. "There's a lot left to do tomorrow."

"I'm off until ten," Savannah said, taking my hand and leading the way to the ladder. "Er, that is... twenty-two hundred."

"Tom assigned the security watch," I said, holding her hand as we descended the steps in the gathering darkness. "He left me and a few others out of it."

She turned at the bottom of the steps and smiled at me, "Yes, I know."

We walked to the foot of the floating pier, then across the clearing as some of the others split off to the bunkhouses, and a few stayed aboard.

"You're... totally, okay?" I asked, as we went up the steps to the deck around our house. "I mean with what we're doing tomorrow."

She stopped at the top of the steps and turned toward me, her back to Trish, who was already on watch.

"No more talk about what will happen tomorrow," she whispered, putting a finger to my lips. Then she smiled and stretched her toes to kiss me. "Let's stick to what we'll do tonight."

# CHAPTER TWENTY-TWO

When I woke the next morning, I had a lot of mixed feelings and my state of being was off-kilter. I was mentally well-rested, and my head was clear, but I was physically worn down.

Savannah had kept true to her word, and we hadn't talked about what would happen today. In fact, even though a lot of feelings and emotions were expressed, very few words had been spoken.

Savannah had left our bed at 2200 and I'd drifted off to sleep, feeling happy and satisfied.

When I opened my eyes, her side of the bed was empty, which told me it was after 0600. I looked at my watch and then grimaced at the narrow shaft of light coming through a crack at the side of the drawn curtains.

The sun had been up for over an hour, and Dink was going to be here soon.

I dressed quickly, then went out into the empty living room, finding the door to Alberto's tiny bedroom standing open, a full pot of coffee in the little galley, and a large Thermos standing beside it.

I poured some of the coffee into a mug and the rest into the Thermos before setting the coffeemaker up for another run. Then I headed to the door.

When I opened it, Chyrel was standing there, just about to knock.

"Breakfast is ready," she said, smiling. "Your friend Dink called

Savvy and said he was on the way. More backup?"

I suddenly couldn't remember if I'd told her who Dink was bringing this morning—Warren Kennedy and Tank. Had I even told her what we'd decided on for a name? I must have.

"Dink's bringing a new family member," I said. "Our new puppy."

She smiled up at me, but her eyes glistened slightly. "Tank?"

"Yeah," I said, as she followed me toward the rear steps. "He's almost three months old now and taking a break from his early training."

"I can't wait to meet him," she said, as we went down the steps. "Is he really as big as Alberto says?"

I stopped and turned to face her. "Just like his namesake," I replied. "Bigger than life."

What had started several years ago as a business arrangement between Chyrel and Owen "Tank" Tankersley had turned into a May-September romance. Or maybe June-November.

Chyrel had never wanted a husband or kids but had agreed to marry Tank so that his pension would continue to help fund his foundation after he passed. He'd been dying of cancer when he came to the Keys shortly after retiring from the Corps, and Chyrel had made a positive difference in his last days.

As her eyes started to well, she hugged me. Then, after a couple seconds, she turned and hurried down the steps, tugging me along by the shirtsleeve. "Come on, I'm hungry."

The others were all gathered around the two large tables. Savannah turned toward me, a plate in each hand and a smile on her face.

She nodded at the end of the table. "Have a seat, sleepyhead."

"I'll get back to it," Chyrel said to Savannah, then headed

toward the comm shack.

As I sat next to my wife on the long cypress bench, she pressed her thigh against mine, and I could feel her warmth through the fabric of her jeans.

"Still hungry?" Savannah asked, moving her hip slightly against mine.

"In more ways than one," I whispered, suddenly realizing I was famished.

There was a lot of chatter around the two large tables, each big enough to seat eight people. Three folding beach chairs had been added near the grill where Jimmy and Naomi sat, still tending the cookfire.

We'd had electricity on the island for some time, but both Jimmy and I preferred cooking on the large stone grill and chimney, and we had a never-ending supply of driftwood that collected on the eastern shore and along that side of the floating dock.

Our power grid consisted of a solar array on the little islet off the northeast shore, separated from the main island by just a few feet.

The array looked like a giant sunflower and behaved the same way, with wedge-shaped panels that unfolded at sunrise like flower petals into a fifteen-foot circle that automatically tracked the sun across the sky all through the day, then folded up at night. The minimal energy used to move the array was nothing compared to what it produced by maintaining an almost perpendicular angle to the sun.

The "sunflower" charged two giant Tesla battery banks housed inside what was once a battery shack with twenty deep-cycle marine batteries on a platform. The Power Walls, as they were called, stored, managed, and provided more energy than the old batteries, lasted longer, and charged faster. And they had a ten-year warranty, whereas the old glass matt batteries had to be replaced every two years.

We hadn't had an outage since it was installed, and the backup diesel generator, which only ran for an hour or so after a cloudy day, had only needed to have its fifty-gallon tank refilled once during all of last year.

I'd nearly finished my meal when Jimmy stood and cocked his head, listening. "Boat coming."

Several of us were on our feet instantly.

"Relax," Jimmy said, looking around at me, Deuce, Tony, Andrew, and Charity. "It's Dink. He's coming up the back way."

I realized then that the wind had shifted slightly during the night and was coming more out of the northeast. It made sense that Dink, who would be in a shallow-draft flats skiff, would avoid Moser Channel and the choppier open water north of the Seven Mile Bridge, and would instead come the longer way and be sheltered in the shallower waters between Cutoe Key and the north end of Big Pine.

"Go ahead, Skipper," Jimmy said. "Y'all go and welcome your new best bud home. We'll get this."

Chyrel appeared at the top of the steps, looking off to the north.

"Come with us, Chyrel," Savannah called up to her, then turned to Maddy. "Can you watch things up there for a few minutes? Just yell on the comm if Chip needs either of us."

Everyone involved had been issued tiny bone-mic communication devices, or earwigs, from the supplies Deuce had brought in on Charity's helo.

Chyrel had everyone on the same frequency, but had remotely powered down most devices, saving the batteries. The comm shack had direct, encrypted satellite communication via Chyrel's computers with Chip or Helen aboard *Ambrosia*, as well as everyone involved in the op.

"I can do that," Maddy said, then sprinted to the steps as Chyrel came down.

She joined me, Savannah, and Alberto, and we hurried to the south pier, where I could now hear the buzz of an outboard weaving back and forth through one of the shallow and unmarked channels that filled and drained the backcountry twice a day.

"He's staying here with us, right?" Alberto said, as we walked out onto the planks.

"Of course he is," I replied. "He's way too young for a lot of boat travel. Puppies get motion sickness pretty easy."

"How do you know?" he asked, looking up at me.

I shrugged. "Google."

We waited at the end of the pier as the sound of Dink's approaching outboard grew louder. Over it, we heard the deep, steady *woof* of a dog.

"There he is!" Alberto exclaimed, as Dink's custom-built skiff made the turn into Harbor Channel.

Warren Kennedy sat beside Dink on the aft casting deck. Dink's boat had no real helm seat, just a shallow recess between wide side decks to put your feet in and a minimal center console. The well was wide enough to seat three and could easily be stepped over while fighting a fish. The hull was red, and the topsides a gray, all-grip surface. A fishing machine that didn't pretend to be something else at times.

Warren had Tank by his collar as the large pup stood in front of him, his feet planted solidly apart, head up, and facing into the wind as he leaned into the turn, barking.

It occurred to me that it was the first time I'd heard him bark. He had a deep voice, even for a full-grown dog, and it carried easily across the water, punctuating the slap of the hull as it entered choppier water.

"He doesn't look seasick..." Savannah said.

No, he didn't, I thought. He looked like a big doofus having fun.

The boat slowed, and suddenly Tank recognized us and began smacking Warren in the ribcage with his tail.

We'd gone up to see Tank every week since the litter was born, and in the last five weeks, to work with him at Warren's training facility for two days each week.

"I thought you said he was only three months old," Chyrel said, as Dink slowed the boat and turned toward my channel.

"Not yet," Alberto replied. "He's only ten *weeks* old."

"Oh. My. God," Chyrel said, breathing the words out slowly.

Tank began tugging at Warren's arm, and the patient trainer leaned over him, said something to him in a low voice, and the dog obediently sat down at his feet, panting.

Then Warren gave him a treat from his pocket.

Dogs pant for a lot of reasons—exertion, pain, happiness, and in this case anxiety. At his age, everything was an exciting adventure. Today was his first day away from home.

Dink already had lines waiting on the fore and aft decks, and Alberto and I only needed to pick them up when he put the twenty-foot skiff smartly against the dock.

"Good morning," Warren said, getting to his feet.

"Hope it wasn't too rough," I said, tying the bow line off to a cleat.

"It was fun, actually," he replied. "And I think Tank liked it."

When I turned around, the giant puppy was staring at me, as if waiting for me to say or do something.

"Hello, Tank," I said, getting a sort of a chuff of a bark in return.

"Up and over, Tank," Warren said, stepping across to the dock.

The puppy clumsily bounded over the low gunwale, then sat beside Warren, again looking up at me.

His fur was dense; a little longer than a Lab's, and dark black, reflecting a purple tint in the sun. He had four white paws and a small white marking on his chest, just left of center. His jowls were longer than a Lab's, hanging over his lower jaw, and he had a higher, more pronounced forehead with a big head and heavy brow.

And then there was his size. At ten weeks, he was almost as big as a grown Lab.

"Welcome to your new home, Tank," I said softly.

He looked up at Warren, who bent down and unclipped the leash from his collar.

Tank rose and walked toward us on feet the size of a bear cub's, then sat down in front of me, glancing over at Chyrel.

"This is Chyrel, Tank," I said. "She is our friend."

He moved over toward her and lifted her hand with his muzzle.

Chyrel dropped to her knees and held his head in her hands, staring into his dark brown eyes. "Oh, this face! I think you're going to like it here, boy."

"Can we go play?" Alberto asked. "I want to show him the whole island."

"Introduce him to everyone, too," I replied, then looked down at Tank. "Go with Alberto, Tank."

The two of them walked toward the foot of the pier at a leisurely pace. I'd noticed during his training that Tank never got overly excited and never put a lot of emphasis in speed. Unlike most puppies I'd seen, he and his littermates seemed more aloof, above all the playfulness and wrestling that most pups enjoyed.

"How big will he get?" Chyrel asked.

"He was thirty-two pounds at yesterday morning's weigh-in," Warren replied. "He's ten weeks today, and just moved into the number two spot in weight, ahead of one of his brothers." He turned to face me and Savannah. "With proper nutrition and exercise, he should gain three to five pounds a week until he's eight months, then just a couple pounds a week until he turns one. Monitor his weight weekly and raise or lower feeding as needed. I brought a hundred pounds. That should last him through next week."

I did the math in my head. "You think he'll be a hundred and thirty pounds at one year?"

"And he eats ten pounds a day?" Savannah asked.

"Two pounds of dry, three times a day," Warren said. "If you want to get some canned food, you can add that for dinner instead of the kibble. He'll need less as he gets older."

Six pounds of food a day? I thought. Good thing I hadn't opted for one of the macerator showers.

"Based on his current growth pattern," Warren continued, "I think one-twenty is a conservative estimate. I also believe, since he's half Lab, he'll probably continue to develop after a year, becoming stronger, as he uses up all the puppy fat." He paused and looked at Savannah. "We will understand if he's too much. Not everyone can handle such large breeds."

"Not a chance," she replied. "This island or our boat will be his home forever."

Dink moved easily around his boat, securing things and raising the outboard before stepping over to the dock and immediately stumbling, almost falling in the water.

He looked over my shoulder. "You got a bunch of people here,

Jesse." He stepped to the side, looking around me. "Is that a *helicopter*?"

Chyrel's hand moved to her ear, and the motion wasn't lost on Warren. Being a former cop, he'd probably used similar communications devices.

"We got him!" Chyrel exclaimed, turning to Savannah. "You made the connection. Chip just confirmed."

"Um, we have to go," Savannah said to Warren, then nodded quickly at me. "Told you we'd get X."

Dink looked back at me. "What's going—"

"I *think*," Warren interrupted, holding up a finger to Dink, "the less you and I know, the better." He gave me a knowing look. "Am I right?"

"We're uh... in the middle of something," I replied. "Or the start, I guess."

Dink grinned from ear to ear. "I knew it!"

Just then, Marty and Kim came around the corner of the house, walking toward us.

"Deputy Phillips?" Warren asked, surprise in his voice.

Marty's eyes went wide as he and Kim both stopped dead in their tracks.

"Lieutenant... Kennedy?" Marty stammered. "What are you doing here?"

CHAPTER TWENTY-THREE

The fact that Warren knew Marty was no surprise. Marty was once a Monroe County Sheriff's deputy and Dade County was just to the north. Even a patrol deputy would occasionally interact with law enforcement in nearby jurisdictions.

After a tense moment, Warren stepped past Kim and Marty, rounding the corner of my house. I didn't stop him.

He looked around at all the commotion, his eyes picking up everything. Trish and Maddy were with Alberto and Tank, near the fire pit. Trish was kneeling and saying something to the pup.

Several others were busy carrying plastic tubs of dishes up to Jimmy's house. His kitchen had a large dishwasher and double sink.

Tony and Paul were out on the north pier, carrying a long crate from Rusty's boat to *Taranis*.

Warren turned and looked at me. "I'd heard rumors, but..."

"This isn't typical," I said. "I'm retired."

That was lame, McDermitt, I chastised myself.

"In fact, Lieutenant," Marty said quickly, "most everyone here is family. This is my wife, Kim. She's Jesse's daughter. We both work for FWC now."

Warren glanced at the bone mic curled around Marty's ear. "That woman with Savannah had one of those." He turned to Kim, then me, his expression neutral and reserved—a cop waiting for the answer to an unasked question.

Out of the corner of my eye, I saw Trish and Alberto leading Tank toward the little beach by Jimmy's place.

Then Deuce and Andrew started toward us, and Warren noticed my eyes move toward them and turned his head.

"I know that man," Warren said, turning back to me. "He was an assistant deputy director of Homeland Security when I was with SWAT."

Deuce stopped. his eyes moving from Warren to Dink, and finally to me. "More friends?"

Warren extended a hand. "We worked together once," he said. "I'm Warren Kennedy, retired lieutenant, Miami-Dade."

Deuce studied his face for a fraction of a second before responding.

"The kidnapping!" he exclaimed, the corners of his mouth ticking up slightly. "You helped us get the girls back where they belonged, avoiding the red tape and media."

I glanced over at Warren. Deuce was talking about a girl named Colby, who'd lived with her mom in a trailer on Grassy Key and just disappeared on her way to work one day.

I knew Deuce must have had help from the cops in getting the girls safely home after Tony, Andrew, Tank, and I extracted Colby and two other girls from a torture house in the Glades using Charity's chopper.

But I never knew who his contact was.

Until now.

Dink extended a hand to Andrew. "Hi! I'm Dink." He looked Andrew and Deuce over, both dressed in tactical pants and T-shirts. "I'm a fishin' guide and a friend of Jesse's."

Andrew shook hands with him. "We've met, Dink. At the Rusty Anchor a few years back. Your boat was squashed by a flying stage."

"Haha! Oh yeah."

Deuce fished into a cargo pocket and pulled out a small box, which he handed to Warren. "Turn this on. There will be someone to explain." Then he tapped his earwig and said, "Chyrel, patch unit fourteen through to our lead asset with Miami-Dade."

I turned toward Deuce and whispered, "Who—"

He held up a hand, one finger extended.

Warren switched his headset on and spoke. "Warren Kennedy here."

His eyes widened as he looked from me to Deuce. "Captain Fallon?"

Dink wandered away a few steps, trying to bypass all the hubbub as Warren stepped the other way and turned to talk quietly to someone on the comm.

Captain *Fallon*, I thought.

Deuce nodded toward Dink. "Do you trust him to be here?"

I glanced over at the fishing guide. He'd been a hard-working man as long as I'd known him, had always been willing to help when needed, and I'd never heard anyone say a bad thing about him. Well, except for the occasional gripes from other guides.

"Completely," I replied. "I'll talk to him." I glanced over to where Warren stood, speaking quietly on the comm. "Who's he talking to?"

"His replacement," Deuce said. "You remember Sherri Fallon? She's now a captain and in charge of Miami-Dade's tactical teams."

Sherri Fallon had been one of the original team members of Deuce's Caribbean Counterterrorism Command under DHS. She'd been the unit's armorer and was very knowledgeable and proficient with a variety of weapon systems. After the team had broken up, she'd returned to her old job at Miami-Dade's armory.

"Thanks to your training with our old team, Sherri applied to and was accepted to the Miami-Dade SWAT team."

Warren turned around and removed the earwig, then handed it to Deuce.

"Is there anything I can do to help?" he asked me. "I'm off until Monday, and to be honest, I was hoping to be invited to spend the night and help get Tank acclimated to his new surroundings."

"That would be a huge help," I replied, as Alberto and Tank came running toward us. "I will have to leave soon."

"Guess what, Dad?"

"I know, I know," I said, as he stopped in front of me, and Tank planted his butt right beside him. "There're twenty-one people on the island."

"Twenty-two!" Alberto exclaimed. "You left out Tank. But that's not it. Guess again."

I shrugged. "I'm all out of guesses, son."

"Tank can swim!" Alberto shouted, raising his hands and hopping up and down.

The pup jumped up, putting big, wet, sandy paws on my clean white T-shirt. At ten weeks.

"He should be an excellent swimmer," Warren said, taking Tank's collar. "Molly has taken all the pups to water several times, and Tank was one of the first to go in with her." He turned to me. "It'll be important when he gets bigger that he gets more exercise in the water than on land. Especially when he's older."

"How come?" Alberto asked.

Warren knelt beside the boy and the pup and glanced up at me. I nodded. Alberto knew.

"He'll be really big," Warren said. "Exercising in water is easier on the joints for older dogs."

Alberto looked down at Tank, sitting next to him, his head as high as the boy's waist. "But he's just a puppy now."

"But he won't be for long," Warren said. "Enjoy it now. He'll grow up very fast. How old are you?"

"I'll be twelve in June."

"Before you become a teenager," Warren explained, "Tank will be a full-grown adult dog. The first year of a dog's life is about fifteen or twenty for us humans. Then their aging slows down a little."

Alberto put a hand on Tank's head, absently scratching him behind the ear, like he'd done with Finn. "How long will Tank live?"

"About eight or nine years," Warren replied honestly. "Maybe ten, if you take good care of him and see that he gets plenty of exercise in the water."

"I will!" Alberto promised.

A double blast from an air horn split the air. It was the signal for everyone involved in the operation to assemble.

Savannah stood at the top of the steps to the comm shack, the horn in her hand. Then she turned and disappeared inside.

"We have to go," Deuce said.

I turned to Dink. "Are you hanging out?"

He grinned. "What? Leave and miss all this?"

"Keep what you see and hear under your hat," I cautioned him.

"Loose lips and all that, man. I get it. Can I help with somethin'? I still owe you big time, man."

"Can you swim?" Alberto asked him.

Dink looked down and nodded. "Everyone can swim."

"Take me and Tank swimming," he said. "I want to show him the dog ramp on the north pier." He looked up at me. "Will that be okay?"

The kid was wise beyond his years. Maybe too much so. He knew what was going on, knew that he wasn't supposed to be a part of it, and that Dink was in the same boat.

"Sure, son," I replied. "Just be careful, okay?"

"I'll go with them," Warren said. "This should prove interesting. He's experiencing so many things for the first time."

Alberto looked up at me. "Don't leave without saying goodbye."

I nodded. "I promise."

Deuce, Andrew, and I trotted across the clearing toward the comm shack and went up to join the others, all fourteen of us crowding into a room no bigger than a one-car garage.

"Mr. X... is Raymond Belsus," Savannah stated, standing beside one of the desks.

A man's image was displayed on the computer screen. He looked to be in his mid-thirties, well-dressed, clean-shaven, and with a fresh haircut—a GQ or Wall Street Journal cover photo.

"He's a prominent Miami businessman with no prior arrest record," Savannah continued, scrolling through her tablet. "He's thirty-eight years old and was born in Miami. His grandparents were Greek immigrants, when his father was a child. His parents owned a real estate firm, which he now owns. He also owns a few other local enterprises, and has a small partnership in a shipping company."

"A *Greek* shipping company?" I asked.

"A Kewpie doll to the tall hunk in back," Savannah replied, getting a few chuckles. "Belsus is the second cousin to a woman in the Greek port city of Piraeus whose husband also owns part of that same shipping company. His name is Jason Pappas."

"Pappas?" Charity asked. "Weren't Jerry and DJ involved in a—"

"Unrelated, as far as we can tell," Savannah replied. "Pappas is a very common surname in Greece."

"Savvy dug into cultural history," Chyrel explained. "A common practice is to buy part of the company owned by someone you want to go into a business deal with. It's one of the reasons the crime syndicates there are so firmly entrenched."

"Everyone's got skin in everyone else's game," Tony said.

"Jason Pappas is thirty-three-years old," Savannah continued. "He's the second oldest of four brothers, and they all jointly own the majority share of a small shipping company of seven container ships."

"But it's the oldest brother's *day-to-day* occupation that we found most interesting," Chyrel added.

"The oldest brother is a boatwright," I announced.

Savannah's eyes went wide. "How did you know?"

It was nice to see that I could still surprise her.

"Moving stolen yachts that are registered with the U.S. Coast Guard is one thing," I replied. "Once they reach a foreign port, they'd be recognized by the manufacturer's hull number, always affixed somewhere in the boat, and they'd be impossible to sell legally."

"I get it," Andrew replied. Being a Coast Guard master chief, I figured he'd make the connection. "A boatwright or shipyard would have access to every manufacturer's hull numbers and know if a boat was sunk or destroyed."

"Exactly," Savannah said. "They simply swap or alter the numbers to a stolen boat to one that they know is out of commission, change the name, and file for a salvage title."

"So, how'd you connect this guy?" I asked.

"Cellular association," Savannah replied, her blue eyes twinkling brightly. "David developed an AI program to follow patterns, given certain search parameters, and through a process of scouring years of cellular and internet communications between

Greece and the U.S., with an emphasis on South Florida, it finally spit out a name. Then we just connected the family tree, looking for someone with the right profile."

"We need to delay the departure," Deuce said. "At least until we can firm this up. Going after a leading Miami citizen could really blow up in our faces."

I looked at Deuce, knowing he was right, before facing Savannah.

"We can chase it to ground from a hundred different angles," she said. "And we will. But the dog's still going to point at this Raymond Belsus, then his second-cousin-in-law, Jason Pappas, and finally to his older brother, Hector Pappas."

"Chase it," I said. "Deuce is right. Taking down gangbangers or thieves is a whole lot different than busting a leading citizen. Besides, it would be smarter to make the crossing under cover of darkness anyway. What's the time difference between here and Greece?"

"Seven hours," Chyrel replied.

"That means it'll be dark here and in Piraeus for five of those hours."

Deuce turned and nodded. "A couple of hours after sunset here would be a couple of hours before sunrise there."

"They came before midnight," I said. "Sunrise in Greece."

"We'll want to draw them out earlier," Savannah said. "At a time of our choosing."

# CHAPTER TWENTY-FOUR

By sunset, Savannah and Chyrel had not only confirmed their suspicions, but they'd added even more evidence, including back-to-back calls made shortly after the attack on *Taranis*, originating from an unregistered burner phone located in north Biscayne Bay.

For most of that afternoon and evening, the burner used to make those calls had been in close proximity to an AT&T smartphone registered to the dead man, Harvey Martinez. Which meant the burner was owned by either the guy with the gun tucked in his pants or the boat's driver.

And most damning of all, the burner had been calling a cell phone registered to Raymond Belsus.

Our target was acquired and had been confirmed.

Before sunrise, Charity would fly out to Homestead with my daughter and son-in-law to meet with Sherri Fallon and two of her best people.

While we worked on setting a trap for the pirates, Sherri would start trying to find a friendly judge to sign off on a no-knock warrant, a judge who would understand the different roles of DHS, FWC, Miami-Dade PD, and the private investigative sector—me, the aged Neanderthal with more money than brains.

Our plan involved us "fishing" for the pirates, moving *Taranis* around Biscayne Bay with the AIS off, and turning it on when we stopped. Kind of like bouncing a jig off the bottom near a coral formation in the hopes of enticing a big grouper out.

The idea was to use the Armstrong satellite to track multiple surface vessels at the same time, looking for any sudden changes in course when our AIS came on, revealing our location.

The goal was to take them down hard and fast, but allow them to slip away, so the satellite could track them.

With any luck, he'd run straight to the boss.

Beyond that rudimentary plan, we had nothing.

Better to just go with the flow—wing it.

As the sun got closer to the horizon, several of us turned Billy's plane around, so it and *Taranis* were pointing windward.

The maneuver wasn't difficult. The floats extended beyond the propeller and, with several people in the water keeping the fenders in front of the floats, we were able to spin her around. Then Billy carried an anchor out to deeper water.

An hour later, with Billy's Beaver out of the way, we slipped the lines at sunset and got underway with quiet goodbyes from the dock.

Aboard *Taranis*, everyone was subdued as we headed south. My ad hoc crew had spent the last day familiarizing themselves with the boat's systems and redundancies, and I'd had a chance to inspect Billy's work in the bow.

Everyone aboard was highly qualified to operate just about any kind of vessel, so nothing on *Taranis* was a surprise.

Thirty minutes later, we passed under the Seven Mile Bridge, and I increased speed as we turned east, angling toward the Gulf Stream to pick up a couple of extra knots.

"Bring the stabilizer online," I said to Tony, who was at the navigation desk. "Wind it up to fifty percent."

Three miles from shore, almost over the horizon, I started the main engine and after a few minutes to warm up, I moved all three throttle controls up until we were making twenty-two knots speed over ground, according to the GPS.

The sea state was pretty calm, and *Taranis's* three bows knifed through the water with minimal disturbance.

Tony lowered the brightness on the red lights, which were all that we had on to preserve night vision, and it looked a little bit lighter outside as my eyes adjusted.

The overhead speaker crackled for a second, then a soft piano solo began, the volume turned low. The lyrics that followed were familiar, but obviously a cover of a Simon and Garfunkel song from the mid-sixties, "The Sounds of Silence."

The singer's voice seemed dark and foreboding.

Hello darkness, my old friend...

How many times had I stalked someone in the dark? How many times had I seen things in the darkness that nobody should see?

And here I was, surrounded by the night, heading toward a rendezvous with a destiny whose outcome I *knew.*

"Twenty-four-point-five knots," Tony said, "speed over ground; we're in the Gulf Stream."

A quick glance at the chart plotter confirmed it. We were six miles south of Long Key and had picked up speed.

We were out of the middle of the Stream, where northbound cargo ships would be, and we were far enough from the edge to avoid southbound vessels, which tended to dodge the great current.

"This isn't Simon and Garfunkel," I said, then glanced back at Deuce and the others. "Y'all should get some rest. It'll be midnight before we get there."

"It's a band called Disturbed," Tony said, as the singer began ramping up the vocals. "Want me to switch it to something else?"

"Wake me and Andrew in a couple of hours," Deuce said, moving toward the steps down to the port ama with Julie.

Andrew just stretched out on the large sofa in the salon as Paul started down the forward steps.

He paused on the first one and looked at me over the dash. "You have misgivings?"

I didn't need his psychoanalytical bullshit.

Besides being a forensic psychologist, Paul Bender was one of the best marksmen with a handgun I'd ever worked with.

That's what I needed him for. To repel possible boarders.

"Of course I have misgivings," I replied, meeting his gaze. "I put a lot of money in this boat. I'd appreciate you doing all you can to not get it shot to shit."

Tony glanced over, then quickly looked down at the chart plotter and radar screen, grinning.

"Like you said," Paul continued, pressing, "it's a long crossing, if you feel like talking about it."

"I'll keep that in mind," I replied, seeing the lights of a large tanker on the horizon ahead. "You got that ship on AIS, Tony?"

He knew I knew what it was, where it was, and where it was headed, but Tony went through the motions of pulling up the ship's AIS display as Paul continued on down the steps.

"Oil tanker headed to Galveston," Tony replied. "Well out of our way, hugging the edge of the Stream and making fourteen knots."

"I've turned off the others' comms so they can rest," Savannah said over my earwig. "He means well, Jesse."

I heard the click of the latch in the forward stateroom. "I know. I just don't need the psychobabble right now."

The song ended and Tony didn't bother playing anything more as we rode smoothly into the dark night, *Taranis* barely making a sound.

CHAPTER TWENTY-FIVE

Savannah knew her husband had conflicting feelings—she could hear it in his voice and see it in his mannerisms. It wasn't just about what they would be doing for perhaps the next several days either. She felt certain that her own departure from the way she'd typically behaved before Mexico had to be weighing heavily on his mind.

For many years, while Flo was growing up, she'd been able to avoid any kind of conflict by remaining wary and suspicious of everyone and everything. She'd used *Sea Biscuit's* ability to move great distances without stopping, as well as her shallow draft, to keep a low profile. Her default response to seeing another boat was to turn away immediately.

She'd often found desolate anchorages in more out-of-the-way places, where they'd often stayed for weeks, even months a couple of times, and had on occasion befriended a few people in the cruising community. But it had been rare. So, her exposure to the darker side of humanity had mostly been avoided.

Until Hoffman's Cay.

It'd been so long ago that Savannah had blocked it from her memory.

Until Mexico.

She hadn't been looking for trouble either of those times, yet people had died, and their blood was on her hands. Nor had she invited the thousands of other crude but less dangerous encounters.

It was in the days after the shooting in Mexico that she'd come to grips with the fact that danger didn't seek Jesse out. It was just there—everywhere—all around us, waiting to lift its ugly head.

He just doesn't take the steps to avoid it that most of us do, Savannah surmised. And why should he? Why should anyone? Why should good people have to take so many precautionary steps to avoid conflict?

Growing up in tiny little Beaufort, South Carolina, she didn't remember deadbolting doors. Dad would always leave his keys in the boat, as did all his captains, to make moving personnel around easier if someone was ill or got hurt.

Back then, Savannah had been shrouded from the bad, simply by being in a community so small that bad wasn't tolerated, and everyone knew everyone's mom and dad.

Jesse's natural tendency to *not* shy away from it had at first seemed exciting to her. In another life, long ago, she'd been the same. Until she'd met him and become pregnant with Flo, her one and only child.

When they'd first met, Jesse not only didn't avoid confrontations, but had intentionally inserted himself, stepping in to protect her and her sister from what later turned out to be sex-slave traffickers. There were three of them, and just Jesse and her and Charlotte's captain.

They'd spent three months with the man, cruising in their parents' boat all the way down the coast from South Carolina, and she couldn't remember his name. Jesse had incapacitated two of the men almost before their captain moved.

She'd spent two weeks with Jesse and had never been able to forget him.

A month after leaving him, they'd seen each other briefly at Earl Haley's trial. Their testimony helped earn the man a twenty-year sentence. Jesse had seemed distant at the trial, not really acknowledging she was there.

At the time, she still hadn't learned she was pregnant.

The newspapers all said Haley had just disappeared into the Everglades after he'd escaped custody while being transferred. He was presumed dead, and his body was never found.

Years later, Jesse told her that after Haley escaped police custody, he'd tracked him down and killed him with his bare hands, deep in the swamps.

Still, today, after all these years, he hadn't spoken of it again, and she still had unanswered questions—parts of what he'd told her didn't make sense and she'd always thought he was covering up for someone. His friend Billy, maybe. Where Jesse said he found Haley wasn't far from where he and Billy had grown up.

His lifestyle had moved from exciting to unnecessarily dangerous, and he'd told her enough that she'd kept her doubts as to who Flo's father was from him for many years.

But what happened in Mexico, even though she was doing everything right, had changed her thoughts on humanity as a whole.

She'd seen it up close. She'd *chosen* not to turn and run, but to do as Jesse would have, and go help a friend. And because of that decision, she'd been the primary instrument in ending a man's life.

At first, it had sickened her, just as the altercation on Hoffman's Cay had. Later, when she'd learned who the man had been and some of the things he'd done, her notions of right and wrong became clouded.

She'd done more than end a man's life. She'd ended the pain and torment that man had inflicted on, and would likely have continued to wreak, on others.

"I'm in," Chyrel whispered next to her. "Full access to all of *Taranis's* systems and controls. I can even run the boat from right here if we need to."

Two monitors above and behind their two laptop screens flickered and came to life, each showing two video feeds, side-by-side. The monitor on the left showed feeds from *Taranis's* port- and forward-facing cameras, and the one on the right displayed what was visible to starboard and behind.

All that could be seen on any of the night-vision camera feeds was the greenish gray of the water's surface, bright flashes of white as spray occasionally passed the screen near the bottom, barely illuminated by the boat's interior lights, and the night sky above the horizon.

A dazzling panoramic display of stars could be seen all the way around. The moon hung just above the horizon in the view over the bow.

Savannah turned her microphone on. "We can see everything you can, Jesse," she said. "Actually, a bit more, unless you're driving by the cameras, too."

"Eyesight and forward-scanning sonar," Jesse replied over her headset.

"Where are you planning to anchor first?" she asked. "The same place as last time would be too obvious."

"I like your idea for Boca Chita Light," Jesse replied. "But with the wind the way it is, it'll probably be more protected down off the seawall on the southwest side."

"I think it's the safest start," Savannah replied. "If they're operating out of the north end of the bay and have AIS on, they might jump at a second chance, and anyone heading toward you after midnight would be pretty suspect."

"When we get there," Jesse continued, "I'm only going to leave the AIS on for thirty minutes. If you don't see movement, we'll shut it down and get some rest before moving closer in the morning."

"Roger that," Savannah said, then muted her and Chyrel's mics and turned to her friend and mentor. "Do you suppose they trailer that boat? The one that attacked us?"

"It was likely stolen," Chyrel replied. "They might've already sunk it or stranded it somewhere and stolen another."

"I wonder where they get gas if they don't have a trailer to take it to a gas station?"

Chyrel turned from her screen and looked at Savannah. "Marina camera footage!"

"And live streams," Savannah said. "Can you apply facial... never mind. Of course you can. Start with the marinas in the northern part of the bay that have cameras at the fuel docks. I'm betting every single one has at least two these days."

"On it," Chyrel said. "But it might take a while."

Chyrel worked on getting into the security camera systems of several marinas in northern Biscayne Bay, accessing historical footage, then running what she could through facial recognition software—child's play for her.

While she did that, Savannah started doing the same thing with any live webcams she could find in the area, and there were hundreds. She didn't need Chyrel's computer skills because the former CIA computer analyst had created an app that would do it for her. All she had to do was open the live stream within the app and attach it.

Fortunately, a lot of them were run through just a handful of live-cam servers, which she could access, allowing her to attach the facial recognition software to dozens of feeds at once.

One by one, she worked through all the live streams she could find, connecting their feeds to the facial recognition software stored on Armstrong Research's cloud-based multi-encrypted technological interface system, or METIS.

An alert tone came from Chyrel's side of the double workspace, sounding like a tiny drop of water in a still pond.

"It's eight o'clock, Chyrel," Chip's voice announced. "What are you working on?"

Savannah continued her own work, tuning Chyrel out as she brought Chip up to speed.

Chip would take over for Chyrel, and in most cases, he was equally adept at the technology side, so he'd be able to finish what she started while Chyrel rested.

Helen would come on at ten o'clock to take Savannah's place and hopefully by then, they'd have every camera with a view of a fuel dock connected to Armstrong's METIS software.

An hour later, after Chyrel had gone to bed, Chip quietly announced that he'd finished the marinas, and that the search would run in the background and alert them of a hit, while he continued to expand to other businesses in the area that were on or near the water.

"There are a lot of red-light cameras, too," Savannah said. "That'll have to wait for Chyrel, though."

"Got a hit," Chip announced, a little before ten. "Recent one, too."

Savannah leaned over and saw the image of a man in a tank top sitting on a bar stool. He had a scraggly beard and greasy-looking long hair.

"That's the guy from the boat that attacked us!" Savannah blurted out. "When was that taken? And where?"

"Two days ago," Chip replied. "Face rec found Ramon "Snake" Martel eating chicken wings at Ted's Hideaway, a place on Second Street in Miami Beach, about six or seven blocks from Government Cut. Time stamp on the video says 5:30 PM. He tipped less than five percent."

"Miami Beach?" Savannah said. "Expensive, even for wings. I would have thought Snake more of a Whopper kind of guy."

As the door behind them opened, Savannah made a quick note halfway down the page on a pad beside her keyboard, knowing there'd be other hits, hopefully more recent.

"Can I get you anything?" Maddy asked, stepping into the room. "Is everything going okay?"

"They're on schedule," Savannah said, muting her mic and looking up at the 360-degree video display around her and Jesse's new boat. "It looks like they have a beautiful night for it, too. Have a seat."

"When Rusty told me about you and Jesse, I didn't believe him," she whispered, sitting down in front of Chyrel's dormant computer while she slept soundly just a few feet away. "I've been sitting here watching things unfold, and I still can't believe it."

Savannah knew when someone was deflecting their true feelings, and Maddy had been quiet most of the day. She seemed troubled.

"Something's bothering you," she said. "What is it?"

"I don't want to..." Maddy paused and looked away for a

197

moment before returning Savannah's gaze. "Sid texted me yesterday. Some strange guy's been hanging around."

"And you think it might be someone... from your past?"

Maddy's parents' marriage, as well as both their parents' marriages, and, going back for many generations, even the marriages of all that progeny, had been carefully planned and orchestrated for hundreds of years. To what end, Savannah had yet to understand. Like Rusty's, Maddy's families' histories were recorded for generations before that, many going back more than a thousand years.

But why? The only thing Savannah had gathered was that a secretive organization was maintaining pure blood lines of hundreds of families, perhaps thousands.

"I think it *is* one of them," Maddy replied. "Sid's description didn't ring any bells, though."

Maddy had said she'd never been approached by the group but had learned a little about them over the last few years, mostly from slip-ups Marshall Grey had made.

But it was enough for her to know that she was targeted for some specific reason.

And Grey coming thousands of miles only proved it.

Madison Thurman could be sure of one thing. Nobody in her family tree was even remotely related to anyone else outside of the family for at least twenty generations—more than four hundred years and over two million individual ancestors.

All meticulously planned and carefully guided, without the use of DNA or computers.

That is, if everything Maddy had overheard and pieced together was actually true. Savannah felt that Maddy believed it was. Which was good enough.

Grey had followed her from Wyoming to the Keys, intent on taking her back to the ranch that'd been in her family for over a hundred and fifty years. And he'd had help. But they'd failed. Or rather, Marshall Grey had failed. He'd failed to take Savannah seriously when she told him she was going to blow his head off.

Maddy sighed. "Sins of the father keep on coming—"

"You can't blame him," Savannah said. "Nor your mother. It was just... how they were raised."

"You mean how they were bred like livestock," she said, her voice tense. "It makes me sick to think about it."

"You mean having a child?" Savannah asked.

"Oh, no," Maddy whispered. "I want kids. But when *I'm* ready, and when I find the right guy. Definitely not on some timetable and with someone I don't know or like."

Savannah responded with a quizzical expression.

"My parents first met on the day they got married," Maddy said. "Same with all four grandparents."

Savannah shuddered. "And your parents never spoke to you about any of it?"

"Dad died when I was eleven," Maddy said. "After that, just the two of us in that big, empty house... Mom just wasn't the same." She paused and looked up at Savannah. "The house is huge—six bedrooms. It was built for a large family, and only two of those rooms were ever used."

"And you don't know anything else about this group or... this organization, or whatever?"

"No," Maddy replied. "Just what I overheard Marshall talking on the phone about or when he or one of the others let something slip. I'm sure I knew four men and two women who are part of it. Doesn't sound like much, but in a town as small as Greybull..."

"He's going to be transferred soon, right?" Savannah asked. "And February is over, so you're out of danger. You should try not to dwell on all the what ifs."

For whatever reason, it had been Marshall's intent that Maddy become pregnant in February, to have a baby in November, near her own birthday.

"They're moving him up to north Florida on Monday," she replied, but didn't seem comforted by the fact.

"Then everything's okay," Savannah said. "There's almost always some creepy guy hanging around the Rusty Anchor. It probably has nothing to do with you at all. Besides, even if you got pregnant now, the baby would be born in December. Wasn't that part of the plan?"

Maddy's lower lip trembled. "A fetus can survive..." She paused, fear gripping her voice. "It can live outside the womb after six months."

Savannah's eyes went wide.

"If I get pregnant before May," Maddy sobbed, "they can just kill me and take the baby. That's all they want!"

# CHAPTER TWENTY-SIX

I kept *Taranis* six miles offshore, and as we neared North Key Largo, I slowly started turning toward the north, following the coastline, but staying far enough away that we wouldn't be sighted from shore.

Tony and I stayed on watch, letting the others rest. I doubted we'd be so lucky as to find the guys tonight, or even in the coming days. So, I wasn't worried about getting my own rest. I was wide awake, even a little jittery, and once we arrived, I could turn things over to Deuce and the others until dawn.

As we made minor course corrections, I began to wonder about how Deuce and Julie handled their home life, doing what they were doing.

Deuce had once been a SEAL, an officer with an entire team under his command. After the Navy, he'd headed a counterterrorism task force during the wars in Iraq and Afghanistan. He'd served as a sub-cabinet member at the federal level, and now worked covertly for Armstrong Research and ran a PI business on the side.

Julie had enlisted in the Coast Guard and still served as a chief petty officer in the reserves. Like her husband, she also worked for Armstrong.

Deuce and Julie had two boys, fourteen and ten, and while they were here, the boys were staying with Tony's wife in Homestead, and she was taking them back and forth to school in Key Largo.

Then again, I'd had two daughters as an active-duty Marine, but that had ended in divorce and me being estranged from my daughters for years.

Deuce and Julie were obviously doing something to make their marriage and family life work with their professional life.

Something that I hadn't. Or Sandy hadn't.

My first wife had changed over the years we were married. She came to hate what I did and hated the Corps for making me do it. She'd become bitter about the deployments and being alone, even though there was a spouse support network in place.

Then one day, she left and took the girls.

But mutual support was one thing I knew my friends had going for them in spades. They were both committed to what they were doing and understood each other's needs. Had Sandy supported me that way, we might still be together.

And I wouldn't have Savannah. Or Flo, or Alberto, for that matter.

"Mid-tide and falling," Tony said, interrupting my thoughts as he studied the chart plotter. "Caesar's Creek is ten miles north-northwest. There's five-foot shoaling at the outer markers, but the channel's deep beyond that, and well-marked."

Cutting inside *would* save us having to go beyond Boca Chita and the sand flat that extended to the north of it and then having to double back.

"You know it?" I asked.

"Fish up here a lot with a friend," Tony replied, looking up expectantly.

"Take the helm," I said. "I'll go up on the bow."

Turning the wheel, I lined the outer markers up on the chart plotter and we switched places, so I could study the narrow passage into southern Biscayne Bay.

I looked at my watch and saw that it was nearly 2300. Savannah would be asleep. I tapped the power button on my earwig twice, waking it up. "Chyrel, are you there?"

"Hey, Jesse," she replied over the comm. "I thought you'd be asleep by now."

"Tony and I decided to take her all the way in," I replied. "Not much chance of catching them tonight, so we'll sleep once we get anchored."

"We've got a ton of leads," she said. "Savvy came up with the idea to tap into fuel dock cameras and run facial recognition. Manuel Woods and Raymond Belsus have been spotted numerous times and they were together at Miami Beach Marina just yesterday."

"What about the second guy from the boat? The guy with the rifle."

"Our man, Snake Martel, was all over the waterfront early last week but hasn't been spotted on any cams for a couple of days now."

"We're taking Caesar's Creek to the inside," I said, moving over to the side hatch. "Please connect me and Tony directly."

There was a click in my headset and Chyrel said, "You have direct comms."

"It looked plenty wide on the chart plotter, Tony," I said, opening the door and stepping out onto the side deck into a bracing wind. "Drop your speed to about five knots boat speed when we're half a mile from the outer markers and kill the main engine. We'll run silent from here on."

"Roger that," he replied. "We should be able to float across the shoals with a couple feet under the keel. But the outer edges of the creek and the sandbars are always shifting. That's why we fish here—anchor on the flats and wade along the drop-off."

Turning, I headed forward, my head down against the cold night air blowing around the wheelhouse, then stepped around the giant sun pad and crossed over to the main hull. Moving cautiously, I walked out to the pulpit, holding the low rails as I went.

I wasn't worried about being tossed overboard by an errant wave; the sea state was much calmer as the water got shallower.

But if we ran aground at twenty-five knots, the boat would stop and I'd keep going, flying ass over tea kettle from the bow.

Once I reached the pulpit, where the handrails rose higher and the gap between them narrowed, I wedged my hips in, standing on a small platform built for just that purpose, then leaned forward into the wind.

My face became the foremost part of *Taranis*, and just by the light of the stars and a rising moon off to starboard, I could see the way the water moved ahead of us and could easily judge where it was deeper.

We slowed, and though the sound of the diesel's exhaust was faint, when it was gone, the only sound was a gentle swish of water ten feet below my ears. The narrow, backward swept bow knifed cleanly through the water with very little disturbance.

Standing way out on the bow at twenty-five knots was an exhilarating experience— no wonder Savannah and Alberto had enjoyed it.

"Looks a little deeper about ten degrees to starboard," I shouted unnecessarily.

The earwig picked up vibrations in the jawbone, not a person's voice, and there was no engine noise to shout over.

"What was that?" Tony asked sarcastically, as the boat began to turn toward a deeper passage ahead. "I couldn't hear you. You're gonna have to speak up!"

Chyrel giggled.

"Straight ahead for a little over a hundred yards," I said, in a much lower tone. "Then head toward the first markers."

We glided stealthily between two shallow sandbars with a good thirty feet on either side.

"Clear of the sandbars," I said, continuing to study the water ahead.

The outer markers were lighted, and Tony steered directly between them, then angled slightly to port to pick up the next one.

"Looks like plenty of depth between the markers," I said. "Zoom in on the plotter and steer the middle of the marked channel. I'll let you know if the sands have shifted and correct you, but it looks good."

Tony followed the middle of the channel, turning slightly after passing each marker to line up with the next. A slight current was against us, which would slow our forward progress, since Tony was keeping *Taranis* at five knots boat speed— meaning how fast the boat was moving through the water. I knew the helm would be super-responsive at that speed.

The glow of Miami's lights to the north diminished my night vision a little, but I found that simply cupping my hand over that side of my eyes allowed me to see the markers clearly.

Ten minutes later, we passed the inner markers and cruised out into the deeper waters of Biscayne Bay.

When I entered the wheelhouse, Tony stepped away from the helm, keeping one hand on the wheel. "She's a lot more responsive on the electric motors than I would have imagined."

I held a hand up as I sat down at the nav desk. "You drive. Just head for the ICW and follow the channel north at eight knots. It's just another hour. *Taranis* has three rudders, all foldable. When power to the ama motors is turned off, the rudders automatically go to neutral and fold up into a recess in the hull, and the props fold into a tapered cone."

"Incredible," he said, checking the chart plotter and adjusting course.

"It came from my half of my and Savannah's 'What if' list."

"What if?"

"If time and money weren't a concern, would it make our life afloat better? Just equal wasn't a trade."

He looked over, obviously puzzled. "How would slippery outer hulls make life better?"

"Ever fly a kite really high when you were a kid?"

He looked over and grinned. "You didn't?"

I nodded. "On a long, downwind crossing, we can run a kite sail up to about five hundred feet and make eight to ten knots without power."

My old laptop was pushed way back on the dashboard. I pulled it onto the nav desk and opened it. When it powered up, I clicked on the *Soft Jazz* icon.

Chyrel's face appeared on the screen, looking off to the side. When she looked back at her screen, she jumped. "How'd you—" She clamped her mouth shut, then smiled. "Oh, you're on your old laptop. I forgot this patch was still on my machine."

"How's Savvy holding up?" I asked.

"She's doing fine, Jesse," Chyrel replied. "And she'll continue to do fine, as long as you don't start second-guessing her." She paused and looked straight at the camera. "But she worries about you."

"I worry about her," I admitted, speaking softly. "It was never my intention to drag her—"

"Do you really think you have *that* much control over her?"

Chyrel cut in. "She's an independent *Southern* woman, Jesse, and she can do anything you can. Maybe not as fast or as hard or as well, but her heart's one hundred percent in it."

I sat back, a little surprised. Chyrel could be outspoken about a lot of things, but she'd never backed Savannah like that before.

"Sorry," she said. "But I believe in her. And she believes in you. You should feel the same."

What we were doing was way out of the norm for most relationships between husbands and wives. Few couples had to worry about their spouse being involved in a gun battle.

If Deuce and Julie could make it work, what was stopping us? Was I just too old and too set in my ways?

"She thinks outside the box," Chyrel continued. "Just like you. She's provided Matt and Mr. Stockwell with a lot of information, and right now, *Ambrosia* is heading east at full speed toward Greece. They'll be in the Greek Islands by tomorrow night."

"They're moving ahead to take down—"

"Thanks to Savvy," Chyrel said. "There's been a lot going on here while you guys have been out enjoying a starlight cruise."

Tony snickered at the helm, but diverted his attention to the horizon when I glanced over.

"Okay," I said, slowly. "What all have you got on these guys here in Miami?"

She smiled again. "Quite a bit. Like I said, using facial recognition and tapping into traffic cameras, private security cameras, and public webcams, we've tracked their movements over the last several days. And we have Woods and Belsus under surveillance now. It's just a matter of time before Martel is spotted on a web cam again."

She paused, as if there was more.

"What are you not telling me?" I asked. "Are Alberto and the puppy okay?"

"They're fine," she replied. "It's Maddy. When I relieved Savannah, she told me that Rusty's wife had texted Maddy about a strange guy that'd been hanging around, and now the girl's worried he's from that group in Wyoming she's been having to deal with."

My mailing address is the Rusty Anchor....

"Chyrel," I said, suddenly alarmed. "I need you to hack into the security cameras at the Rusty Anchor and run that facial recognition."

Her eyes suddenly opened wide with realization. "Snake Martel!"

CHAPTER TWENTY-SEVEN

Research Vessel Ambrosia
Mediterranean Sea

The two men and one woman on duty on the bridge went about their business normally, communicating with one another only when needed, and without unnecessary chit chat.

Travis Stockwell liked that. Fewer distractions meant sharper focus.

He stood behind the bridge crew, a coffee mug in his left hand as he quietly observed. He knew the ship was traveling at forty knots, and he could feel a slight vibration through the soles of his shoes and an occasional sideways shift to the deck beneath his feet, but other than that, there was no real sense of movement. It felt almost like riding on a train.

Stockwell had been an Army Airborne colonel before retiring and moving to Homeland Security after 9/11. His position with Armstrong Research was a lot easier. And nobody was shooting at him.

Usually.

Only one of the three crewmembers with Stockwell on the bridge was prior military. Still, they worked together as if they were a cohesive combat unit. A trait left behind by *Ambrosia's* former skipper, no doubt.

Stockwell took a drink from his mug. Hurtling across the surface of the Mediterranean Sea at forty knots was a bit disconcerting to him.

"How far are we from land right now?" he asked the first officer.

"Twenty-four nautical miles south of the southernmost tip of Malta," Val McLarin replied. "We'll be in the Greek Islands just after sunset."

The sky ahead was still black. It was an hour before dawn, and the lights on the bridge deck were subdued, with only minimal red lighting and the soft red glow from several instruments, to maximize the crew's natural night vision.

Turning, Stockwell went aft through the open hatch joining the bridge to the command center. Three of his analysts were at work, one talking quietly to someone on her computer screen.

Travis had always been an early riser and had never needed much sleep to be fully rested. He could close his eyes and go to sleep during an artillery barrage and wake up clear-headed when he wanted to.

His being on the bridge or in the command center before dawn was nothing new to the crew. He'd been nearly a permanent fixture for several years.

The woman talking was Helen Shaw, an Irishwoman who'd joined the crew a year earlier after retiring from Interpol. She was the senior of the three analysts on duty and they were all working very closely, though remotely, with Armstrong's top analyst, Chyrel Koshinski, as well as Savannah McDermitt, who was the overall handler for her husband's side of Armstrong's two-pronged attack on the pirates who'd been preying on expensive yachts.

"Updates?" Stockwell asked, once she'd ended her communication.

"That was our contact with the local police force," Helen replied, her Irish accent matching perfectly with her auburn hair, porcelain complexion, and green eyes. "Captain Fallon will be meeting with a federal judge in his chambers first thing in the morning."

"That fast?"

"She cautioned it won't be, sir," Helen replied. "This judge will want to review everything, and will likely take several hours, but Captain Fallon feels sure she'll have her warrant by midday."

"That'll be sunset in Piraeus," Stockwell said, thinking aloud. "We'll reach the Greek Islands by then. That doesn't give us much time to get into position."

"No, sir. It does not." Helen paused, then turned and looked up at Stockwell. "Captain McDermitt doesn't think they will be able to force the two parties together that soon, anyway."

"He's probably right," Stockwell said, nodding his head as he thought about it. "We may be obliged to hang around and play tourists for a day or two. If we get the chance, want to get dinner ashore?"

Helen looked up at him, her green eyes sparkling. "Dinner ashore in the Greek Islands? That would be lovely, Travis."

Stockwell had been drawn to the woman right away. Aside from the chef, she was the only one aboard even remotely close to his age. She'd been a security analyst for Interpol until her husband died of cancer at fifty-four and she'd quietly retired from that service.

"Where is McDermitt now?" Stockwell asked.

"He's moved his yacht into the southern part of Biscayne Bay," Helen replied, all business once more as she brought a live satellite image up on her screen.

"*Taranis* is the orange lightning bolt icon, here," she continued, pointing at the screen, then moving her manicured nail up the screen slightly. "They plan to anchor here, near a small island called Boca Chita Key, which they should reach in less than thirty minutes."

"Why is it a lightning bolt?" Stockwell asked, puzzled. "Why not an arrow or a boat?"

"Taranis was the Celtic god of thunder," she replied with a bright smile. "He always carries a lightning bolt, and as I understand, the McDermitts' yacht is electric powered."

"Boca Chita is where he's going to start chumming the air waves with his identifier?"

"Only for a very short time," Helen replied. "METIS is already tracking all surface targets in the bay and is watching for a sudden change in direction. McDermitt wants to wait and go full active in daylight—moving quickly around the bay, turning his AIS on and off, as if it might be malfunctioning."

"His idea?" Stockwell asked.

Helen looked up at him. "Savannah came up with it."

A corner of his mouth ticked up and Helen smiled.

She'd been first to ask him to dinner not long after she'd come aboard. It was just a shared meal in the ship's galley, but that had led to another date at an outdoor restaurant in the Azores, which led to an eventual weekend getaway in the south of France.

Stockwell leaned over her shoulder, pretending to look closer at her screen. "What time will you get off?" he said, in as low a voice as he could.

"With any luck," she whispered back softly, "shortly after I'm relieved here."

Stockwell gulped and his face flushed, caught completely off guard by the same crude joke he'd heard countless men tell.

"Well, then," he began, straightening. "We should—"

One of the other analysts sat bolt upright in his chair, staring at his screen. "It's him!" Troy shouted. "Chyrel found Snake Martel!"

Stockwell moved behind the young man and looked at his screen.

The image on it was sharp and detailed, not like most security cameras. It showed the inside of a restaurant in a wide angle, covering the entire room.

The young analyst zoomed the image in on one man sitting at the bar, looking just to the left of the camera and slightly above it. He was smiling up at someone tall.

"Are you sure it's him?" Stockwell asked.

Troy typed on his keyboard, and lines appeared around the face of the man, with circles at the eyes, nose, and chin. Then a second image appeared—a mug shot from a year earlier.

"One hundred percent, sir," Troy replied. "Chyrel changed the search parameter just a moment ago, and METIS got a hit almost instantly, from just two hours ago."

"Where?" Stockwell demanded, then turned to Helen. "Get this intel to Fallon and McDermitt, ASAP."

Troy looked up from the screen. "It was in Marathon, Florida, sir. A place called the Rusty Anchor."

CHAPTER TWENTY-EIGHT

The rattle of the chain over the pulpit must have awakened Deuce and Julie in the portside aft guest cabin. I knew it woke Paul in the forward cabin. As quiet as *Taranis* was, there wasn't anything between his bed's headboard and the powerful drum winch in the bow except a mostly empty storage area and two bulkheads.

Andrew had risen from the settee just as we'd moved into position to drop the hook, just a couple hundred yards from the seawall.

"Everything's done," I told everyone as they all gathered in the wheelhouse. "Feet up, anchor down."

"You didn't wake us," Deuce growled.

"Is he always this grumpy when he gets a chance to sleep in?" I asked Julie.

She gave me a wry grin and headed to the nav station.

I checked my watch. "It's past midnight," I said. "You and grumpy Gus have the con. The rest of y'all can hit the rack. Nothing's going to happen here tonight."

Paul disappeared first, then Tony headed down to Alberto's cabin, and Andrew went back to his spot on the couch.

Julie sat down next to me at the nav desk and looked at the chart plotter as Deuce took a seat right behind her on the lounge, rubbing his face vigorously.

"Savvy dug up a lot of intel on past movements of the guys who attacked us," I told Deuce. "She used facial recognition software and public webcams to put together a timeline from before the attack until now. One of the tangos, Snake Martel, disappeared a couple days ago." I glanced over at Julie, bent over the chart plotter. "Chyrel's checking another location for me."

Julie looked up from the screen. "Your AIS is on."

"I turned it on just before we anchored," I replied, adjusting the helm seat to face them. "The eye in the sky has been tracking every boat in the bay and adjacent waters for the last couple of hours, so right now, we're waiting to see if METIS notices if any vessels suddenly change course or head toward us." I shrugged. "It's a long shot, I know. We're barely in range of the northern part of the bay."

Deuce nodded in agreement. "A long shot, yeah. But to do what Savannah suggested means operating in daylight, and I know you prefer darkness. This bay has a lot of shoals, and we don't need to hang your pretty boat up on one while trying to outmaneuver our target. It's still worth a shot while we sit here and rest up, though. How was the passage?"

"You *slept* through it," I replied with a grin. "Easy passage-making is what *Taranis* was designed for."

"You're uh... waiting up for Savannah to come on?"

"That, yeah," I replied. "And I wanted to talk to the two of you."

Julie turned and faced me. "About what, Jesse?"

"How do you reconcile... this? What you do?" I asked, leaning toward them with my elbows on my knees. "I mean being married and having kids."

Deuce sat back and put his arms across the width of the lounge seat as he let out a breath. "That's a big, loaded question if I ever heard one."

"Savvy thinks it might be a good idea if I did some flatfoot work," I said, lifting my head and looking around the wheelhouse before bringing my gaze back to Deuce. All three of us were armed, and Andrew's sidearm was in a cubby behind the couch. "She said nothing dangerous, but here we are."

Julie turned in her seat and put a hand on Deuce's arm. "This is different, Jesse. This op involves family. I'm sure this isn't what she meant. And I'm equally sure she's as committed to family as all of us."

"You'll have to go back to wearing the mask," Deuce said. "And be able to switch from investigator to father in half a heartbeat. And back again. But if you want my opinion, having the support of your spouse in everything you do, and being completely open and honest about *what* you're doing, is paramount in a relationship like this."

"I don't usually go with him," Julie added. "When Jack sends him to do a job, I usually stay home with the boys. But like I said, this time, it's family. It does help me cope at home, knowing exactly where he is and what he's doing. I know he has all the training, ability, and backup he needs to get it done and come home safely to us."

"Honesty and communication above mission," Andrew's low voice rumbled from the couch. "If she says no, decline the job. And make sure *she* knows she can do that for any reason."

"I'd say that's it in a nutshell," Deuce said, as both our phones began to make noises and vibrations.

His was on the table, face up. "It's Colonel Stockwell."

He stabbed the screen with a finger and switched to speaker as I pulled my phone out.

Stockwell was calling us both at once.

"I'm here with Deuce," I said, hitting the *Decline* button on my own phone. "What's up?"

"Koshinski did as you suggested," Stockwell began. "And she got a hit almost instantly. Martel was at your friend's restaurant two hours ago. I had Troy send you the details."

"Chyrel told me he disappeared the day after the attack," I said, mostly to Julie. "It wouldn't take a grad student to get my mailing address from the boat's Coast Guard registration."

"I have two assets en route from Miami," Stockwell said. "And one of our people in Key West is headed there, as well."

"You want me to tell Rusty?"

"He's on your island, right?"

Julie was already busy texting on her phone. "I got it, Jesse," she said, without looking up. "Maddy is on watch right now. She's going to wake Dad."

"Thanks for letting us know, Colonel," Deuce said. "What's the situation there?"

"We're going too damned fast," Stockwell grumbled. "We'll reach Crete in about twelve hours. Another two to move up near Athens. After that, we sit and pretend to ogle the scenery until you make your move. You feel certain you can get the goods on the Greek boss in Miami?"

"If we do it right," I replied. "One of them will go running straight to him and that's when Miami-Dade will execute the warrant. If they get one."

"There's a lot riding on things happening on your end," Stockwell said. "Make this happen, Jesse, and I owe you one."

Deuce's screen changed to the lock screen as Stockwell ended the call.

Julie's phone rang in her hand, and she answered it immediately.

"Dad, you need to get home. Now."

She put her phone on speaker, and we heard Rusty say, "...hell's going on?"

"Are you with Maddy?" I asked.

"Yeah, she's right here."

"The text she got from Sid had nothing to do with her. Snake Martel was at the Anchor two hours ago, and it was probably him who Sid saw for the last couple of days and was texting her about."

"What's going on?" I heard Charity ask in the background.

I leaned closer to Julie's phone. "Charity, do you think you can land in the yard at the Rusty Anchor at night without a ground marshal?"

"You know I can," she replied, obviously closer to Rusty's phone.

"Take Rusty, Kim, and Marty to the Rusty Anchor. You can move up to Miami from there just as easily as on the island, and Billy can fly down to the Anchor in the morning to be ready with Rusty in case we need them. Stockwell has backup inbound from Miami and Key West."

"We're on the way," Rusty said. "I'm calling Sid now."

Julie's phone also went to the lock screen.

I looked over at her. "We both know there're still a lot of people around after closing. If anything's happened, someone would have called your dad. They *should* be safe."

We'd all been right. This first guy was just a feeler. He was sent down our way the next day, looking for me. They'd keep coming until they got what they wanted—the prize *and* revenge.

Deep in the pit of my gut, I felt a cold, dark rage beginning to build.

# CHAPTER
TWENTY-NINE

It wasn't my first encounter with people like this. Those who live on the wrong side of the law make their own rules, and not knowing their rules didn't make innocent people safe from retribution should they accidentally cross a line. I'd violated one of those rules in killing the man with the rifle, Harvey Martinez.

I hadn't asked for this fight. Savannah and I were preparing *Taranis* to take us somewhere that didn't have the ugliness that seemed to be crowding in closer and closer around us every day. But in the minds of Martinez's criminal cohorts, I was the aggressor and Martinez the victim. Never mind the fact that he was about to fire on a boat with innocent people aboard—my family.

I knew these people wouldn't stop and they wouldn't go away.

As the four of us waited for news from Rusty or Charity, one of the monitors in the overhead came on without prompting, then Savannah's face appeared.

I checked the clock. It was 0100.

"Charity is on approach," she announced. "She says to tell Julie that she didn't see anything unusual on the flyover except a couple talking at the end of the dock, probably Sharon and Dan. They'll be on the ground in two minutes."

"This Snake guy was just one," I said, staring out over the bow. "It's not going to stop, Savvy. They're going to keep coming for us."

There was silence for a moment.

"I know," Savannah said softly.

With those two simple words, she'd released me from my promise.

I didn't have to tell Savannah these people would never go away on their own. There were far too many sheep to prey on. She knew that. And she knew that I, along with the people now aboard *Taranis*, could *make* them go away. Permanently.

"I've got something else," Chyrel said, her camera cutting in. "Face rec just picked up Martel passing a toll booth on the Rickenbacker Causeway."

"Relay that to Charity," I said.

When Rusty called ten minutes later, he reported that Sid had seen Martel hanging around the last two days, and when he was there earlier that evening, he'd asked her about me.

"Sid figured that since he knew where to come looking for ya, she might as well not hide it, and said she only knew your name, that ya got your mail here, and visited from time to time. You know, as vague as possible with enough truth."

"How long was he there?" I asked.

"She said he got a call about a half hour before closin', paid his tab, and took off in a hurry."

I looked over at Deuce. "Ninety minutes ago. That'd just about coincide with when I turned on the AIS."

"Sid said at first, she was relieved when he asked 'bout *you*, bro," Rusty continued. "She was worried it was that bunch from up in Wyomin', but now, she's just pissed that we woke everybody up."

I thought for a moment. If Martel had been looking for me, it was obvious he'd gotten my details from the boat's AIS and registration.

"He has someone else watching AIS," Julie said. "METIS was

looking for a *boat* to suddenly move toward us, but he's in a *car*."

"Kill the AIS," I said, rising and turning the helm seat back. "Get everyone up."

"Ya think that call was tellin' him where ya are?" Rusty asked.

"Yes, I do," I replied, starting the diesel. "Y'all try to get some rest, Rusty. We're about to move."

"Good fishin'," he replied, then Julie ended the call.

"Where are we headed?" Julie asked, as I activated the windlass.

"Diagonally across the bay," I replied. "About ten miles northwest of here. Look for Cutler Channel."

"Got it," she said, as Tony and Paul came up on deck. "Eleven nautical miles northwest." She looked over at me just as the hook came up. "Five-foot flats extend way out to a rocky peninsula."

"We only draw four," I said, locking the anchor clamp and moving the throttle control forward. "Those rocks will be our shield."

I pushed the throttle forward, running only the diesel. We didn't need to move quickly; nobody was headed our way and there wasn't another boat in sight.

Taranis reached eighteen knots and the hull began to lift slightly higher out of the water.

"We're tracking a boat coming out of Miami Beach Marina," Savannah announced on the overhead. "It's a thirty-foot walk-around with a small cabin, currently headed south."

Deuce moved up to sit next to Julie. "Can you overlay its course onto our chart plotter?"

Julie tapped a couple of icons on the screen, then touched our current location and the marina near the mouth of Government Cut.

A line appeared on the chart, showing the most direct course between the two spots.

"How far will that course line be from where we're going?" Deuce asked.

"About seven-and-a-half miles," Julie replied, then looked at me, realization in her eyes. "This boat's air draft has to be close to twenty-five feet, Jesse. With his radar height, if he has one, he'll be able to see us on radar."

Tony jumped to his feet. "This boat's only sixteen feet tall with the top down," he said. "And that's just the radar arch, lowered flat on the roof, right?"

"You studied the layout and controls up there?" I asked. "Can you handle it?"

"I did," he replied, headed aft. "And I can."

"Do it in order," I shouted over my shoulder after him. "Masts first, then the radar arch before the top. You'll have to crawl back to the deck hatch."

"Got it," he called back, sliding the hatch open and disappearing.

"The top goes down?" Deuce asked.

"Some of the canals in the south of France have low clearances," I replied with a shrug, as *Taranis* reached twenty-two knots—slightly above cruising speed on the main. I throttled back slightly to maintain speed.

"It's probably just a fisherman getting an early start," Paul said.

"Except it's almost low tide," Julie countered. "Night fishing, yeah. Low tide fishing, sure. Going night fishing on a low tide? No. That'll mess up your bottom unless you're very familiar with the waters."

There was a hum of hydraulics from above as Tony lowered the masts onto the roof.

"The radar's range is going to diminish slightly when he lowers the arch," I said. "Even more when he lowers the roof."

"Target boat is continuing south in the ICW," Savannah said. "It's more than twenty miles from you, so he's out of radar range. But shouldn't he also be out of VHF range?"

She was right. And AIS used VHF radio waves to provide information to other mariners.

"Someone on shore, maybe?" Paul asked. "With a VHF receiver and he's relaying our position?"

"More than likely a computer or phone, connected to the internet," Andrew replied. "Lots of websites display AIS ship information."

The sliding door in back opened and Tony returned. "I can see how being able to lower the top will be handy," he said. "But come on. Sitting at the helm, with that roof all closed up around you... It's like being in one of those single-seat, open-wheel racecars."

We made our eleven-mile crossing far sooner than the boat METIS was tracking covered the fifteen-mile run south. When we arrived at one of the spots I'd picked out for its shallow water and natural protection from wind and prying eyes, I energized the electrical systems and put *Taranis* in station-keeping mode.

She slowly turned into whatever combination of wind and current were pushing against her, and the electric motors turned very slow revs to keep us in exactly the same spot.

Under most conditions, *Taranis* could remain stationary in water that was too deep to anchor for up to a full day without sunlight or the generator being started.

The motors barely turned more than two revolutions per second, 120 RPM, about a fifth of the slowest speed a diesel engine could idle at.

The far-left monitor came on, showing an overhead, oblique view of a boat underway.

"The satellite isn't directly overhead," Savannah said. "It's parked over a spot about forty miles east of your current position. We're hoping to see who is aboard."

We waited, watching the satellite feed.

It was an older-looking boat, beamy, with a small, covered helm area, and a raised cabin in front of that, with plenty of deck space to walk around it. The cockpit was uncluttered and big.

It was a boat made to take a lot of people out bottom fishing, so probably wouldn't have the muscle of a sportfishing machine like *Gaspar's Revenge.*

The boat was making twenty knots and was probably capable of a little more, but I wasn't interested in racing him. We'd use the technology Armstrong had at its disposal to play cat-and-mouse until everything was in place.

"The target is perpendicular to you," Savannah said. "Range is 8.1 nautical miles."

"We're lost in the back scatter," I said, knowing that due to the curve of the Earth, if he saw anything at all on his radar, it would just be the upper part of the flybridge deck, and we'd look like part of the small limestone ridge sticking out of the water just to our east.

Even in the moonlight, I could see the sharp rocks were pocked with holes from urchins, meaning they were submerged at least part of the time.

I checked the depth. The bottom was a little more than a foot below the main hull's keel. Shallow water and rocky outcrops. A place for most boats to avoid.

I'd picked certain places in the bay that looked extremely inhospitable on a chart but had a uniform and shallow bottom contour or a challenging maze of at least two cuts to reach. What *Taranis* might lack in speed, I knew she made up for in maneuverability.

Unlike most boats that squatted at the stern during sudden acceleration, *Taranis* simply launched forward. Which meant that we could go from zero to twenty-five knots in just a few seconds, whereas most boats would have to accelerate very slowly, so as not to displace the water from under the stern, dropping the hull into it and possibly damaging a prop.

Or, as the guy had done the other night, tilt the motor up and shoot a giant rooster tail while trying to get away.

We had a lot of options in this spot, even if we drew him in close, due to the shallow flats that extended far from shore.

"He's slowing and turning toward Boca Chita," Savannah said.

"I still think it's someone on shore, relaying information," Andrew said, stepping closer to the monitor and studying the boat, which was now at our previous anchorage and turning around the southern tip of Boca Chita. "I don't see any kind of satellite dish or StarLink receiver on the roof for them to have internet. Just the radar and radio antenna." He looked over at me. "Can they be using cellular way out there?"

"Not very reliable," Julie said. "And definitely no good for a large data site, like marine traffic."

"Hit the AIS again," I said, looking at the monitor and hoping one of the clowns would step out and look up. "And somebody start a stopwatch."

Julie turned on the Automated Identification System, broadcasting our location and data for anyone to see if they were within about six or seven miles.

We all watched the boat on the satellite feed. It was now turning back around the southern tip and heading up the west side toward the lighthouse.

"If it is the same guys," Deuce said, "I don't think they're very bright."

Julie huffed a light laugh. "Yeah, that island's what? Three feet high? With another ten feet of mangroves and bushes? They're looking for a haystack hiding behind a needle."

Suddenly, the boat turned and accelerated, heading northwest.

"Kill it when I say," I said, starting the main engine and taking the electric motors out of station-keeping.

I didn't want to turn the AIS off instantly, not right after they started moving—that would look suspicious.

I spun *Taranis*, using the electric motors at full power in opposing directions.

"Hang on," I cautioned, as I moved both motor controls to full forward and jammed the main engine throttle to the stop, heading due south out of the cove.

"Cut the AIS," I ordered, as we cleared the rocks.

Julie turned it off, paused for a few seconds, then turned it on again. She waited until *Taranis* had moved completely out of the cove, was already up out of the water, and passing twenty knots, flat and level. Then she killed the AIS again.

I'd chosen my spots carefully, making sure that whichever direction a pursuing boat might be coming from, and whichever direction I planned to go next, we wouldn't get within eight nautical miles. Any closer, we'd become more than just a whitecap or small boat on their radar screen.

Biscayne Bay was huge, but it wasn't so big that there was room for error. I'd spent hours with Julie and Kim, locating suitable spots and putting them into the chart plotter's memory.

"Another boat came out of Miami Beach Marina," Savannah reported. "It just crossed Government Cut and is heading southwest at nearly thirty knots."

"Two boats?" Deuce asked, rhetorically.

"We don't know that," I said. "Keep an eye on the second one, Savvy. If he turns toward the spot the first one's headed, then it's probably an accomplice. Two boats is better than one."

Deuce turned toward me, wide-eyed. "Better for *them*! At least one of those boats can outrun us."

I looked over at him for a second. "Exactly. One of them needs to get away, remember? A fast boat is a better getaway than swimming."

But with the possibility that we might have two boats trying to intercept *Taranis*, I wanted distance. These guys had rifles. Not that we'd be unprepared, but a lucky shot only needed to happen once.

Plus, we had to wait until Sherri Fallon could get a judge to sign off on a warrant, and for *Ambrosia* to get into position in the Med.

We would have way too many delays starting this early. I'd wanted to wait until morning, at least. Tomorrow night, at best.

But it was what it was.

"Changing course," I said, turning to port. "Tony, I'm gonna need you on the bow. We're running Caesar's Creek at speed, then head up to Stiltsville on the outside."

"At *what* speed?" Tony asked.

I glanced down at the knot meter and shrugged. "Twenty-two knots? Give or take. The tide's about the same as before, and we know where the sandbar is on the outside. I'll follow our previous track. You just shout if you see any small boats out night fishing."

"Yeah," Tony replied, moving past Julie to the side hatch. "Unless the tide rearranged the bottom."

# CHAPTER THIRTY

The phone call from Manny had caught Snake in the middle of a late dinner. It was just as well. He'd been asking all around Marathon about the big, tri-hulled yacht and wasn't getting anywhere close to finding it, or the owner, or where he kept it.

When he'd first arrived, he'd walked the docks at the address the guy had on his Coast Guard registration. Even if all the other boats lining both sides of the canal were to leave, Snake didn't think the big tri-hull could even get in. And there weren't any empty dock spaces.

The Amazonian bartender hadn't been much help. All she'd told him was that the guy sometimes visited and only got his mail there.

By the time he got to the dock in Miami, Manny and the new guy, Kurt something-or-other, had already left.

The boat they'd used previously and abandoned at the dock was still there. The cops had put yellow tape around it to keep people off, but Snake had the keys to the boat.

It was dangerous. The cops knew that boat.

He looked off to the south. Manny was out there somewhere. And so was the asshole on the three-hulled yacht.

It was after two o'clock, no lights were on in any of the boats around him, and everyone was sleeping. He looked toward shore and saw several people on the well-lit streets.

At least the people here on these boats are asleep, he thought, as he strolled casually toward the center console.

At the end of the dock, he ducked under the tape and quickly boarded the boat, digging the keys out of his jeans pocket as he dropped down between the seat and the console.

He paused and looked back toward shore.

He knew that stealing a stolen boat was just plain dumb, but what else could he do? He wanted to be there when the guy on the fancy boat got what he had coming.

He looked all around once more. Nobody had noticed him.

Snake put the key in the ignition and turned it. The engine caught and settled into a quiet idle.

He jumped up and quickly untied first the stern line, then the bow, and pushed it away from the dock, then hurried back to the helm and put the boat in gear.

In seconds, he was moving away from the dock at a high idle in the re-stolen boat. When he was outside the lights from the docks, he mashed the throttle and headed south.

Once Snake had made it across the main ship channel, he called Manny on his cell phone.

"Where are you, *jefe*?" he asked, steering with one hand as he entered the ICW.

"On the west side of the bay," Manny replied. "What took you so long?"

"A wreck on one of those damned bridges, man."

"Mr. Belsus said the yacht's AIS has come on twice in the last two hours," Manny said, his voice sounding frustrated and strained. "Both places, nothing!"

"Turn on your Friends Locator," Snake said. "I'll come to where you are."

"You're in a boat?"

"The one we abandoned," Snake replied. "I thought it might be a good idea to have two boats."

Manny didn't say anything for a moment. "You're right, Snake. Good thinking. I don't like the feel of this, man."

"Why? What's goin' on?"

"The boss says it just came on here," Manny said. "We get there and it's not there. Then he says it's over here, just twenty minutes ago. We get here, and *nada*, man."

"Remember, I told you, man," Snake said. "Those websites can be wonky as fuck sometimes. Or it could be a legit electrical problem. It's a brand-new boat; shit always breaks."

"You should have my location now," Manny said. "Get here as quick as you can."

Snake ended the call and crammed his phone into the crease of a tightly strapped life vest wedged behind the windshield on the small dash. They'd used that tactic several times to keep track of one another when they used more than one boat to follow yachts they wanted to steal.

His phone showed Manny's location as a circle with an M in the middle. All he had to do was steer straight toward it. Unless he got within half a mile of shore, most of the bay was plenty deep.

He kept the M at the center of the top of his screen and pushed the throttle all the way, letting the outboard scream.

There wasn't anyone around to hear it.

Fifteen minutes later, Snake slowed as he neared the western shore of the large bay. His depth finder still said six feet, but he didn't want to come suddenly up on a sandbar in the dark, or worse, Manny's boat.

Snake had already had to dodge a few things floating in the water.

Finally, he spotted the boat Manny had stolen up in Fort Lauderdale a week earlier and angled toward it.

They were drifting just a couple hundred yards from shore with the motor off, so when he got close, Snake cut his, as well.

"What do we do now?" Snake asked.

"I don't know," Manny replied. "It's like this thing's a ghost come back to haunt my ass."

"Their AIS has gotta be malfunctioning," Snake suggested. "Where was it the first time Mr. Belsus saw it?"

"A little island way out on the edge of the bay," Manny said. "Southeast of here."

"Okay, so maybe he came into the bay there," Snake suggested, offering an alternative explanation. "And if their AIS is blinking out, then reappearing here, that could mean they're just heading up the coast north of here."

The boats drifted closer together and Snake tossed a line to Kurt, while Manny paced the back of the boat.

"An expensive boat," Manny muttered. "At night. With busted equipment. Why wouldn't they just lay low until morning?"

"Those new yachts," Kurt said, shaking his head. "They got fancy navigation equipment and shit. They don't need daylight."

Manny's phone, lying on the dash, started playing a rap song and he snatched it up. "It's Mr. Belsus."

He pushed the *Accept* button and held the phone to his ear. "No boat here either," he said. "Snake just got here in the other boat."

Snake watched Manny in the darkness.

"Where now?" he asked, shoving Kurt toward the side of the boat as he signaled Snake with a winding motion of his hand. "Take Kurt and the rifle. Your boat's faster."

Snake went to the console and started the outboard as Kurt

stepped over with the rifle, then they both quickly untied the lines.

"No way," he heard Manny mutter. "How could he... Mr. Belsus, he would have had to pass right between us."

Snake waited as the boats drifted apart.

Finally, Manny ended the call and returned to the back of the boat. "You're not gonna believe this, man."

"What? Did he see them on the AIS again?"

"He said he was screwing some bimbo flight attendant he picked up," Manny said, unable to hide his amusement. "I could hear her cursing him in the background. He didn't see the boat on *AIS*, man. He saw it out his bedroom window while he was *doin'* her."

CHAPTER THIRTY-ONE

Stiltsville had once been a whole community of homes and businesses built on stilts a mile south of Cape Florida. The community was situated in a part of the bay called Safety Valve, a shallow sand bank that protected the open bay.

Almost a hundred years ago, there'd been more than a dozen structures standing out there in the ocean, with land barely in sight.

The first one was a gambling house. Back then, state law said gambling was legal a mile offshore. The legislators of the time were, of course, thinking gambling *boats*, but "Crawfish" Eddie Walker had a different idea.

Then came the Calvert Club and Quarterdeck Club, and more. They were mostly wood structures on wooden stilts, but some later ones had been built on concrete pilings instead of wood.

Stiltsville had been the playground for Miami's rich and infamous after the war and all through the fifties and early sixties.

The structures had been mostly abandoned since Hurricane Betsy in 1965, and one by one, they'd fallen to the elements until only seven remained. Then, just three winters ago, Leshaw House went up in flames, leaving only six.

The one we were approaching had a covered deck around it, ten feet above the water. A set of rotted stairs ended just a few feet down from the deck, and the underpinning was an extensive network of stilts, beams, and reinforcement. The low peak of the roof was probably no more than twenty feet above the surface.

"I need you back topside, Tony," I said, using the joystick control to maneuver *Taranis* around the structure. "Raise the radar arch. Let's see if it can look over this house."

"They've been sitting there a long time," Deuce said, looking at the satellite feed, then glancing at his watch.

"They haven't had a reason to move," I replied.

The overhead clock showed that it was 0349. It was mid-morning in Greece—at least eight or nine hours before Stockwell could put his team in place.

Savannah's idea had worked, but it'd worked too well and too quickly. Would we be able to keep this up for fifteen hours?

"Fool me once, shame on you," Pap often said. "Fool me twice, shame on me."

Fifteen hours?

The guys on the two boats wouldn't fall for it that long, chasing an electronic shadow all over a four-hundred-square-mile bay.

Was it really necessary, anyway? People who got arrested weren't immediately allowed their one phone call. They had to be interviewed first, get fingerprinted, and have mug shots taken. In a few hours, Sherri would have her warrant. She could arrest Belsus and sit on him for hours before he or anyone else they managed to snag would be processed.

Stockwell could hit the boatyard in Piraeus, and Belsus would still be waiting to get his phone call.

"We can't keep this up indefinitely," I said. "Three times in four hours is pushing our luck."

"We could pull off," Deuce suggested. "Run twenty miles offshore and come back tomorrow night."

"What do you think, Savvy?" I asked, looking up at her in the monitor. "Neither of us expected things to escalate this fast."

The little red light beside the wheelhouse camera was on; she could see us.

"I spoke with Captain Fallon an hour ago," she replied, "apprising her of the quick developments. She contacted the judge and he agreed to meet her at six... zero six hundred. Sherri said she could have Belsus in custody an hour later and it would be no earlier than mid-afternoon before he'll be through booking and allowed to call a lawyer."

"We can roll the dice," I said, turning to Deuce. "That'll be well after sunset in Piraeus. Can Stockwell deploy that quickly when they get there?"

We both knew that Belsus's first call would be to his lawyer and before the suit arrived at the jail, he'd have made calls to Greece, alerting the boatyard.

But would they even consider the arrest of an underling, even a distant relative, who was seven thousand miles away, as any kind of threat?

"Let's find out," Deuce replied, turning to face the camera and monitors. "Please get Colonel Stockwell on the comm."

Savannah immediately bent over her keyboard and her image quickly disappeared, replaced by the Armstrong Research logo. A moment later an attractive, auburn-haired woman appeared. "Hello, Captain McDermitt," she said in a decidedly Irish accent. "Mr. Stockwell is on the way. Please stand by."

The logo reappeared, and I put the controls into station-keeping mode on the east side of the structure.

The whine of hydraulics could be heard, and I looked over at the radar screen in front of Julie. The wall of backscatter to our west suddenly disappeared just before the whine stopped.

"Good," I said. "The radar's no longer blocked by the house. We can use the structure to keep them from picking us up on theirs."

"For about two or three more hours," Andrew said. "It'll start getting light soon. You gotta be tired."

"I'm fine," I said. "It's not the first time I've pulled an all-nighter."

"In the last decade?" Tony asked, coming back in through the rear hatch. "'Cause I'm younger than you and my ass is whooped."

The overhead monitor flickered for a second, and then Stockwell's face appeared. "Sit-rep."

"They'll soon be onto us, sir," Savannah said, taking the lead. "The first time Jesse turned on the AIS just before midnight drew them out, and they've moved *Taranis* twice since then. There are now two boats in the search. None of us thought things would escalate this quickly, but they did. At most, I thought someone might try spying on us from a distance. But they came straight in hot."

"It's not something we can keep doing, Colonel," Deuce said. "At least one of those boats is faster than we are."

"We're still eight hours from being in position to even think about deploying assets," Stockwell growled.

"Can you be in position in ten?" I asked. "We have an idea."

"Ten hours?" he asked, turning to his left.

"Ten on the outside, aye," someone off-mic said.

It was a voice I recognized. "Is that you, Matt?"

"Aye, Cap'n," my former first officer replied, his voice betraying his roots in Cornwall, England. "Our team can start kickin' down doors exactly ten hours from right now."

"What's your idea?" Stockwell asked, turning back to the camera.

"If we wait until daylight, we're a sitting duck," I said. "I only wanted to hit the AIS for a few minutes when we got here, but never expected it to get a bite. We can move far offshore and lay low until tomorrow night, or implement Savannah's plan now, end this tonight, and when the rats go scurrying back to Belsus's house, Captain Fallon will have her warrant and make the arrests."

"She assures me," Savannah added, "anyone arrested at that time on a Sunday morning won't get a first phone call to a lawyer until the middle of the afternoon, and she could probably push that to dinner time."

"That'll be the middle of the night in Piraeus," Stockwell said, a crinkle forming at the corners of his eyes. "Do it. We'll be ready."

The Armstrong logo returned and was then replaced by the live video feed from Savannah.

"I think you should all try to get some rest," she said. "We'll give Captain Fallon a couple of hours, and Chyrel and I will watch over you and the two boats until sunrise. They'll feel more confident with the coming of dawn."

"You're right," I said. "We've all been running on adrenaline and it's wearing off. Forty winks will do us all good. And it will pad Sherri and Matt's time a little more. They'll try a third, but I think anyone cagey enough to steal yachts won't be fooled a fourth time."

"You're sure the boat will keep itself in place without anyone on watch?" Paul asked.

"Yes," I replied, certain of *Taranis's* abilities. "But since you've had the most rest, you can stand watch for a couple of hours."

"What do I do?" he asked.

"Sit here and look back there," I said, pointing at the dilapidated structure twenty feet off our stern. "If it gets too close," I continued, as I pointed to the electric motor controls, "push both these handles forward and wake me up."

"That's it?"

"Nothing to it," I replied. "Thanks for volunteering."

The idea of a power nap, no matter how short, pulled me toward the hatch to my stateroom behind the helm as everyone else headed to their bunks.

Getting rest amid chaos was something we'd all had to do before, even Julie. She'd gotten two rambunctious boys through the "zoomie" stage and into adolescence. All the rest of us had ever done was to sleep during combat.

As I lay back on the empty bunk, clearing my mind, my phone buzzed. A video call from Savannah.

"Hey," I said, when she appeared.

She was standing outside the comm shack on the little porch.

"I just called to say goodnight," she said. "Get some rest. Tomorrow will be busy."

"It's already tomorrow, babe. How's Alberto and the pup?"

"They fell asleep exhausted hours ago," she replied, then turned her face away.

I could tell by the light that she was gazing up at the moon, which she often did. The moonlight was very kind to Savannah's features, showing high cheekbones, and a firm set to her jaw.

Finally, she looked back at her phone. "If all goes well, nobody will be hurt." She paused and glanced back up at the moon. "But if someone must be, I want you to make sure it's them."

# CHAPTER THIRTY-TWO

It felt as if I'd been asleep a long time when suddenly *Taranis's* air horn blasted twice, causing me to sit up so fast, I nearly pulled a groin muscle. Then, from below, I heard the big Caterpillar wake up.

"What the hell?" I heard Paul shout just outside the hatch.

I grabbed my holstered Sig, pulled it free, and chambered a round in one fluid motion, then flung open the hatch and stepped into the wheelhouse, the muzzle of the Sig leading the way.

Paul's eyes were wide. "I didn't do—"

"Stand down, Jesse!" Savannah shouted. "I need everyone up and alert, right now. I've already started the engine."

I pushed past Paul and put my Sig in a cupholder. "What's going on, Savvy?" I asked, as I glanced at the instruments and confirmed the big diesel was idling down below.

One by one, all the other systems came online. Savannah was remotely getting us ready for a quick departure.

"The two boats started moving thirty minutes ago," she replied, a little rushed, but sounding on top of things. "We decided they were giving up the hunt, since they were moving at just ten knots, back toward the marina. When they were five miles from you, they turned suddenly and accelerated. Range is now three miles due west and closing fast."

The others appeared and I yelled for everyone to hang onto something as I pushed all three controls forward at once, praying the diesel gods would forgive me for not allowing a proper warmup.

The electric gods were ambivalent. *Taranis* was one of them.

We were already facing into the wind, waves, and the rising tide, and there was nothing ahead of us except the sandbar and the open Atlantic Ocean. I knew that sandbar was a good six feet deep, even at low tide in the trough of the minimal waves. We should clear it.

Taranis launched forward, ignoring the elements pushing against her, seeking only two things—speed and open water.

"Andrew!" I shouted, as the knot meter passed twenty. "Comm up and get out in the cockpit! Deuce, you're with him. Tony and Paul, head forward through Paul's cabin and be ready on the bow. It's go time!"

Julie moved over to the nav desk and sat down. "How did they know? They couldn't have seen us or picked us up on radar."

I glanced over to Cape Florida in the distance, and the houses and condos that lined the western shore of Key Biscayne up beyond the state park.

"Dammit," I grumbled under my breath. "We were spotted from shore. Probably how they picked us up the first time."

"Sandbar in half a mile," Julie said. "Speed over ground is twenty-two knots. I'm switching over to forward sonar."

"It's plenty deep," I assured her. "Just let me know if there's any submerged debris echo."

Sandbars were notorious for collecting waterlogged trees that were completely submerged and waiting to rip open the bottom of a speeding boat. And something like a denuded tree didn't present much of an echo, but I knew Julie was very well versed in working with sonar equipment; her current billet with the Coast Guard Reserves was as an ST1, or sonar technician chief.

"All your comms are activated," Savannah advised.

"The sandbar's free of debris," Julie called out, then switched to radar.

I glanced at the knot meter. "We're at maximum speed," I stated calmly. "Twenty-six knots, speed over ground."

"I have two radar contacts coming from astern," Julie said. "Target one is two miles back. Closure rate is seven knots. He's slightly to the north of our current course and running parallel."

"We have both on satellite imaging," Savannah said. "Jesse, it looks like the same boat from the other night."

"That one's your's, Andrew," I said calmly. "We take out the closer boat first, then let the other one get away. Wait until Savannah's order."

"Target two is slower," Julie said, "but still overtaking us by about one or two knots. He's two point four miles back."

I slowly turned *Taranis's* wheel just a little to starboard, veering slightly away from the closer, faster boat.

"Everyone be ready," I said calmly. "I'm going to do some weaving to keep number one on the outside and force him to go the long way around. That'll get us a little farther offshore."

"At his closure rate," Chyrel said over the comm, "target one will be within two hundred yards in fifteen minutes."

Two hundred yards was all I was willing to give them. *Taranis* was as big as a barn and even a blind man could hit a barn at that distance.

I wanted as few holes in our new boat as possible. Preferably none.

"And in fifteen minutes," I added, "we'll be eight miles out to sea."

The screen directly above my head came on, displaying a slightly grainy, light-enhanced view astern, zoomed in on the same center console that had attacked us before.

I grinned.

"That's it," Savannah said, sounding almost relieved. "We've got them. Your camera is locked onto it now, Jesse. He's crossing your wake."

"Can you reverse that image?" I asked, looking up at the monitor.

Instantly, the image flipped, and the monitor became my rearview mirror.

Taranis didn't leave much of a wake, especially at speed, but for a good distance back there were three of them, so it was enough bumpy water that the pursuing boat would feel it.

As soon as he recovered from the beating, I turned the wheel slightly to port, forcing him to the outside once more.

"We're ready up here," Paul said from the bow, where he was working with Tony. "Just give us the word. Damn it looks like we're flying from up here!"

The boat on the monitor turned back quickly to cross our wake once more, and again, I calmly adjusted our course to make him take the longer route. He was faster, but keeping him always on the outside would mean more time. I wanted distance. Far enough from shore that we wouldn't be observed.

"We're ready, too," Deuce said, his voice coming through the open aft hatch as well as my earwig.

I realized we could probably do everything we were doing without any comms. It was very quiet on the bridge, even with the back door open.

I looked over at Julie, as she kept a close eye on the radar screen, and ahead of us. "Hey, Jules," I whispered.

She looked over, surprised.

"Can you pull up Tony's playlist from last night?"

She tapped a few buttons, then looked up. "Disturbed?"

I grinned. "Why not. It's too quiet for the conditions. It feels weird. But not too loud."

With a heavy-metal background thumping throughout the boat, we continued changing course back and forth for the next ten minutes, keeping the pursuing center console on the outside, as both boats slowly got closer and closer to us on calm waters. We no longer had the advantage of rough seas to force the other boats to slow down.

I was right. Silent chaos was distracting. The chaotic hard-charging sounds from the speakers, though turned down low, seemed to build tension, heighten everyone's awareness, including my own.

Our pursuers didn't seem to be paying much attention to the fact that while they were both overtaking *us*, the distance they were from one another was getting *greater*.

The center console was not only faster than us, it was faster than his buddy's.

"Target one is within a quarter mile," Chyrel said over the comm. "I have the message composed."

"Send it now," Savannah said. "We don't want them within two hundred yards."

"Message sent," Chyrel confirmed.

The text message we'd agreed to send, since we had Manuel Woods's burner phone number, was short, meant to piss him off, and worded to make him think there might only be one person aboard.

Break off now or I will be forced to defend myself! —Taranis

CHAPTER THIRTY-THREE

The faster boat stayed outside as I continued turning very slightly toward the south. It could outrun *Taranis*, but not outmaneuver her. I could easily turn completely around, and he'd lose a quarter mile, having to slow down even to turn wider.

Taranis's maneuverability at speed meant these guys had zero chance of getting close enough for more than a lucky shot.

It was clear the closer boat didn't want to try jumping our wakes this close, where the water bulges were much higher. It was trying to outrun us, forcing us inside, toward the other boat, which was now angling to intercept. Maybe they realized they were getting too far apart.

Unfortunately for whoever was in the faster boat, his friends were much too far back now to be of any help.

On the monitor, I could see there were two men aboard the nearer boat, and now it was just a couple hundred yards off our port quarter, but we still didn't know how much backup they had on the slower cuddy cabin.

I heard a cracking sound overhead, just a microsecond after seeing the muzzle flash on the screen.

Woods had received Chyrel's message.

"Shot fired!" Tony called out over the comm.

"Light him up!" was Savannah's instantaneous reply.

The Browning M-2 machine gun, or "Ma Deuce," as it was

affectionately called by Marine infantrymen, began hammering hard from back in the cockpit, the sound not all that dissimilar from a nail gun in the hands of a competent roofer. Only a hell of a lot louder.

I held the wheel steady, giving Andrew as stable a platform as he could expect on a boat, and watched the monitor.

The .50-caliber tracer rounds found and began chewing up the stern of the outboard-powered center console, punching thumb-sized holes in both gunwales, the transom, and whatever else the bullets encountered along the way.

There was a sudden puff of flame and Andrew instantly ceased firing as the boat nosedived, dead in the water.

"Splash one tango!" Deuce yelled.

"Hard turn to starboard!" I warned, then turned the wheel quite a bit more.

Taranis responded like a slot car on steroids, turning so sharply that the starboard ama came completely out of the water. I could feel the strain and vibrations through the wheel.

"It's all on you, Tony!" I shouted, seeing the cuddy cabin come into view on the monitor a mile ahead of us.

Before I finished the turn, a long string of fire pierced the darkness ahead, erupting from way out on the bow. It was accompanied by a shrieking sound that could only be described as a continuous loud rip of heavy-duty Velcro.

The long line of what looked like flame was actually only the tracers, loaded every five rounds in the ammo belt attached to the electric Gatling gun.

The fiery whip worked its way across the water as if in the hands of Satan himself, and the buzz from the minigun Billy had mounted in the forward storage compartment vibrated the whole boat.

The rounds fell short of the second boat, hitting the water a couple hundred yards in front of it, and creating over five hundred individual 7.62-millimeter geysers per second. The boat turned around as quickly as possible and began running back toward shore at full throttle, only about a half mile ahead.

Easily within range of the minigun.

The laws of physics dictated that it would take as long for us to get back to Stiltsville as it took to move eight miles offshore, about fifteen minutes. And by the time we arrived, the second boat would again be over two miles in front of us.

We needed him to extremely frightened, as if some horrible creature were trying to devour him.

The electric Gatling gun didn't have even half that range. At least not effectively. But would those in the other boat be aware of that?

I knew from experience the terrifying effect the minigun had on enemy troops, especially at night, demoralizing them and crippling them with intense fear. I'd seen one mounted in a chopper put so many rounds into an Iraqi bunker, the sand all around it caught fire and was melted into glass, entombing the bodies of several Republican Guard troops.

"Take your time, Tony," I advised. "But make it a long, scary ride back to shore for him."

Andrew and Deuce rejoined us in the wheelhouse as Tony let fly with several well-aimed bursts every few seconds, making swirls and loops of fire on one side of the fleeing boat or the other.

The fiery whip came very close to the boat, which was well within range, and if we wanted to hit it, Tony could easily vaporize the cuddy cabin and everyone aboard.

That wouldn't suit our plan, though, and would be a waste of a perfectly good boat.

"How many rounds does he have?" Andrew asked, watching Tony

firing with glee from the forward hatch.

"If you guys brought it all," I replied, with a grin, "he can play for quite a while."

When the M-134 was employed at night, it became a more formidable weapon than just a gun that could fire up to 60,000 rounds per minute. When that stream of lead was coming at you, it was damned frightening, especially if you knew that what was seen was only the tracers, and there were actually four more projectiles between each tracer. The minigun fired so fast, the tracers looked like a stream of molten fire.

At night, it was as much of a psychological weapon as it was a deadly one.

I checked the time. Our nap, if you could call it that, had only been about an hour long, and the sun would be up in another hour.

"Try firing at a higher angle," Paul suggested, when the boat was out of range. "See if you can aim by the splashes."

Deuce moved to the windshield beside the stairwell rail, watching the minigun's arcing fire. The tracers burned out before making impact, but we could easily see the hundreds of splashes nearly a mile in front of us, and well ahead of the other boat. Not effective shooting, but it definitely got the point across.

"Looks a little like a baitfish explosion," I heard Tony say over the comm.

During a baitfish run, it was common to see hundreds of them jumping out of the water when a large predator swam through the school.

Just then there was another short burst that came fairly close to the escaping boat, causing it to veer sharply.

"Oops," Tony said.

"Yeah, oops," I replied. "We want *that* one to get away."

CHAPTER THIRTY-FOUR

The helicopter's turbine made a clicking sound as it cooled, while sitting at Nixon Helipad on the west side of Key Biscayne. It was dark, but the sky to the east had been getting lighter when the helicopter had touched down, ten minutes earlier.

Charity Styles sat alone in the cockpit, checking over her post-flight list, but not shutting everything down. She might need to fly again quickly.

She'd landed with Kim and Marty, and they were waiting for the warrant. Charity couldn't help but think it'd be a lot less trouble and time if she just slipped in alone and dragged a blade across the men's throats as they slept.

Outside, Kim and Marty were talking to two uniformed cops beside a pair of squad cars. Police made Charity nervous. Her credentials were excellent, but they were also fake. Kim and Marty were both in uniform, as well.

An obvious unmarked police car came through the gate and stopped.

Charity got out of the helo and walked toward the two plain-clothes officers. One was a friend she hadn't seen in a long time.

Sherri held a manila folder up in her left hand. "We have the warrant. What's the status on our friends?"

"Hello, Sherri," Charity said, removing her cap and letting her hair fall down over her shoulders. "It's been a while."

Sherri Fallon stopped in her tracks. "Charity? What... what are you doing here?"

"Whatever you and Savannah need me to do," she replied, accepting a quick handshake and hug. "Homeland Security will help in any way we can. You're looking well. And a captain, I hear."

Sherri stepped back and appraised her former co-worker. "And you haven't changed a bit."

Marty and Kim approached, and Charity introduced them to her old friend.

"You're married?" Sherri asked.

"Yes," Kim replied. "And the captain of the boat is my father, Jesse McDermitt."

"You're Jesse's dau—" She paused and looked Kim over a little more closely. "I see it now."

"Roger that," Marty said, holding a finger to his ear, then turning to Sherri. "They've had to move up the timetable, as you and Savannah discussed. One boat has been disabled and the second one is nearing Biscayne Bay. Looks like he's running straight to Belsus's dock."

"Then let's get going," Sherri said, and turned to Charity. "Care to provide a diversion?"

Charity grinned. "I thought you'd never ask."

"I'm with you, then," Sherri said, handing the folder to the other detective. "Phil, take Joey and Frank to serve the warrant. There are two more unmarked units parked near the house and they'll join you when you roll up." Then she turned to Marty and Kim. "You two will go with Detective Conners and take flanking positions on either side of the house. This is a federal warrant issued by a Dade County judge, so you are backup *only*. Is that understood?"

"Yes, ma'am," Marty replied. "Thanks for letting us join the arrest."

Sherri smiled. "We'd never have the evidence if it weren't for you and your 'friends.'"

Marty and Kim got in with the detective, and the two uniformed cops followed in the patrol cars as they drove through the gate.

Charity climbed in the right side of the helo and began the startup procedure, putting her headset on in the process, while Sherri climbed into the copilot's seat and buckled up as the rotors began to turn.

"May I?" Sherri asked, after donning a headset and reaching for the radio.

Charity nodded as the turbine fired and the rotors sped up. Sherri got emergency takeoff clearance and requested controlled airspace all around Cape Florida and Key Biscayne.

Moments later, they were climbing toward a rising sun, then, once they were out over the water, Charity peeled off to the south.

She kept the bird low, under five hundred feet, as she flew along South Beach toward Key Biscayne. The police cars would take several minutes to get there, even though they were running lights and sirens.

"There it is!" Sherri said, pointing.

"And there's *Taranis*," Charity added, spotting the sleek trimaran giving chase.

She was coming out of the sun like an osprey hugging the surface as it prepared to snatch a fish out of the water. A stream of fire erupted from her bow.

Taranis didn't need to catch the boat; she only needed to drive it toward home, where Kim, Marty, and Sherri's troops would be waiting.

"What is that?" Sherri asked, as Charity banked left and climbed.

"That's Jesse and Savannah's new boat," Charity replied. "Or did you mean the minigun being operated by DHS agents aboard her?"

She climbed to two thousand feet, then came back around to the west at a slower speed as they watched the boat Jesse was chasing pass Cape Florida Light and turn into the channel.

The trimaran was more than a mile out, still.

Charity lifted her left headphone and tapped her earwig twice.

"What do you have, Charity?" Savannah asked.

"We're high overhead," Charity replied. "Sherri's with me, command and control, and we're waiting for her team, plus Kim and Marty, to get into position. The boat is headed straight for Belsus's house, and we'll create a diversion once whoever is in it goes inside, so Sherri's partner can serve the warrant."

"Be careful," Savannah said.

"If everything goes the way you planned," Charity said, "this will all be over in an hour."

Far down the bayside shoreline of upper Key Biscayne, Charity saw the three police cars turn onto the street and shut off their flashing lights.

Sherri pulled her phone out and put it under her headphone before saying, "Okay, watch us. When we make our move, roll up on the house and use the cover of the sound from the helo to breach the front door when we hover over the backyard."

Charity moved her Huey sideways, keeping an eye on the boat, which was now slowing and pulling up to a dock behind a private residence.

Sherri put her phone away and looked over at Charity. "They're ready. Do some of that crazy pilot shit, girl!"

Charity pushed the cyclic forward and increased power, putting the helo into a steep dive toward the water. Out of the corner of her eye, she saw the police cars begin moving, two unmarked cars pulling in behind them as they passed.

Fully loaded, Charity's bird had a top speed of a little over 130 miles per hour. It wasn't loaded, and plunging to just five hundred feet, they were going well over 140 as Charity pulled back on the cyclic and aimed the nose at the sea wall behind the house, just as the man from the boat ran across the patio and disappeared inside.

Charity knew that, at their speed, they would arrive before the occupants of the house even heard them coming.

Until she brought the bird to a stop. That, they were certain to hear.

The Huey was a big, heavy aircraft and the beat of the rotors as it turned hard or flared and stopped suddenly was deafening. The rotor wash could push small cars around.

"Whoo-hoo!" Sherri yelled. "God, I miss this!"

Charity pulled back hard on the cyclic while she pulled up on the collective at the same time, flaring the chopper and creating a horrendous noise as the rotors beat the air hard and brought the big aircraft to a stop.

In the backyard, potted plants and statues were toppled by the sudden blast of wind from the rotors.

Charity leveled off, hovering with her skids brushing the palm fronds of the trees surrounding the backyard. The patio itself was now being buffeted by a sudden hurricane-force downdraft, scattering things even more and throwing sand up.

Two men stood staring out through a wide set of glass sliding-door

panels, while behind them, the front door came crashing in, and two uniformed cops ran into the room with guns pointed at the suspects.

CHAPTER THIRTY-FIVE

We'd been anchored for over an hour, watching the cops moving around Belsus's house and yard. He and another man had been taken into custody, but it wasn't Manuel Woods.

The two men on the disabled boat, floating far out in the Gulf Stream, were picked up by the Miami-Dade Police water rescue squad, and neither of *them* was Woods.

Snake had somehow slithered away.

Taranis sat in the shallows across the channel from Belsus's house, just north of No Name Harbor, where we'd stumbled into this mess days earlier. Where we'd anchored had been in full view of the Greek crime boss.

"They've completed a thorough search," Savannah said from the overhead monitor.

She looked as tired as I felt.

"Still nothing?" I asked, dejected. "He's gotta be there. The other guy with Belsus had short, blond hair. The guy in the cuddy cabin had long, dark hair."

"I know," she replied. "Manuel Woods somehow slipped away."

"Do we think he has any contact with Belsus's people in Greece?" Deuce asked.

"Highly doubtful," she replied. "The Greek mob is very, *very* closed to outsiders."

"Is there any reason for us to stay here?" I asked, anxious to get moving again.

Movement equaled distance.

"Come on back to the island," Savannah said. "Kim said she and Marty would ride with Detective Conners back to the helipad, and Charity will bring them back here."

"How's everything at the Anchor?" I asked, activating the drum windlass.

"Nothing at all happened," Savannah replied. "Billy said he and Trish were going to stay there through tonight, to talk about their plans to open the submarine tomorrow, and if we wanted to take part, we should join them."

Just like that, I thought.

A father and son killed, a mother, daughter, and tutor kidnapped, another man dead at my hands, one bad guy missing, and a possible raid on a yacht theft ring thousands of miles away.

And all for what? So we could forget about it, gather around the fire ring, and laugh and get drunk?

The anchor came up, and I activated the clamp when it was in the pulpit. Then I turned the knob on the joystick, causing *Taranis* to begin to spin on her own axis. As the bows came around to the south, I moved both ama motor controls forward, watching Belsus's house slip slowly, silently past, the sun rising over the red-tile roof.

I looked forward toward the markers, but something odd had caught my eye. I looked back again, studying the house much more closely.

What had I seen?

The yard and landscaping had a Mediterranean look, or it had before Charity rearranged things, and the house could go either way—South Florida or the Med. The neighborhood was affluent, the properties all worth well into seven or eight figures. All neatly subdivided into quarter acre lots, with massive homes sitting just ten feet apart from one another.

Everything neat, tidy, and wreaking of money.

So why was there a wall mounted air-conditioner in the gable?

"Savvy! Patch me through to Sherri!"

I stopped the motors and put Taranis in station-keeping, then moved to the port hatch, along with Deuce.

"What is it?" he asked.

There were several clicks, then Sherri answered. "What's up, Savvy?"

"Go ahead, Jesse," Savannah said, looking up at the camera. "I patched your comm into my cell phone."

"Sherri, you've overlooked something," I began, remaining calm and speaking clearly. "There is an air-conditioned space in the attic over the south side of Belsus's house. It's over the main living area."

"We checked the attic," Sherri replied. "But it's on the north side, a pull-down stair."

"Look for an attic access in the living room area," I said. "Maybe in a closet ceiling or something. There's a wall-mounted air conditioner in the gable end on the south side of the house. A box unit in this neighborhood?"

"Thanks, Jesse," Sherri said. "We'll look again."

I saw her step outside and wave. Then she walked around the patio and looked up at the air conditioner.

"Are you going to wait around?" Savannah asked.

"No," I replied, looking up at the red dot next to the camera. "We're headed home. You did good, babe."

"Why don't you get some rest," Deuce offered. "We can get us back home."

I turned *Taranis* east, rounding the cape, and pointing her toward the open water. "No, I'm good," I said. "Anything from Stockwell?"

"Matt's leading the raid tonight," he replied.

My head jerked up. "What?"

"Don't worry," Deuce said. "Stockwell's best people will be with him. Seriously, man, you look wiped out. Nothing's going to happen there for several hours. You'll be home before anything goes down. Go get some rest."

I nodded and turned the helm over to Julie. "Wake me if you hear anything."

Stretching out on our bunk, I looked out through the expansive glass wall at the water passing by. I could see the far shore of Biscayne Bay, but knew it was only the tops of tall trees I was seeing at that distance.

Forward, I could see Boca Chita Key, and beyond it, the tops of trees on North Key Largo.

Just as I was about to doze off, there was a light knock on the hatch.

"Yeah?"

It opened slightly, and Deuce looked in, grinning. "You probably want to come hear this."

I sighed deeply and rolled out of bed and to my feet.

When I entered the wheelhouse, I could feel a different vibe in the air. Everyone was looking at me, as if expecting me to say something.

"What's going on?" I asked.

"Jesse," Savannah said. "I have Kim on Facetime and Chyrel is patching her through."

My own mood changed to one of concern. "What's wrong?"

The screen flickered and a camera feed appeared, looking down at Belsus's house. The loud and familiar noises were from inside a helicopter.

"Dad? Can you hear me? Are you seeing this?"

I stepped closer to the bank of monitors. "I hear you, Kim. What's going on?"

"They found Woods in the attic, Dad!"

Three people were being helped into an ambulance, all three with MDPD jackets over stooped shoulders.

"It's the Hoaglands, Dad!"

 # CHAPTER THIRTY-SIX

I sat alone on the aft part of the flybridge deck, my feet up on the rail, a cold Red Stripe in my hand, and the sun almost to the horizon.

The double murder had happened more than a month ago. All along, I'd felt certain that Hoagland's wife, daughter, and the teacher they'd hired to homeschool their two kids had been sold into the black market sex trade. It happened so often, and the victims were never found, that it was surprising that Belsus would hold onto the captives so long.

It'd been a long twenty-four hours since we'd pulled away from my little island in the backcountry, moving swift and silent in the direction of chaos.

I was beyond tired. I was so exhausted I knew it would be difficult to fall asleep right away. At least that was what I'd told Savannah.

The truth was, I needed to hear from Matt or Stockwell. I needed to know we hadn't just cut the tip of the finger off, but the head of the snake.

We'd done our part. Belsus, Woods, and the third guy, who it turned out was Belsus's attorney, were still being processed ten hours after being cuffed.

I heard quick feet coming up the steps. It was Savannah.

"I have good news," she said, sitting down beside me. "Travis just called. Matt and the team from *Ambrosia* uncovered two yachts that were in the process of being re-identified, and they rounded up all the players involved, tied them all to the mainmast of a stolen ketch, along with all the evidence of both thefts."

"So, it's over?" I asked, as Alberto came up the steps, the puppy following him carefully.

"He's still not used to steps," Alberto said, as Tank sniffed around the outdoor kitchen. "He acts really clumsy."

"Yes," Savannah whispered. "It's over. There isn't anyone going to come after us."

I smiled at Alberto. "He's only eleven weeks old, son. Times seven, that's... um..."

Alberto rolled his eyes. "Seventy-seven, Dad."

"He's clumsy on steps because he's still a toddler."

The puppy loped toward us, his jowls pulled back slightly in a goofy Lab smile as he panted.

"Hello, Tank," I said, when he lumbered up onto the sun pad.

The pup sat at my feet, looked at me and made a chuffing sound, not quite a bark.

"You like it here, boy?" I asked, leaning forward and scratching the side of his neck.

He chuffed again, lurching to his feet, then turned and walked cautiously to the edge and looked down through the rails. Then he stood and put his paws on the top rail, his big chest puffed out, and barked twice.

In that moment, I saw my old friend, Tank Tankersley, standing on a parapet wall in dress blues, looking down at a mob at the gates of the embassy, chastising and cursing them loudly, and daring them to pick up the fight with him, knowing that his Marines, situated all around him on that rooftop, would respond instantly and with deadly accuracy, should they desire to escalate things.

I scooted to the end of the sun pad and stood next to him, just like on that day many years ago, offering up my own life beside Tank to protect others.

There was movement on the stairs, and I looked over to see Kim coming up.

"I just got off the phone with your friend, Captain Fallon," she said, striding across the deck. "She had some interesting things to say about the people you work for."

"*Used* to work for," I corrected her, as I rubbed the side of Tank's neck. "I'm retired now."

She moved closer, then glanced back at Alberto.

"I think it's time for Tank to eat," Savannah said, picking up on Kim's body language. "Would you like to feed him?"

"Yeah!" Alberto exclaimed. "Come on, Tank."

"I'll go with you," Savannah said, rising and following the boy and puppy.

Kim joined me at the rail, both of us looking west toward the setting sun. Then she looked up at me. "You didn't seem very retired earlier today."

"Well, I am," I replied, though I didn't want to admit it, even to myself.

"Captain Fallon said she'd been working with Armstrong for several years." Kim said. "While still working for Miami-Dade. She put me and Marty in touch with a man named Charlie Bremmer. Do you know him?"

The sun reached the water, and, in my mind, I could hear the sizzle.

"He was the one who recruited me, Deuce, and Charity," I replied, turning to face her. "Are you leaving FWC?"

She looked back toward the setting sun, and my eyes followed her gaze. "No," she replied. "But Marty and I agree we can make a bigger difference working with them." She paused as the lower half of the sun disappeared.

"There was a hidden stairway behind the TV in Belsus's living room," Kim continued. "Sherri also told me that Amanda and Emma Hoagland, as well as the teacher, Destiny Douglas, are all going to be okay." She paused again as the sun sank lower and lower. "But it will take a while. All three of them are very traumatized, Dad. They witnessed the murders of Ron and Ronnie Hoagland."

I didn't want to ask, and I certainly didn't want to hear the answer, but found my mouth moving on its own. "How bad was it for them?"

"Dehydrated, malnourished, beaten... raped."

The blood in my veins boiled, then instantly turned to ice as the sun disappeared below the horizon.

"They'll all be locked away for a long time," Kim said. "They won't hurt anyone else."

I knew from experience that others would rise up to take Belsus and Woods's places before the sun came up again.

The criminal world knows no vacuum.

I couldn't get my head around the anguish and agony the mother and daughter suffered, or the brutality of being used like that after witnessing the murders of the father and son.

Prison was too easy. My idea of punishment would involve a burning shed, a vice, and a dull, rusty, butterknife.

Kim looked up at me, my face beginning to contort with the rage at the thought of how easy those men would have it compared to what they'd put their victims through.

"Are *you* okay, Dad?"

I could feel the strain building in my forearms as my hands gripped the rail, the tension moving up to my shoulders and down my back, muscles flexing as I tried to snap the rail I was holding in both hands.

The sub-human part of my brain, that part that controls our instinctive reactions, the fight or flight response, wanted to stomp, slash, and break bones.

Innocent people were out there, falling victim to evil people every day. Cops reacted to the crimes but were constrained by the rules of a civilized society and overwhelmed by the sheer numbers. All too often, the bad guys got away with their crimes because their victims had nobody to turn to.

"Dad?" Kim asked, softly. "What are you going to do?"

I released my grip on the rail, took a deep breath, and turned to face my middle daughter. "I'm not finished yet."

AFTERWORD

For a long time now, I've been following this young couple on YouTube, Riley and Elayna. They have a channel where they have been chronicling their lives at sea aboard their sailboat La Vagabonde for over eight years. I first found their channel when they'd released the eighth episode of their first season as they were crossing the Atlantic Ocean, from the Azores to the Bahamas, in a Beneteau 40. I binge-watched the first seven episodes and haven't missed one since.

Several years back, they moved up to a catamaran, had two children, both boys, and continued releasing even better videos on their channel, showcasing the places they visited using underwater cameras, drones, and now a remote production staff. And I continued to watch every new episode, becoming a fan and, by Season Two, a patron of their channel.

Lenny and Darwin are now five and three, and the family has recently moved aboard La Vagabonde III, a brand-new, custom-built, Rapido sailing trimaran. Riley contributed to the design, having now logged tens of thousands of sea miles and knowing just what he wanted in a blue-water passage-maker suitable for family life.

The seed of an idea was planted in my head then. And in subsequent videos, they shared more about what they were building and the technology and performance ability they designed into Vaga

III, which is nothing short of incredible.

She actually sails faster than the wind....

Three years ago, as Riley started laying out his ideas for a new boat, built specifically for them and what they do, then began talking to Rapido, and adding information about the build on their channel, I got to wondering.

What would Jesse put into a custom boat?

So, I've been designing Taranis, using only words for over two years. Whatever spare time I had, or whenever I'd get an idea, I researched, learned, and created an outline for Jesse and Savannah's new boat.

If money wasn't a concern, and for Jesse and Savvy it isn't, what would they both want, and what concessions might each of them make to appease the other?

I didn't even have a name for their new boat until I started writing this story. Then I kind of needed one. And since Jesse and Savannah's ancestral origins are in Northern Europe, Taranis, the Celtic god of lightning and thunder, seemed an appropriate name. And she even has a "Thunder" button, in tribute to how Taranis carried his lightning bolts.

The Taranis bio is now tens of thousands of words—a fourth of a novel. Yes, I create "biographies" for Jesse's boats, planes, and of course, The Beast. They're characters, too.

Jesse's bio is even longer, including every major life event, deployment, promotion, and now, slots for new Young Jesse books, coinciding with pivotal points in his life.

In short, I know every square inch of Taranis's three decks, roof, and hull. In Weigh Anchor, I got to introduce you to her, and now in Swift and Silent, we've seen what she's capable of.

Special thanks to one of the many very intelligent and learned individuals in my core reading group, Drew Mutch, MIT grad and former deputy program manager at Maritime Applied Physics Corporation, where he specialized in—you guessed it—multi-hull design and engineering.

After a lot of back and forth with Drew, I don't think there's any need for readers to suspend disbelief about what Taranis can do.

She's been vetted, and I only had to make small adjustments to my design biography. Mostly about speed. I wanted thirty-eight knots, but Drew convinced me that wasn't possible with the setup I had. This became one of the concessions that Jesse made.

As far as looks are concerned, I'm working with a graphic designer, and we may have something to show you soon. In fact, we hope to include it in the new T-shirt design coming this spring or summer to my online Gaspar's Revenge Ship's Store.

But until then, if you were to look at a Leen 56 power trimaran, then imagine it several feet wider, with longer wave-piercing hulls, you'd have a fair idea of what Taranis looks like.

Thanks also to my other core readers, Mike Ramsey, Dana Vilhen, Deg Priest, Katy McKnight, Kim DeWitt, Glenn Hibbert, Jason Hebert, and Alan Fader, who all received the manuscript before it went to my editor, then provided great insight and contributions to the story. Without their expertise, this story might not be nearly as enjoyable.

Greta and I had a quiet Christmas with our two youngest kids, Richard and Jordan— oh, and Milli, the Night Fetcher, or Lil Big Dog, who would bite my arm off if I didn't mention her.

All the wrapping paper and boxes were piled neatly in the middle of the living room but were quickly dispatched to the far corners by this playful pup.

I call her Night Fetcher because she has really good night vision and loves to play fetch in the dark, often showing off by circling around me and dropping the ball between my feet from behind. Lil Big Dog is self-explanatory if you were to meet her. She's obviously part dachshund, with short, stubby legs and long, hound-dog ears, but at almost forty pounds, she's clearly mixed with a larger breed. We think maybe a black-mouthed cur. At ten months, she's nearly full-grown and she's a big dog, but only shin tall. One of our neighbors calls her Cujo, because of the "big dog" sound of her voice.

Greta loves this little big pooch, and I am so happy we decided to adopt a puppy from a rescue shelter late in our lives. To see the smile on her face whenever Milli says or does something off the hook is infectious. I love to see my wife smile and hear her laugh. And yes, all our dogs have talked to us. And we, to them.

There are a lot of people who determine how my stories turn out. My editor, Marsha Zinberg, doesn't just correct my high-school English, but she explains why she's making a change. And I take my time to learn what she teaches. After all, she's been a professional editor for several decades. Marsha has now worked on twenty-four of my forty books, including two non-fiction titles; our relationship goes back to late 2018, and *Rising Charity*. We'd met at a NINC conference a few months before, and I asked her if she'd be willing to add me as a client. She didn't know the genre very well, but as it turned out, that didn't matter. In fact, it helped enrich my stories because if she didn't understand something, odds were the average reader might not.

The same goes for my audiobook narrator, Nick Sullivan. He was the 63rd to audition for my first audiobook back in 2015, and I'm glad I kept the auditions open.

Nick has recorded every single word I've written, and along the way, we've become friends, fellow authors, and even co-authors of a couple of Tropical Author collaborations.

After he records a new book, I listen to it and read along, stopping often to make a change in the text, because what he recorded was better. He also points out dozens of things that would sound better in audio, and thus read better.

These two people have changed the way I write.

Thanks also to Sam, Ash, Cam, Jen, Mel, Amy, Adriane, and Brian, my team of virtual assistants at Aurora Publicity. They do a lot of the grunt work to bring my books to market, including formatting, cover design, advertising, computer work, and even my newsletter. It's thanks to Aurora that I haven't had to give up writing time to run my business.

And then finally, you've now gotten to meet Tank.

Thanks to my friend Mary, and her almost one-year-old pup, Ignacious, for providing me with some valuable insight. Iggy is a Tibet mountain dog and probably the most easy-going, chill dog I've ever met. And why not? Due to their sheer size, Tibet mountain dogs have no natural fear of anything. They were bred to protect flocks of sheep from packs of wolves. Packs! So, when Iggy first met me, a big, bearded guy, in dark sunglasses and USMC cover, instead of growling or barking, he walked right up and sat down in front of me, just as friendly and non-threatening as you could imagine. I said, "Hey, Iggy," and we were friends.

If only we humans could meet one another like Iggy does.

Since Tank would need to be a swimmer, he had to have some Lab traits from his mother, and all the clues are there. When he's fully grown, he'll look like a black Lab with big jowls... until something is placed beside him for size comparison. A big Lab would be eighty pounds, like Finn. Tank will be that, and half again—as big as many grown men.

And lastly, I want to thank you, my readers. I'd write the stories if you weren't there, but it wouldn't be as much fun. It gives me such a huge thrill knowing so many enjoy my work. Thank you.

Also by Wayne Stinnett

The Jerry Snyder Caribbean Mystery Series

Wayward Sons   Voudoo Child   Friends of the Devil

The Charity Styles Caribbean Thriller Series

Merciless Charity   Enduring Charity   Elusive Charity
Ruthless Charity   Vigilant Charity   Liable Charity
Reckless Charity   Lost Charity

The Young Jesse McDermitt Tropical Adventure Series

A Seller's Market   Bad Blood

The Jesse McDermitt Caribbean Adventure Series

Fallen Out   Rising Storm   Rising Tide
Fallen Palm   Rising Fury   Steady As She Goes
Fallen Hunter   Rising Force   All Ahead Full
Fallen Pride   Rising Charity   Man Overboard
Fallen Mangrove   Rising Water   Cast Off
Fallen King   Rising Spirit   Fish On!
Fallen Honor   Rising Thunder   Weigh Anchor
Fallen Tide   Rising Warrior   Swift and Silent
Fallen Angel   Rising Moon
Fallen Hero   Rising Tide

Non Fiction

Blue Collar to No Collar   No Collar to Tank Top